NOBLE SANCTION

WILLIAM MILLER

NOBLE SANCTION

Book and Cover design by www.LiteraryRebel.com

First Edition: July 2019

Dedication and special thanks:

I owe a great debt of gratitude to former CIA field officer Andrew Bustamante for teaching me spycraft and helping me get the facts right.

I'd also like to thank the early readers for invaluable insight and feedback. Every book is a labor of love and your input was instrumental in bringing this one to print.

"I look inside myself and see my heart is black."
~ Mick Jagger

CHAPTER ONE

ELIŠKA CERMÁKOVA WAS STRETCHED OUT OVER THE engine block of a Dodge Charger. She had a wrench in one hand, straining against a stubborn bolt on a dead alternator. A vein stood out on her neck and beads of sweat glistened on her forehead. The muscles in her arms bunched. A giant fan cooled the sweat on her skin into a sticky shell. Rock 'n' roll blasted from a stereo in the corner. Metallica was hammering through *Seek and Destroy*. The smell of rubber and motor oil filled the garage. The bay door was up and hot South African sunshine reflected off an asphalt parking lot. The shop didn't have a name, just a sandwich board out front that advertised, "*Full Service Auto Repair. Brakes—Tires—Ice-Cold Air!*"

Eliška wore a grease-stained tank top and cut-off shorts. Short blonde hair framed a pretty face. She gripped the wrench and flexed until she felt like she was about to give birth to her colon. The bolt refused to give. She let go with a frustrated sigh, straightened up, and palmed sweat from one cheek, leaving a dark streak on pale white skin.

"Need help?" Nelson asked. His name was stitched into the pocket of work-stained coveralls. He was a tall black man—six-foot-seven—with skin the color of eggplant. He had a Hyundai up on the lift and spoke without taking his eyes off his work.

"I got it," Eliška assured him. She dropped the wrench on a rolling cart piled with tools, picked up a flathead and rummaged around until she found a small sledge. She braced the screwdriver against the bolt and tapped it with the hammer. That done, she grabbed the wrench and was about to try again when she felt her phone vibrating against her left butt cheek. She fished the mobile from her back pocket, recognized the number, and thumbed the green button. "When and where?"

"Café Organica," her contact said in a rasping American accent. "One hour."

Eliška glanced down at her grease-stained tank top. Damp cotton clung to her modest breasts and her nipples poked through. She said, "Can it wait? I need to change first."

"Time is a factor."

"You know I don't like to be rushed," Eliška told him.

"Don't keep me waiting," he said, and the line went dead.

Eliška pocketed the phone and cursed.

Nelson was shaking his head. "They call and you jump. Who is this new employer of yours?"

"You know better than to ask questions," Eliška told him. In truth, she had no clue. The American had contacted her six months ago and, despite her best efforts at uncovering his identity, he remained a complete mystery. He paid top dollar though. That was enough for Eliška. She said, "I'm going to need a clean set of wheels."

"Take the Lexus." Nelson unzipped his coveralls to reveal a nickel-plated revolver stuffed in the waistband of his pants. "Need this?"

Eliška hesitated only a second before shaking her head. "No. I'll be alright."

"Be safe."

She grabbed a heavy canvas jacket covered in old oil stains from a hook by the door. The keys to the Lexus hung on a peg board. She shrugged into the jacket as she stepped outside. Heat clobbered her and the thick jacket only made it worse. The black IS 350 was parked around the side of the shop. Eliška thumbed the fob. The doors unlocked with a chirrup. She climbed inside and headed west, into the heart of Johannesburg.

———

Forty-five minutes later, Eliška backed into an empty spot across from a bustling shopping arcade dedicated to free trade and sustainable living. The sun was a shimmering yellow disc in a cloudless blue sky. Eliška edged the gleaming black Lexus up to the curb and killed the engine. The car turned into a sweat box as soon as the air conditioner cut out. April in South Africa is arid and hot with little rain and less shade. The altitude makes skin cancer a major concern, especially for someone as pale as Eliška.

She checked for traffic before climbing out. Long legs

carried her across the quiet boulevard, past a vinyl shop and a bonsai nursery, to a fair-trade coffee shop. A pair of black women, arms weighed down with shopping bags, gave her a nasty look as she passed. The American sat at an outdoor table shaded by a large canvas umbrella. A cigarette dangled from one corner of his mouth. He wore a beige summer-weight suit over a black button-down. A copy of the *Johannesburg City Press* lay on the table next to a cup of coffee with enough cream and sugar to make a spoon stand up straight.

Eliška took a seat across from him.

He pushed back his cufflink and glanced at a Rolex Submariner. "You're late."

"You're lucky I'm here at all," she told him. "I don't like being called across town for a meeting last-minute. Especially now. A couple of whites downtown are just asking for trouble."

The American was a cool customer. He didn't seem disturbed by the crowd or the hostile looks. White farmers in South Africa were being slaughtered by angry black mobs, but the American lounged in his chair like he didn't have a care in the world. He said, "They never should have ended apartheid."

"You didn't call me out here to discuss race relations," Eliška said. She wasn't concerned equal rights in South Africa. Whites had mistreated blacks for decades. Now blacks were mistreating whites. Round and round it goes. Where it stops? Nobody knows. Probably, it would end when some fool launched a nuke and blew up the world. Not Eliška's problem. She said, "What have you got for me?"

"One last job."

"I'm listening."

The American—Eliška had come to think of him as Bob —slid a tablet computer across the tablecloth. She woke it up and found a black-and-white headshot of a middle-age man with a bad comb-over and fleshy jowls.

Bob said, "You'll find the relevant details on a file folder. The target's name is P. Arthur Fellows. He works for the Secret Service. We need it to look like an accident."

Eliška was already shaking her head. "No way. You know the rules. I don't take jobs in America."

"We're prepared to triple what we paid you last time." He took a thick envelope from his pocket and laid it on the table. "Half up front, of course."

That got Eliška's attention. She sat there, staring at the black-and-white, trying to think of all the reasons *not* to do it. Bob, and whoever he worked for, were good clients. They paid promptly in dollars and didn't ask questions. But Eliška only had a few hard rules: No children, and no jobs inside the United States. America's law enforcement was too well-connected, and they took contract killing very serious. There was too much chance she would end up on the FBI's most-wanted list. She put the tablet back on the table and shook her head. "Sorry. The answer is no. Find somebody else."

"We want you," Bob said. He leaned back and breathed smoke.

"The answer is still no." Eliška stood up to leave.

He took the cigarette from his mouth and said, "That's unfortunate, Ms. Cermáková."

Eliška's blood ran cold. She hadn't used that name in

eight years. She looked around to see if anyone had heard before lowering herself back into the seat. "How the hell do you know my name?"

"I know everything about you," Bob said. "Maybe the Czech Republic would be interested to know where you've been hiding these last few years?"

Eliška leaned across the table and jabbed a finger into Bob's chest. "Make another threat, and I'll spill your guts all over the sidewalk."

"I really hoped it wouldn't come to this," he said and managed to look disappointed. He put a hand inside his jacket, brought out a grainy surveillance photo and dropped it on the table.

Eliška picked up the photograph with trembling fingers. It showed an old man with an oxygen tank hobbling up a sidewalk in Prague. She whispered, "Damn you to hell."

"The choice is yours, Ms. Cermákova," Bob said. "The carrot or the stick? You're going to eliminate P. Arthur Fellows for us, or dear old daddy will have an accident."

Her throat clutched. She managed to croak out, "Leave my papa alone!"

"That's entirely up to you."

Eliška stuffed the picture in the pocket of her grease-stained work coat. She wanted to rip the American's throat open with her bare hands. Instead, she said, "I'll do it, but this is the last job. You understand me? After this, we're through. Tell your employer to find somebody else."

Bob inclined his head. "Show me proof of death, and you'll never hear from me again."

"And I have your word my father will be left alone?"

"I swear it."

Eliška knew he was lying. As long as she was alive, her father would never be safe. She didn't know how the American had learned her real name. In the end, it didn't matter. She needed to kill P. Arthur Fellows and then find a way to disappear or spend the rest of her life at Bob's beck and call. She grabbed the envelope with the cash and the tablet computer. "I'll let you know when it's done."

A smile played across Bob's weathered face. "I look forward to hearing from you."

CHAPTER TWO

Forty-eight hours later, Eliška Cermákova touched down at JFK International. Tires shrieked on the tarmac and the fuselage rattled hard. A handful of passengers applauded the successful landing. Eliška arched her back and rubbed sleep from her eyes. A yawn tried to split her jaw in two. She covered her mouth with the back of one hand. She had spent the last two days cooped up on airline seats. From Johannesburg, she had flown to Egypt, Egypt to Paris, Paris to Turkey, then China, Vancouver, and finally into New York—all on a series of fake passports.

While the airbus taxied to the terminal, Eliška stood up, stretched, and reached for her bag. She was no longer blonde. Now she had long chestnut curls and a beauty mark on her left cheek to match her Canadian passport. She checked herself in a compact mirror while she waited for the plane to marry up with the exit ramp and then followed the rest of the passengers to customs. She flashed a smile at the young immigration officer and his rubber stamp came down with a *thump*. He told her enjoy her stay. She could feel his eyes on her butt as she walked away.

So far so good, Eliška thought. From there, she followed the signs to long-term parking. A gust of cold air hit her as she stepped off the elevator. Fluorescents reflected on the roofs of the cars and cast the empty lot in a sickly green glow. The smell of rubber and urine mixed together in a pungent cocktail.

Long-term parking is the perfect place to pick up a clean set of wheels. The owners are out of town and ticket stubs are clearly displayed. A gunmetal-grey Camaro near the elevators caught her eye. It had only been there two days. She threw a quick glance around, reached in her backpack, brought out a laptop and set to work hacking the Camaro's CAN bus system.

Modern cars are basically computers on wheels. Everything in the vehicle is controlled by an electronic control unit. Anyone with a laptop and a little bit of know-how can remotely access the system and send commands to the ECU. Eliška balanced the laptop on one knee while she pecked at the keys. It took less than three minutes to pinpoint the Camaro's CAN bus and override the access codes. The doors unlocked with a *chirp*.

Five minutes later, she was pulling out of the long-term lot onto the Belt Parkway, headed west toward New Jersey. She hit Newark at rush hour and crept through traffic until she made it onto the New Jersey Turnpike. From there it was a four-hour drive to DC. She reached into her bag for her phone, queued up some heavy metal, and stuck one headphone in her ear. The sun was going down in the west and a bank of dark clouds was crawling up from the south, promising rain.

Eliška pulled into a roadside motel somewhere north of Baltimore. She had heard stories of Mobtown. None of them good. The motel was a squat concrete bunker of fading paint with doors that opened onto the parking lot and a flickering neon sign advertising vacancies. Eliška paid cash and parked the stolen Camaro outside the door to number twenty-seven.

The room was depressing, with walls so thin she could hear the couple next door. She put the chain on the door, took a rubber wedge from her bag and jammed it in place, then used the toilet before her bladder exploded. She had been holding it for the last two hundred miles. With that taken care of, she stretched out on the bed. She didn't bother to undress. She wasn't going to be here long. She took out her cellphone, dialed a number by heart, and hesitated before pressing send.

Do it, she told herself. *Make the call.*

Her thumb tapped the green button and the call went through.

The old man picked up after a dozen rings.

Eliška said, *"Dobry den, Baba."*

"Eliška?" he spoke in Czech. "Is that you?"

"It's me, Papa. How are you feeling?"

She heard him take a hit of oxygen. "How much trouble are you in?"

"No trouble," Eliška lied. "I'm just checking up on you, Papa. Has anyone come by the apartment lately?"

"No." He cleared his throat with a loud hacking noise. "No one comes here. The only company I get is a man from the hospital. He stops by once a week to drop off new tanks. Are you sure you aren't in some kind of trouble?"

"I'm fine, Papa. I was thinking to come by and visit with you. Maybe sometime next week, but I have a few things I need to take care of first."

He made another loud hacking noise, trying to work phlegm from his throat. "Eight years you've been gone. Now you want to visit? I don't know what kind of trouble you're in, but don't bring it to my doorstep, Eliška."

The line went dead.

She dropped the phone on the bed and wiped tears from her eyes. He was still alive and ornery as ever, Eliška told herself. That was something. The old man had never forgiven her for walking out on him, and Eliška couldn't very well explain why she had left. She closed her eyes, took in some air, and reached for the tablet with the target's info.

He was middle-age, with a wife and a teenage son. Eliška ignored that information and scrolled through the rest of his profile. P. Arthur Fellows worked for the US Secret Service and was utterly predictable in his habits. Every Thursday, he worked late, then picked up dinner at his favorite sushi restaurant before driving home. He walked the dog at eight o'clock and spent the rest of the evening on the sofa with his wife, watching television.

Killing Fellows would be simple. He was set in his ways. Predictable people are easy to kill. Getting away with it is the hard part. Everything inside Eliška told her to forget the name P. Arthur Fellows and take the first flight out.

Operating in the United States was too risky. But Bob knew where her father lived. He knew her name. He knew everything about her. She had to deal with Fellows, or Papa was a dead man.

CHAPTER THREE

Eliška Cermáková walked into Sushi Gakyu on Thursday night, a redhead in a slinky green dress and heels. A generic Asian melody struggled to give the place authentic atmosphere. The tables were packed with a mix of millennials and government workers. The chef was a Japanese man of indeterminate age, slicing fish with deft flashes of a *yanagi* knife. P. Arthur Fellows sat at the bar, a cup of sake in front of him, along with stacks of xeroxed pages. The chef passed a plate of sushi over the glass partition and Fellows accepted with a muttered, "*Arigato gozaimasu.*"

"That looks delicious," Eliška said. She took the stool next to him and let the dress ride up her thighs. "What is it?"

Fellows paused with a slice of fish halfway to his mouth. His eyes flashed to her thighs and made the trip north. The cold wedge slipped from his chopsticks and hit the plate with a small *splat*. An embarrassed smile tugged at his lips. He cleared his throat. "Yellowtail."

"Any good?" Eliška asked.

"Ota makes the best sushi in town," he said and turned back to his fish.

Seducing a man can be deceptively hard work. Fellows thought the conversation was over. After all, what would a woman like her want with a man like him? Fellows was middle-age, balding, and going to fat. Eliška looked like she had just stepped from the pages of a fashion magazine. She said, "Do you come here often?"

"Every Thursday," Fellows told her as he captured another slice of fish with his sticks. His ears were turning red. "What about you?"

"I just moved here. I'm still learning my way around the city." She stuck out a hand. "My name is Becca."

"Arthur." He put his chopsticks down and shook her hand with a slightly moist grip. Pink spots formed in his waxy cheeks. "Where are you from, Becca?"

"Holland," she lied.

They were soon deep in conversation. Arthur told "Becca" a little about himself, leaving out the fact that he had a wife and son. She talked about her dream of becoming a veterinarian. At one point, she reached for the soy sauce and Fellows casually slipped the wedding band off his finger.

———

The CIA's Deputy Director of Operations, Albert Dulles, sat in a corner booth with his back to the wall. He liked to sit where he could keep one eye on the room and he saw the honeypot cozy up to the chubby accountant type. He saw the man slip off his wedding band and heard the girl laugh just a little too loud.

Nicknamed the Wizard, four decades in the spy business had hardwired tradecraft into his brain. Alarm bells were going off inside his head as he watched the scene at the bar. The girl was obviously a pro, but the mark was all wrong. *Why him?* Dulles wondered. His clothes and shoes said strictly middle-class government worker in a dead-end job. There were better-dressed men in the room. And better places to pick up a john, for that matter. Why not the Waldorf or the Trinity just a few blocks away? Why troll for bottom feeders in a middling sushi joint when she could hook senators in a high-class hotel? It didn't make sense.

"Are you even listening to me?" Chelsea Dulles asked.

Wizard blinked and turned his attention back to his youngest daughter. "Of course I was listening."

Chelsea sat back and crossed her arms over her chest. Blue eyes flashed in a stormy face. She was dressed in a conservative business suit with a starched white collar. Her dun-colored hair was cut in a shoulder-length bob. "What was I just talking about, Albert?"

Albert. He was always Albert. Never Father or even Dad. Certainly not Daddy. Just Albert. Wizard had made a complete hash of his family life. It was no secret and not something he tried to sugarcoat. He was too old to be anything but honest with himself. His job wasn't conducive to family life. Wizard had made peace with that fact. What he did was more important.

He patted his coat in search of cigarettes while trying to recall the last thing he remembered hearing.

"You can't smoke in here," Chelsea reminded him.

Wizard abandoned the search. "You were telling me about this David fella you've been seeing. And I don't think it's a good idea for you to be dating a member of the Iranian government. You work for the State Department. If word of this gets out, it's going to look bad. Your position would be compromised."

She shook her head. "First of all, his name is Dawoud, and I don't recall asking your opinion. You don't get a say in who I date. You lost that privilege a long time ago. And second, I was talking about the president rattling his saber. He can't pull that bull-in-a-china-shop routine with the Iranians."

"Why not?" Wizard asked. "Seems to be working with the Norks."

"Iran is not North Korea," Chelsea said. "It's a totally different situation. We've been working for months to get things smoothed out over there, and it's going to blow up in our faces if the president tries wading in like John Wayne."

"Sometimes a strong show of force is exactly what these countries need."

"Not Iran," Chelsea shook her head. "It's not going to work. The Iranians are a proud people."

"What have they got to be proud of?" Wizard asked.

"Oh God, you sound just like him." She closed her eyes and breathed through pursed lips. "There are factions inside the Iranian government working toward change."

"Like this Dawoud fella?" Dulles asked.

"My point is"—she went on as if he hadn't spoken—"we

can't convince the Iranians to disarm and adopt democracy if the president is threatening more bombs. Talk to him. Help him see that diplomacy is the only path forward. He listens to you."

"That's a stretch," said Wizard.

"Fine, he listens to your boss. You need to tell him to back off. Tone down the rhetoric and let us do our job."

"My job is to give the president the most accurate information I have available."

"What's that mean?"

"You aren't the only one with assets inside Iran," he told her.

Chelsea leaned in. "You have someone inside Iran? Who?"

He shook his head. It was a small side-to-side movement, barely noticeable unless you were looking for it. "You know I can't tell you that."

She sat back and frowned. "Well, I don't know what information you are getting, but my sources are good. In ten years, Iran will be the new UAE."

"I'll believe that when I see it," Wizard said and watched the hooker as she headed for the door with her john in tow.

CHAPTER FOUR

THE JOB WAS DONE. P. ARTHUR FELLOWS WAS DEAD. The Secret Service agent hung in the closet with his own belt looped around his neck and his tighty-whities around his ankles. The other end of the belt was attached to the hanger rod. His face was a bloated purple radish. A swollen white tongue lolled from his open mouth.

Eliška, dressed in a black thong and high heels, stepped back to observe her handiwork. She had used the belt to strangle him, then wrestled his dead body into the closet. It was heavy, back-breaking work. Arthur was no pixie. Sweat glistened on Eliška's bare skin. She took a deep breath and pushed a lock of red hair out of her eyes.

Killing was the easy part.

Now she had to erase the evidence. She crossed to the bedside table for her purse, donned a pair of nitrile gloves, took out a thumb drive with a lightning connector and attached it to the dead man's phone. A spinning hourglass appeared on the screen, followed by a long series of code as the hacking software cracked the phone's encryption. Within twenty seconds, the device was unlocked and Eliška searched the web until she found an autoerotic asphyxiation website. She quickly downloaded several photos, left the website open, and tossed the phone into the closet at Fellows's feet. That should keep the authorities from digging too deep. The investigating officers would unlock the phone, find the porn, and rule it accidental death by asphyxiation. Case closed.

Eliška reached to the bottom of her purse and brought out a tightly folded leotard, along with alcohol swabs. She pulled on the skin-tight bodysuit and went around the hotel room, wiping down all the surfaces.

When that was done, she made the bed, stripped out of the leotard, and donned the green dress. She paused in the entryway, fanning out the wig so it concealed her face, before letting herself out of the room

She hung the "Do Not Disturb" sign and made her way to the stairwell, where she used her hip against the push bar to avoid leaving fingerprints. There was still a chance the authorities would review the surveillance footage. They would see that P. Arthur Fellows had checked in with a prostitute. DC police would make a token effort to track down the girl, but even a streetwalker is smart enough to skip town when a john croaks.

Eliška reached the ground floor, took a pair of Jackie O. sunglasses from her purse, and slipped them on before crossing the lobby. She let herself out the front door of the hotel and disappeared into the night.

CHAPTER FIVE

WIZARD STOOD AT HIS KITCHEN ISLAND, SCANNING intelligence reports and smoking his first cigarette of the day. He was dressed in a threadbare bathrobe. A plate of toast and jam sat untouched. The first gray light of morning filtered in through the curtains. The Deputy Director of Operations rarely slept and when he did, it was hardly deserving of the name. He spent most nights in his easy chair, puzzling through a tangled labyrinth of classified information. He would smoke one cigarette after another, searching for links in seemingly random events. He usually drifted off sometime after three in the morning and woke before the dawn.

As he stood there paging through a report out of Iran, the morning edition landed on the front step with a soft *thump*. Wizard checked an antique Rolex on his boney wrist before shuffling to the door. A breath of cold air hit him as he stepped onto the porch.

Dulles lived on a seven-acre plot of land in the wooded

hills north of Langley. The closest neighbors were a half mile down the road. They had no idea Dulles worked for the Company or that the edge of his property was guarded by infrared cameras and state-of-the-art motion sensors. The neighbors had a nine year old little girl liked to cross the property lines in the pursuit of rabbits and frogs. She made life hell for Wizard's security people.

As Wizard bent down for the paper, ash drooped from his cigarette and the breeze carried it away. He scooped the paper off the porch steps and straightened up with a tired groan. Simple things like bending over were getting harder and harder.

The neighbor drove past on his way to work. He honked once and waved. Wizard raised the newspaper in salute before shuffling back inside. He returned to the kitchen island and his uneaten toast and shook the morning edition out of its green plastic sleeve. The headline article was politics. Isn't it always? Below the fold was a story about a Secret Service agent found dead in a hotel room, apparently the victim of accidental strangulation. Wizard's joints might be getting old, but his eyes were sharp as ever, and he recognized the face in the picture.

CHAPTER SIX

Ezra Cook and Gwendolyn Witwicky occupied a corner cubicle in the basement at Langley, where action figurines decorated the desks. A long banner near the elevators declared, *"We Are Groot!"* The hum of computer fans and the smell of overworked processors hung in the air, along with a whiff of cheap body spray. Several fake windows showed rolling green pastures meant to provide a sense of openness, but the denizens of the basement felt right at home under the electric blaze of high-resolution monitors.

Witwicky wore Coke-bottle glasses. Her mousy brown hair was pulled back in a ponytail. She was still on crutches, recovering from the car crash that had left her in the hospital with a severe concussion, two broken ribs, and a fractured shin. The computer ninjas who worked in the basement rarely got out in the field. For most, their biggest concerns were paper cuts and high cholesterol. The attempted murder had turned Gwen into a minor celebrity.

She had been forced to tell the story over and over, until she was thoroughly sick of hearing herself talk. She had just finished a shortened rendition of the crash that morning, standing next to the coffee maker in the break room, and the audience had stared wide-eyed, like she had single-handedly planted the flag at Iwo Jima.

Ezra Cook had a video gamer's complexion, with a hooked nose and a head full of black hair that stuck up at odd angles. A pair of noise-cancelling headphones were clamped over his ears, blasting *Goo Goo Muck* by the Cramps. Over the last month, Ezra had carved five pounds of extra fat from his frame courtesy of karate lessons taught by a sixth-degree Shotokan black belt. He had signed up for classes after Gwen's near miss. He was also taking his gun to the range and getting pretty good. Well, he hit the target more often than not, anyways. That was a start. Seeing Gwen clinging to life in a hospital bed had made him sick to his stomach. Worse, he hadn't been able to do a thing about it. Ezra never wanted to feel that helpless again. More importantly, he wanted Gwen to know he could protect her.

He glanced up from his work. The clock on the wall pointed to 11:30. Ezra checked his computer, which was synced to the atomic clock in Boulder, and found it was actually 11:32. Not even noon and his stomach was already rumbling. He used to skip breakfast and sometimes lunch. Now that he was getting some exercise, he seemed to be hungry all the time. He stretched and tugged the headphones off. "I'm starving," he announced. "Want to head up to the cafeteria?"

"You're always hungry," Gwen said. She was wearing corduroys and a Gryffindor sweater today. She looked like

Hermione all grown up. She said, "And you never get any bigger. In fact, I think you've lost some weight. What's your secret?"

He grinned. "Good genes, I guess."

He wasn't ready to tell Gwen about his new extracurricular activities. Just yesterday, Ezra's sensei had announced that he was almost ready to test for his yellow belt. Ezra wanted to surprise Gwen. In his daydreams, they were having drinks after work when a couple of meatheads started harassing her. Ezra would single-handedly, and spectacularly, dispatch all three goons. His fantasies always ended at Gwen's apartment where they both confessed their love for each other.

"Maybe you've got a tapeworm," Gwen said and reached for her crutches. "You should see a doctor."

"Need help?" Ezra asked.

He always asked. She always said no.

"I got it," Gwen said as she levered herself out of the chair onto the crutches.

The internal line on Ezra's desk lit up and he reached over to press the intercom button. "Ezra Cook speaking."

"Mr. Cook, this is DDO Dulles's secretary. Is Ms. Witwicky with you?"

"Uh ..." said Ezra, wondering why the Deputy Director of Operations would be calling him. "Yeah."

"I'm right here," Gwen said.

"The Deputy Director would like to see you both in his office."

"Are we in some kind of trouble?" Ezra asked.

"Report to DDO Dulles's office right away," the secretary said and the line went dead.

Gwen chucked him on the arm.

"Ow." He rubbed his bicep.

"What did you say that for?" Gwen asked.

He shrugged. "Can't hurt to ask."

She scowled and shook her head.

They made their way to the elevator together. The doors closed and the car started to climb. Gwen said, "Why would the Wizard want to see us?"

"How does he even know who we are?" A knot was forming in Ezra's belly. He felt like a man headed to the gallows.

"I haven't done anything lately," Gwen said.

"Me neither."

The elevator let them out on the ground floor and they navigated the busy entryway. Ezra grabbed the door for Gwen. Boiling gray clouds gathered overhead and thunder muttered in the distance. The air felt like rain. Ezra had to go slow so Gwen could keep up. They left the New Building and crossed the grounds to the Old Building, making the shelter of the overhang as the first heavy drops landed on the sidewalk connecting the two campuses. A moment later, the skies opened up.

"April showers bring May flowers," Gwen said.

"I doubt there are any flowers where we're going."

They rode the elevator up to seven and passed a sea of cubicles to the inner sanctum, arguably the nerve center of the CIA: a suite of offices which house the Deputy Director of Operations (DDO), the Deputy Director of Intelligence (DDI), and the Director of Central Intelligence (DCI). The reception area is a wide-open space with pale-blue carpet underfoot and plenty of seating. A trio of secretaries act as gatekeepers. There were no flowers, but two potted plants stood in the corners, adding a splash of color to an otherwise austere space.

Dulles's secretary peered at them over half-moon spectacles. She was a formidable black woman with streaks of early gray in her hair. "He's waiting for you."

Something in her tone sent a shiver up Ezra's spine. The knot in his stomach turned to a hard lump. His legs felt like wet noodles. He wanted Gwen to go first, but she was too slow on the crutches, so he summoned up his courage and raised a fist to knock.

"Go on in," the secretary said. "He knows you're coming."

Ezra turned the knob, feeling like a small boy invading the sanctity of his father's bedroom.

The office looked like the private chambers of an eccentric genius or a madman—maybe both. The overpowering stench of cigarettes clung to every surface, despite Langley's strict policy against smoking. One entire wall was a spider's web of red string tying together a collection of intelligence reports and newspaper clippings. At the center of the vast web was a black-and-white silhouette with a question mark. The rest of the office was buried under piles of reports with handwritten notes in Wizard's spidery scrawl. The DDO was old school. He eschewed computers in favor of his own private system, which seemed to include a lot of sticky notes. Top secret information was strewn about the office on yellow stickies and three-by-five cards. It was such a profusion of raw intelligence, staffers jokingly claimed they would have to burn the office to the ground to prevent security leaks when Wizard finally retired.

Dulles sat hunched over his desk, a chain-smoking vulture, half hidden by tottering piles of paperwork. His suit had gone out of style with Elvis Presley and a Chesterfield dangled from one corner of the gash that served as his mouth. He waved them in without looking up from a report he was reading.

"Have a seat," he rasped.

Ezra had to move a stack of dossiers out of a chair for Gwen. He started to pile the folders on top of a filing cabinet but Wizard said, "Not there."

Instead, Ezra balanced them on the corner of Wizard's desk. Gwen lowered herself onto the seat. Ezra stood. He wasn't sure what to do with his hands. First he hooked his fingers in his pockets, but decided that might be disrespectful and clasped them behind his back instead like a soldier at parade rest.

Wizard took the cigarette from his mouth, exhaled a cloud of smoke, tapped ash into a cut-glass tray full of butts and returned the cigarette to his lips, without ever taking his eyes off the report. His unruly brows pinched and his mouth moved silently as he read, causing the glowing tip of the cigarette to jump and dip.

They waited.

He finished reading, closed the file, noticed a spot of ash on his tie and brushed it off before looking up. "How're you feeling, young lady?"

"Good." She pushed the glasses up the bridge of her nose. "I'm feeling just fine, sir. Thanks for asking."

Wizard scratched one eyebrow with a nicotine-stained fingertip. "I understand you two were instrumental in uncovering the illegal operations of Frank Bonner and Paris Station."

"Yes, sir," Gwen and Ezra answered in unison.

"And that you hacked the database in the process."

Ezra swallowed hard. "We were ordered to do that, sir."

"We thought we were acting under authorization from acting DDO Coughlin," Gwen added.

"No one's ever done that before," Wizard muttered to himself while rifling a stack of papers. "Technically, it's a federal crime."

"Sir," Gwen scooted to the edge of her seat. "The director cleared us of any wrongdoing."

Ezra tried to speak up but the words refused to come out. He felt rooted to the cigarette-burned carpet.

"Relax, Ms. Witwicky." Wizard waved away her concern. "I didn't bring you up here to discipline you. I'm putting together an operation and I need a couple of bright young go-getters like yourselves."

Ezra let out a breath. Gwen gave a nervous laugh that died on her lips.

Wizard brought out two sheets of paper and passed them over the desk. "Here are your new marching orders. Sign and date them."

Ezra scrawled his signature on the bottom without looking, added the date and passed it back, feeling like a man who'd just got a second lease on life. Gwen, of course, read over the whole document. While she examined the fine print, Ezra's attention strayed to the wall. He asked, "What is all this, sir?"

Wizard leaned back and studied him for a long moment before saying, "That, young man, represents my life's work."

CHAPTER SEVEN

WIZARD CRANKED HIMSELF OUT OF HIS CHAIR WITH A series of tired grunts, like an old engine struggling to turn over. He jabbed the glowing tip of his cigarette at the wall. "What you see here represents nearly forty years of counterintelligence work. Four decades of sifting the truth from all the lies and disinformation. To the untrained eye, it looks like so much randomness—that's the way it's meant to look — but there are clues hidden in there for the careful observer.

"For years now, I've been seeing a pattern in world affairs—a connecting thread tying together seemingly unrelated events. It all started in '79 with the Ayatollah Khomeini's rise to power. That's when I first began to suspect there was a guiding hand, an unseen force, manipulating events from the shadows. But to what purpose, I couldn't fathom. He's a master of subtle manipulation, whoever he is, and he plays a long game. Some of his machinations take years, even decades, but I've learned to recognize his fingerprints in the smallest details."

The DDO went on talking, more to himself than Ezra or Gwen. His steely gaze roamed over the wall while ribbons of smoke trailed from his cigarette. A rope of ash dropped to the threadbare carpet unnoticed.

Gwen watched the bent and wizened old figure, wondering if he was coming unglued. He wouldn't be the first operations officer to lose his marbles. The world of covert intelligence was a complex labyrinth of lies and deceit, a wilderness of mirrors, where no one was above suspicion. Play the game long enough and you start seeing double agents in every shadow. Every scrap of information is possible disinformation. When that happened, it was time to pack it in, but crazy people rarely know they're crazy. Some had to be forced into retirement. Others had to be institutionalized. Rumor had it there was a top-secret CIA nut house for spooks who lost their grip on reality. According to legend, some of the Company's top spymasters spent their twilight years in padded cells. Gwen didn't want to offend Wizard—she had tremendous respect for him—so she chose her words carefully. "And you think this... criminal mastermind... is behind all of these events?"

A smile hitched up one side of his weathered face. "You're wondering if Wizard has finally scrambled his noodle."

Gwen shook her head. "I didn't say that."

"You wouldn't be the first." Wizard noticed his cigarette had burned down to the filter and he stabbed it out. "A lot of people think I've outlived my usefulness. Foster thought I should be put out to pasture. He wasn't alone either. Of course, he was convicted of conspiracy and treason. It goes to show you..."

What it showed, Wizard never did say. He crossed behind his desk and lit another cigarette. "Starting now, you two are going to be working directly for me. I'm taking you off whatever you had going, effective immediately."

Ezra's relief at not being in trouble quickly evaporated. He glanced at the tangled web of intelligence reports tacked to the wall and said, "What exactly is it you want us to do, sir?"

Wizard handed them a newspaper article about a dead Secret Service agent. Ezra and Gwen put their heads together and read. The agent, P. Arthur Fellows, had been found hanging in a closet of the Hamilton Hotel on K Street. Authorities were ruling it an accidental death.

Gwen said, "Looks like he strangled himself."

Wizard brought them up to speed on his sushi dinner before passing a folder across the desk. The tan cover was marked with a red slash and stamped EYES ONLY. "I had our people in IMGINT scour the traffic cams around the hotel. They came up with this."

IMGINT is short for image intelligence. The experts who work in the IMGINT shop can look at satellite photos from space and tell you if an Arab man in baggy pajamas has a gun in his pocket or just a roll of dinars. During the Cold War, they were instrumental in keeping track of Russia's missile trains. The shop had diminished with the advent of heat signature and X-ray technology, but they're still a highly valued department within the halls of Langley. Ezra opened the folder and found a grainy photo of a woman leaving the Hamilton.

"The same woman I saw him with at Sushi Gakyu," Wizard told them.

Gwen said, "And you think she killed him?"

Wizard blew smoke. "She might be a prostitute. DC police are checking into that. It's possible this whole thing is coincidence. Maybe her john died, she got scared and split. But if she did, she hung around forty minutes and cleaned the room first. The coroner puts the time of death at 7:20 in the p.m. She didn't leave until almost eight."

Ezra asked, "Was his money still in his wallet?"

"No, she cleaned him out," Wizard admitted. "But that doesn't prove anything. If she's a pro she would take his money out of desperation, and a hired assassin would take the money to make it look like she was a hooker."

"So either way, she could still be an assassin," Gwen said.

Wizard nodded. "I want you two to walk back the cat on this mystery woman."

Gwen took the grainy traffic-cam photo from Ezra and puffed out her cheeks. "Where do you want us to start, sir?"

"Until we know otherwise, operate under the assumption that she's a hired assassin," Wizard told them. "Dig through FBI and Interpol databases. See if you can find a match. I want to know who she is and where she went after she left the hotel."

"Understood," Gwen said.

"We're on it," Ezra assured him

"It goes without saying, but this is considered top secret. Don't breathe a word of it to anyone outside this circle," Wizard told them. "Find an unused operation room and set up shop. I want regular updates."

"Yes, sir," they chorused before making their way down the hall to the first available mission control room. Ezra swiped through the door and Gwen swatted the light switch. Buzzing fluorescents flickered to life. Manhattan efficiency apartments have more square footage. The over-ripe smell of mold was enough to make Gwen's eyes water. A grime-encrusted coffee machine stood on a table in the corner and a bloated ceiling tile looked ready to give birth. The water-stained tile signaled a leak that had yet to be repaired. Probably hadn't even been reported. Protocol dictated Ezra and Gwen alert maintenance staff, but that meant repairmen coming and going while they conducted a top-secret operation. Instead they ignored the leak, powered up the computer terminals, and logged on to the server.

The last team to use the room had made off with the seating so Ezra had to steal a pair of rolling chairs from a nearby break room. Gwen leaned her crutches against her work station and plopped down in front of a computer. "Why do these things keep happening to us?"

"You feeling the same way I do?" Ezra asked.

She nodded. "Like we just stepped in it."

Ezra said, "Wizard is either a certifiable genius or just plain certifiable."

"I'm leaning toward the latter," Gwen said. "The guy is ancient. He should have retired a decade ago and taken up golf. Instead, he's got us chasing ghosts."

"Let's just ID this hooker and be done with it," Ezra said.

CHAPTER EIGHT

NOBLE SAT IN A PEW OF THE FIRST UNITED Methodist Church in downtown Saint Petersburg, staring up at a stained-glass reproduction of *The Last Supper*. The drowsy smell of incense hung thick in the air. Late afternoon sunlight—or was it early morning?—filtered in through the stained glass and combined with the eerie stillness to give the place a surreal, almost dreamlike, quality. Noble had been there since yesterday, or maybe it was the day before. His thoughts were jumbled. Time seemed to lag and leap. He propped his forearms on the pew in front of him and laced his fingers together. Stubble covered his cheeks and shaggy hair scraped the collar of his polo shirt. He had shed fifteen pounds since February—fifteen pounds he couldn't afford to lose—and dark eyes stared out of deep sockets set in a gaunt face. He fixed his gaze on the reproduction of Da Vinci's masterpiece and his mouth twisted into an ugly frown.

Why her? Noble asked. *Why her? Why not me?*

Silence was his only answer.

Noble had come here every morning since Sam died. He sat in the same hardwood pew, asking the same questions, and got the same answers. He drank himself to sleep most nights and woke up the next morning with a splitting headache and a hole in his chest where his heart should have been. He knew what he was doing was wrong. He knew he was only numbing the pain. Sooner or later he would have to deal with it, but he couldn't. He wasn't strong enough. Sam's death had left an emptiness deep inside him, a dark vacuum sucking up all the light. He needed to confront her death and find a way to cope but the wound was too raw.

Every time he closed his eyes, he saw her in those last precious seconds before she died.

Noble pinched the bridge of his nose between thumb and forefinger. "Don't go there."

He tried to pull himself out of the tailspin, but it was no good. Before he knew it, he was back on the river, feeling the deck roll beneath his feet and the icy spray hit him in the face. He saw Sam appear around the corner of the pilothouse. He tried to yell, tried to warn her, but he was too late. He heard the sharp whip-crack of the pistol and saw her eyes go wide. Then she was tumbling over the railing and into the dark waters. He heard the splash. It was like an invisible knife ripping his heart open.

Noble raked a hand through his hair and took a few deep breaths. He tried to force the images out, but they refused to go. The picture of Sam's face just before she fell was etched into his memory. Tears welled up in his eyes and doubled his vision. He didn't bother to wipe them away.

They'd just keep right on coming. He turned his attention back to the stained-glass image of Christ.

Why? Why did you let this happen? Why did she have to die? Speak to me!

His phone started vibrating. He dug it from his pocket and answered with a blunt, "Noble."

"Jake? Albert Dulles here. How you holding up, son?"

It was an effort to keep his voice steady. "Okay, I guess." After a beat he admitted, "I've been better."

"I was sorry to hear about Samantha Gunn," Wizard croaked out. "She was a good soldier. I wish I had been there. Maybe things would have turned out different."

Noble couldn't find any words. A thorny fist had a grip on his vocal cords and he fought back a fresh wave of tears.

Wizard took a drag from a cigarette—Noble heard the paper crackle—and exhaled. "You can't blame yourself, Jake."

"With all due respect, sir ... I'm the only one to blame."

"I been where you are, Jake. I've lost a lot of good men. In Nam, I gave the orders that sent twenty-two soldiers to their deaths. I lost seven more during the Cold War. I'm not going to tell you it gets easier. It doesn't. You've got a choice to make: You can get back in the saddle or spend every night on that boat, drinking yourself to death."

"How did you—" Noble started to ask.

"I told you," Wizard cut him off. "I've been there. I know what you're going through. I know all the guilt and the doubt and the anger and confusion. I know what it's like to drink yourself to sleep every night and wake up in the morning wondering if you've got the courage to eat a bullet, because that's the only thing that will make the pain stop.

But you can beat this, Jake. I know you can. You just have to get back in the game."

Noble passed a hand over his face. Everything Wizard said was right but hearing it only pissed Noble off. He said, "You didn't call to check up on me."

"I've got a job for you," Wizard said. "You interested?"

Noble sat there thinking. He was in no condition to work. He said, "I'm not your guy, sir. Find someone else."

"A Secret Service agent named P. Arthur Fellows was murdered three nights ago," Wizard told him. "The killer made it look like an accident. DC police have already tied off the investigation."

Curiosity got the better of him and Noble asked, "You got a line on the killer?"

"She's an international assassin known only as the Angel of Death."

"Sounds like a comic book character," Noble commented.

"She's wanted for six murders in six different countries and suspected of a dozen more," Wizard said. "I need someone who can run her to ground and find out who paid her. I want to know who had Fellows killed and why."

Noble's mind was already ticking over the problem. There was a puzzle in front of him—a mystery in need of an answer. Instinct did the rest. He asked, "Who's running point on this?"

"I've got operational command."

"Congressional oversight?" Noble asked.

"Not yet," Wizard admitted. "I want something solid before I climb the Hill for approval."

"I've been down this road before," Noble told him.

"She'll be long gone by the time those spineless turds on the Hill motivate themselves to action," Wizard said. "I need someone who can move fast and bend a few rules. I'll give you all the support I can, but I've got to know right now: Are you up to it?"

Noble chewed the inside of one cheek. He didn't feel up to anything. He'd spent the last two months drinking, but maybe this was the answer he was looking for? At the very least it would keep him busy and right now, he needed to get his mind off Sam. He let out a breath. "I'm in."

"Pack a bag," Wizard said. "There's a ticket under your name leaving out of Tampa International at 1:30."

"What time is it now?" Noble asked.

"11:15," Wizard informed him and rang off.

CHAPTER NINE

Twenty minutes later, Noble passed through the doors of the Wyndham Arms in downtown Saint Pete. It was like walking into an oven. An old man with cloudy eyes sat in a wheelchair close to a fake fireplace that radiated real heat. The lobby smelled strongly of Bengay and talcum powder. Brochures on the front desk advertised, "*A Safe Place for Active Seniors—We Treat Your Family Like Ours.*" The brochures didn't mention the cost of room and board, which could only be described as highway robbery.

Jake scrawled his signature in the visitor's log and went in search of Mary Elise Noble. He found her in the art room, hunched over a ball of wet clay on a spinning wheel. Frail, arthritic fingers worried at the soggy lump, but it kept collapsing in on itself. An art teacher, not much younger than the *"students,"* was busy making her own pot and giving instructions about how it was done.

Noble leaned over his mother's shoulder. "I don't think it will hold water."

"Well hello, stranger!" She let the runny mass of clay melt and the wheel slowed to a halt. "I'd be happy if I could get it to hold a *shape*."

Noble followed her to a sink. She rinsed off the clay and dried her hands on a towel before wrapping him up in a hug. "I was beginning to think you had forgotten about your old mother."

"Been busy," Noble lied. "How are you feeling?"

She stepped back and studied him with narrowed eyes. "I should be asking you that."

Noble got the feeling she could see right down into his soul. Mothers are like that. At least his was anyway. She always seemed to know just what he was thinking. He shifted his weight and stared at a spot on the floor, not sure how to start. He had come for advice but there was a lump in his throat the size of Rhode Island and he couldn't get his words out. His brow pinched.

She threaded an arm through his. "Let's take a walk."

Noble allowed himself to be led out into the sunshine of a small garden populated mostly with cacti and other succulents that can survive the harsh Florida summers.

His mom said, "What's up, bucko?"

Noble thought about how to answer that without divulging classified information. The job of covert intelligence doesn't lend itself to idle chat. Spooks can't go home at the end of the day and discuss work. It's a problem for the people who make their living as spies and an even bigger problem for the government agencies that deal in secrets. Human nature is to talk. Sooner or later, even the most battle-hardened spymaster has the urge to rehash the past.

For that very reason, the Company has several retirement communities scattered around the nation—places where former spooks can sit around the clubhouse and relive the glory days without exposing government secrets to the wrong person.

"I lost a soldier," Noble said at last. It was close enough to the truth. "An operation went bad. Someone died."

" 'There is a time and a season for everything,' " she quoted. " 'A time to be born and a time to die.' We don't get to choose when we go. God calls us home in His time."

"Well, it wasn't this person's time to die," Noble told her. "I planned the operation. I put her in harm's way. She's dead because of me."

"And you blame yourself?"

"There's no one else to blame," Noble said.

"Is that why you've been drinking so much?"

He nearly missed a step. "How'd you know?"

"I'm your mother," she said, as if that explanation alone should be enough.

"What's the Bible got to say about good people dying while evil people live?" Noble asked. It was a sign of how desperate he was. Normally he avoided any mention of God or the Bible around his mother. Once she got started, she could go on for hours.

"God sends rain on the just and the unjust alike."

Noble shook his head. "I don't want to hear that, Ma. A good person is dead. I want to know why. Aren't you the one who always tells me God works everything out for good? Where is the good in this?"

" 'And we know that God works all things together for

the good of those who serve Him, who are called according to His purpose,' " she quoted. "His ways are higher than ours, Jake. Sometimes we don't understand it. Often times we don't like it. But we can't see very far on this side of eternity."

Noble bit back an angry reply.

"Are you mad at yourself or at God?" she asked.

He thought about it. "Both, I guess."

"Have you tried talking to Him?"

He thought back over the last two months, every day sitting in the hardwood pew talking to God without answer. A bitter taste filled his mouth. "Yeah, I did, actually."

"And?"

"Instead of a word from God, I got a call from Langley."

"Maybe that's your answer," she told him.

They continued their lap of the garden and his mother said, "When do you leave?"

Noble checked his watch. "Couple of hours."

"When should I start getting nervous?"

He shook his head. "It's nothing dangerous."

She didn't believe the lie and let him know it without saying a word. "Be careful."

"I'd rather be lucky," Noble told her.

Every soldier is careful. Sam was careful. And she was dead. Another hard lump formed in his throat at the thought of her body lying at the bottom of the Seine. He fought back another onslaught of tears.

His mother turned to face him and took both of his hands in hers. Her skin felt like dry parchment paper. She said, "Would you like me to pray for you?"

The sadness evaporated in a hot flash of bitterness and anger.

"Sam prayed," Noble told her. "Right before she died. It didn't seem to help."

He slipped his hands free and made his way to the exit.

CHAPTER TEN

On the top floor of the Apollo Fund, headquartered in Bern, Otto Keiser pushed his wheelchair up to an expansive conference table of immaculately polished African blackwood. His top staff had gathered around the table, laptop computers open in front of them. Beyond the windows lay the stunning panorama of the Swiss Alps. The sawtooth ridges were capped with snow, but Keiser wasn't interested in the view. He studied a half dozen flat-screens showing a continuous stream of stock tickers and candlestick charts.

Steve Fellers was pitching a tech stock that had taken a hard dip over the last month. "This is the lowest it's been since the IPO and it has nowhere to go but up. Sources inside the company promise me they've got a new chipset that will rival Intel, but we need to move on this before they make a public announcement and everyone starts buying."

Keiser nodded. His double chins worked like a pair of fleshy bellows beneath pouting lips. "Buy a seven percent stake and increase it by a quarter percent every day until they announce the new hardware. Anyone else?"

A hand went up at the end of the table. Keiser waved for the young man to speak.

"Sir, Pelax Corp has taken a shellacking. Our analysts expect them to post an eight point two percent loss."

"How much have we got invested?" Keiser questioned.

"We have a three and a half percent stake in the company," the young man prompted.

"Sell it all."

"All at once, sir?"

"No reason to wait," Keiser said. "Soon as they post their yearly earnings, the stock will take a hit and we'll lose money."

"If we sell off all our holdings, it'll cause a panic, sir. Other stock holders will rush to sell and Pelax will go bankrupt."

"That's Pelax's problem," Keiser told him. "I'm not running a charity."

The young man rapped keys. Within moments, the sell order would go through. Other investors would see that Apollo, the largest private fund in the world, was dumping Pelax Corp. There would be a race to unload as average investors tried to pull out before Pelax hit rock bottom. Larger shareholders wouldn't be able to sell their stock in time and a handful of millionaires would find themselves bankrupt. Years ago, Keiser would have watched it happen, like a scientist injecting a virus into living tissue to observe the effects through a microscope. But bankrupting a handful of millionaires had lost its thrill. Watching an international company crumble was no more exciting than watching paint dry. Corporations rose and fell. Keiser was above it all, observing with casual disinterest, like an apathetic god viewing the machinations of man through the eons. He only reached down to move mountains when it benefitted him.

On the wall of flat-screens, Pelax's price fell from twenty-seven dollars a share to twenty-four, then twenty-two, twenty-one, twenty. After that, it went into a free fall. Investors unloaded as fast as they could and the price of the company plummeted, bottoming out at four dollars and twenty-seven cents a share.

Steve Fellers made a low whistle that ended with an explosion. Someone else chuckled.

Keiser had already turned to more important matters. He checked the figures on his private work station and said, "Short another hundred million in US dollars."

Linda Bhakti's hand shot up. Bhakti was the newest edition to Keiser's team of analysts. She had recently graduated from the Hong Kong School of Finance and showed real promise.

"Speak," Keiser barked.

"Sir, Quantum Fund has been shorting a lot of dollars lately. So much so that IBD and other sources are starting to speculate."

"What of it?" Keiser grumbled.

"Well, sir, there are no indicators of trouble in the American economy and no one expects the dollar to go anywhere but up."

Unruly grey brows bunched together over the bridge of Keiser's nose. "Is that a question or a statement, Ms. Bhakti?"

"Sir, we've shorted over three hundred trillion in the US dollar in the last few weeks." Bhakti paused to adjust her glasses and continued. "The prevailing opinion on Wall Street is that we are buying in anticipation of a sell-off."

"What's your point?"

"We have a duty to protect our clients' investments, sir." Bhakti said, "If you are wrong, you'll bankrupt the fund."

Keiser slammed a beefy fist down on the tabletop and levered his bulk out of the wheelchair. Spindly legs trembled under the strain of holding up his corpulent mass. Keiser kept himself on his feet through sheer force of will. His face turned red. His eyes bulged. "Don't tell me how to run my own fund! I made my first billion in this business before you were even a wish in your mother's heart. Nations rise and fall because I allow it. I don't need you to tell me what's at stake!"

The meeting room sat in stunned silence at the sudden outburst.

Keiser thrust one trembling finger at the door. "Clear out your desk."

Linda Bhakti sat there, her eyes magnified by her glasses, unable to speak.

"Now!" Keiser barked.

She got up and fled the meeting.

Otto Keiser settled his corpulent body back into the chair and adjusted his tie. "Anyone else have a problem with the way I run things?"

The question was met by silence.

"Then we're done for the day," Keiser said. "I want you all here bright and early. Remember, money never sleeps!"

The meeting room cleared out and Keiser took a

moment to compose himself. Though he hated to admit it, Bhakti was right about one thing: People were starting to speculate. He would have to lean on the editor at *Investor's Business Daily*. It wouldn't do to start a panic. Not yet anyways.

His phone chimed and Keiser checked the caller ID. It was an encrypted line. Only Keiser's closest associates had the number. He thumbed the green button and put the phone to his ear. "How is our latest venture coming along, my young friend?"

"Everything is just fine. That little problem in Washington has been taken care of."

"Excellent," Keiser said. "Then I think our contract employee has outlived her usefulness at this point, don't you?"

"Agreed."

"You will make certain she doesn't violate her nondisclosure agreement?"

"Consider it done."

"I'll leave the details up to you," Keiser said and hung up.

CHAPTER ELEVEN

Noble landed in DC just after three o'clock. He picked up a rental from the airport and crossed Key Bridge toward Langley. Rain was coming down in sideways sheets that tried to rip the little Hyundai right off the highway. Noble motored along the George Washington Memorial Parkway to Dolley Madison Boulevard and almost missed the turnoff to CIA headquarters. Pranksters had carried off the sign again. Nice to know some things never changed.

As a non-official cover operative, Noble had no credentials and no parking pass. He was forced to join a line of cars at the main gate where a guard, dressed in black fatigues with an MP5 slung across his chest, inspected driver's licenses. Another man used a mirror on a stick to search for explosives. A pair of German shepherds sat on their haunches, soaked to the bone and seemingly oblivious to the rain. Their yellow eyes watched the vehicles, noses twitching and ears perked. The taillights in front of Noble winked and flashed as the line crept forward. When he got to the front, Noble switched off his wipers, buzzed the window down and gave the guard his name, along with a prearranged code phrase.

The guard, water dripping off the bill of his cap, plugged the information into a handheld tablet and waited. Icy droplets blew in through the open window, landing on Noble's shoulder while the guard compared Noble to his photo in CIA database. His eyes narrowed at the gaunt figure in the rental car and then went back to the Company photo.

"I've been sick," Noble lied.

"Uh huh." The guard didn't sound convinced, but waved Noble through.

Rain continued to lash the windshield as Noble swung into an empty parking space and switched off the engine. He double-timed it to the front entrance. It was a wasted effort. He was thoroughly soaked by the time he reached the safety of the overhang.

Inside, he went through another round of security checks before crossing over the CIA emblem on the marble floor. He stopped at the memorial wall. Three new stars had been added in the last twelve months. One for Torres. Another for Sam. The third represented the corrupt Frank Bonner. Noble paused and stretched out trembling fingers to touch Sam's star. The simple impression struck in the stone was the only testament to her sacrifice. Battery acid filled his mouth. His stomach wanted to empty its contents all over the floor. He took a few deep breaths. He was struggling for control of himself when he caught a whiff of smoke.

Wizard stood near the bank of elevators, looking like the

specter of death in a slim black suit and a knitted tie. A cigarette dangled from thin lips and a file folder was clamped under one spindly arm. Sharp blue eyes studied Noble from beneath scraggly gray brows.

People muttered under their breath about the presence of a cigarette in a clearly marked no-smoking zone. Others, who knew better, remarked on the sudden appearance of the legend in the flesh. "They call him the Wizard," someone hissed. "... since the Cold War ... " someone else was saying. "... spymaster ..."

Wizard ignored the whispers, crossed the floor and stuck out a gnarled hand. He had a surprisingly strong grip for a man of his age. "Good to have you back, Jake."

"Thank you, sir."

"I wish it was under better circumstances."

What could Noble say to that? *If wishes were horses, beggars would ride.* That's what his mother would say. Noble simply ducked his head. "Thanks."

"Let's not waste time shooting the bull." Wizard jerked his head at the bank of elevators.

The crowd edged away, giving them a car to themselves, and Noble realized not all the whispers were about Wizard. Some were about him. "... Jake Noble ...," he heard someone say. "... wiped out the Los Zetas Cartel ..." And "... took down Frank Bonner ..."

The corrupt chief of Paris station was classified top-secret/eyes only, so naturally everybody at Langley knew. It was surprisingly hard to keep secrets in a place where keeping secrets was a part of the job.

Wizard thumbed the button for seven and the doors

rolled shut, sealing out the crowd. In a casual tone, he asked, "How's our friend Sacha Duval?"

"Safe," Noble told him. "How's the director handling it?"

Wizard shrugged. "She's coming to terms with it."

Armstrong hadn't asked about the infamous hacker since the fallout in Paris. Duval was still on America's most-wanted list. If the Company knew where he was, they would be forced to do something about it. Noble had stashed Duval and ordered him not to make contact unless his life was in danger.

Wizard passed Noble the file folder he'd been holding. "Here's everything we have so far," he said. "Friday morning, a Secret Service officer named P. Arthur Fellows turned up dead in a hotel room on K Street. DC police are still operating under the assumption it was an accidental death, but we have reason to believe he was killed by this woman."

Noble flipped open the folder and found a grainy traffic cam photo of a knockout in a slinky green dress leaving the Hamilton. Her face was hidden by Jackie O. sunglasses and a curtain of red hair. Noble leafed through the file. The assassin had landed on the CIA's radar when she murdered a Bolivian colonel. She was the prime suspect in a dozen other high-profile assassinations over the last decade. Noble turned to her profile page at the very back:

Name: *Unknown*
> *Alias*: ANGEL OF DEATH
> *Age*: *Unknown*
> *Height*: *Unknown*

Weight: Unknown
Sex: Female
County of Origin: Unknown
Ethnicity: Unknown
Family Background: Unknown

"That's a lot of unknowns," Noble remarked.

Wizard agreed with a grunt. "My team of analysts has spent the last three days putting together a profile and tracking her movements. We now know she works out of South Africa and we've got a line on her cutout. I'll let the analysts fill you in on the rest."

The car stopped on seven. Wizard, trailing smoke, led the way to a situation room. He used his laminated ID card on the door. It unlocked with an electronic chirp and the deadbolt released.

Noble recognized the pair of analysts from a run-in they'd had down in Mexico City and, judging by their expressions, they remembered him as well.

"This is Gwendolyn Witwicky and Ezra Cook," Wizard was saying.

The computer nerds froze like a pair of mice who had just spotted a cat.

Wizard took in their expressions and said, "Looks like you three already know each other?"

"We've crossed paths," Noble said.

"Good," Wizard said. "You're going to be working together."

CHAPTER TWELVE

Gwen felt like she had just stepped into a cage with a hungry lion. Jake Noble had been a dangerous fugitive the last time they had met. Gwen and Ezra had been sent to Mexico to apprehend him. It was their first real field assignment, and it didn't end well. Noble had taken away their guns with the ease of a man reaching for toilet paper and left them stranded. Gwen and Ezra had spent the next six months in the Company doghouse, debugging lines of code.

They both managed awkward nods in his direction.

Noble acknowledged them with the barest thrust of his chin. "Give me the short version," he said. "What do we know about her?"

Gwen turned to her computer and started rattling off information. "She's responsible for six deaths that we know of and we suspect her in twelve more. She's not your run-of-the-mill trigger for hire. She makes all her kills look like accidents. That's sort of her specialty."

"Anything I can't get from her jacket?" Noble asked and slapped the file down on a nearby desk.

"We're working to collate info on her now." Ezra rapped keys and brought up a number of surveillance photos. "We scoured the streets around the hotel where P. Arthur Fellows was killed and came up with a number of surveillance photos. We showed these images to our guys—"

"And girls," Gwen interjected.

"And girls," Ezra added, "down in IMGINT. Based on height, weight, and bone structure, they believe she's Eastern European."

"That narrows it right down," Noble muttered.

"She's also got an ankle tattoo," Gwen said. She brought up an enlargement on her screen and pointed with her pinkie. "You can just make out the dark mark on her left ankle in this shot."

Noble leaned over her shoulder and Gwen edged away. Her heart began a rapid tap dance in her chest. It was like having a jungle cat crouched on her shoulder. "The IMGINT techs assure us the red hair is a wig," Gwen managed to say. "You can tell by the—"

"I'll take their word for it," Noble said. He stood up and crossed his arms. "What else can you tell me?"

"Age anywhere between twenty-six and thirty-three," Ezra supplied. "Weight approximately one-twenty. Height five-ten. We think she might—"

Noble cut him off. "I just need to know where to find her."

"You start in South Africa," Wizard rasped. He took a bottle of pills from his coat pocket, shook a pair into his open palm and dry-swallowed. Tears welled up in his eyes, but he went on talking. "I spoke to the Chief of Station down in JoBurg—woman by the name of Hadley—she's been working that desk for a decade now. Nothing happens down there without her knowing about it. Her intel suggests Angel operates out of Johannesburg, but that's about all we have."

"Johannesburg is a big place," Noble remarked.

"We've collected surveillance footage from all the major airports along the East Coast," Wizard said. "Cook and Witwicky are going to walk back the cat, see if they can't find out when and where the assassin entered the country and then retrace her movements. Hopefully, they'll have something by the time you land.

"The boys downstairs in the Alibi Shop are putting together a legend for you as we speak. You're an American businessman living in Australia. You've got a rival you need out of the picture. Think you can handle it?"

"Shouldn't be too hard," Noble said. "Have we reached out to the Secret Service? Found out if P. Arthur Fellows was working on anything that might have gotten him killed?"

"They're not cooperating," Wizard said. "Head of the Secret Service is busy trying to sweep the whole thing under the rug. He doesn't want the press finding out one of his investigators was a pervert."

"Not even if helping us would clear Fellows's name?" Gwen asked.

"This is DC," Wizard said. "No one remembers the retraction, only the headline. I'll keep trying, but I doubt the Secret Service is going to hand over Fellows's case files."

Gwen shook her head in frustration.

Wizard handed one of the new surveillance photos to Noble. "Take a good look. That's your target."

Noble held the photo up to the light and chewed the inside of one cheek.

"And remember, this operation is EYES ONLY," Wizard said.

"What's the op name?" Gwen wanted to know.

"MOUSETRAP," Wizard supplied. It was impossible to know if he had already run it through the database that assigns random code words or came up with it on the spot. He turned to Noble. "You're wheels-up in ninety minutes. Head downstairs to the Alibi Shop to collect your ID and pocket litter."

"Weapons?"

"Hadley has arranged everything. There'll be a package waiting for you at the hotel in Joburg."

Noble nodded and let himself out of the room. When he had gone, Wizard turned to Ezra and Gwen. "Keep a close eye on him."

CHAPTER THIRTEEN

ELIŠKA CERMÁKOVA STOOD UNDER A HOT SHOWER, letting the warm water relax her aching muscles. She arched her back and ran her head under the spray. It was good to be out of the wig. When she had used up every bit of hot water, she twisted the knobs and reached for a towel. She had flown out of Dulles International before P. Arthur Fellows's death had even hit the morning edition and hopscotched around the globe until she made her way back to Johannesburg.

She lived in a modest farmhouse northeast of the city on a few acres of mostly undeveloped land. It was a rugged affair, with flagstone floors and exposed beams. The furniture was all secondhand and, except for the kitchen, in a generally sad state. An assortment of wigs, makeup, and a few prosthetics filled a spare bedroom. Eliška had a card that listed her as a member in good standing with the South African film industry. The few neighbors within visiting distance were under the impression that she worked in wardrobe design, which explained her odd hours and long absences.

A wolf dog provided security. When Eliška wasn't home, he lived on field mice and jackrabbits. She hadn't bothered naming the beast, knowing one day she would leave and not come back. But the dog was always happy to see her and it was nice having someone to come home to.

Eliška dried her hair, wrapped the towel around herself and walked into the living room, where patio doors looked out over rugged scrubland. The sun was a bright-orange disk in the west. Dust motes danced in the spill of warm sunlight. The wolf dog trotted past the doors with his tail in the air and his nose down, on the trail of a curious scent.

She did a cursory check of the mail. The house was owned by one of her fake identities and rented out to another, so it was mostly junk and circulars. She tossed the whole pile into the bin, opened the refrigerator, and poured herself a glass of dark-red wine.

Her first instinct had been to fly to Prague directly and check on Papa, but her employer probably had eyes on the old man. He would expect her to do just that. Instead, Eliška had returned home while she worked out a plan. She needed to keep the American off-balance.

She carried her glass into the living room and covered the ratty sofa with her towel before sinking into the soft leather. She had spent the whole flight considering her next move. Now she went over the plan in her head. It wasn't perfect. There were a lot of moving parts—a lot could go wrong—but it was the best she had. She put her glass down on the coffee table, reached for the burner phone and dialed the preset number.

Bob picked up after a dozen rings. "I was wondering when you'd be calling. I saw the papers. Good work, as usual."

"I want the rest of the money and then I'm out."

"A deal's a deal," the American told her. "Meet me at the café. I'll be there in two hours with the rest of your wages."

"Tonight is no good," Eliška told him. "I'll be there tomorrow at noon."

He hesitated only a fraction of a second. "That works for me."

Eliška hung up without saying goodbye.

A laptop sat on the scarred oak coffee table. Eliška booted the machine, opened a web browser, and brought up a series of websites. She was searching for something very specific.

CHAPTER FOURTEEN

Lucas Randall sat beneath the shade of an umbrella, sipping coffee loaded with cream and sugar from a ceramic mug. The South African sun beat down, turning the sidewalks into shimmering white mirages that played tricks on the eyes. April is a fall month in Johannesburg, when the heat of summer gives way to milder temperatures and cool nights, but the elevation and a subtropical climate keep the UV index high.

Randall wore a linen suit, hat, and shades to protect his skin from the brutal sunlight. A phone lay on the table next to his coffee cup. He scanned a newspaper article about redistribution of farmland as reparation for apartheid being proposed by the South African government, while keeping one eye on the street. A gleaming black Cadillac backed into a parallel spot and the driver's side door hinged open. Randall brought the paper up to cover his face and peered over the top. A tall blonde in a short red skirt, thick denim jacket, and Jackie O. sunglasses climbed out. She was hard to miss, even from half a football field away. Randall lifted the phone and dialed. He heard the connection and said, "Blonde hair. Red miniskirt."

Cermáková looked both ways before starting across the boulevard. She was in the middle of the street when a Ford Explorer swung out into traffic and gunned the engine. The assassin glanced over her shoulder in time to see the SUV barreling down on her. She disappeared under the front grille with a muffled *thump* that got lost in the high-pitch scream of terrified onlookers. The Explorer hurtled through the intersection, mowing down two more pedestrians. An unlucky bicyclist went sailing over the hood, limbs splayed out like an aerial acrobat before crash-landing in a heap on the asphalt.

The crowd at the outdoor café stood up with a collective gasp. Several people had their phones out, dialing emergency services. One woman broke down in hysterical sobs. Traffic backed up as motorists got out to administer first aid.

The blonde in the red miniskirt lay in a tangle of shattered limbs with her head turned the wrong way on a broken neck. The Jackie O. sunglasses had landed in the gutter. Blood pooled around her mangled body and her face was fixed in a frozen scream.

Randall lit a cigarette as he strolled away from the café. That took care of Cermáková. He didn't feel particularly good about the death of Fellows, or the assassin for that matter, but you have to set the world on fire if you want to reshape it. And that's exactly what Randall meant to do— set the world on fire so he could remold it closer to the heart's desire. Fellows and Cermáková were simply the first two dominoes in complex effort to lead humanity into a better tomorrow. Sacrifices had to be made.

Randall left the shopping arcade and cut across two blocks to a waiting Jeep Cherokee. Eric Veers was in the driver's seat with his jaw set and his knuckles white on the steering wheel. He was a former *Bundesmarine* Captain with short-cut hair slowly turning to grey and deeply tanned skin. He waited for Randall to shut the passenger door before motoring away from the curb.

Sirens were blasting in the distance.

Eric spoke German, "It's done?"

"It's done," Randall told him.

"And the driver of the van?" Eric asked.

"A two-bit hood," Randall said. "Can't be traced back to us, if that's what you're worried about."

"That's not what's bothering me," Veers said. "I didn't sign on for murder."

"She was a cold-blooded killer," Randall told him. "The world is a better place without her."

"And the American policeman?" Veers asked.

"Secret Service agent," Randall corrected him and then said, "Collateral damage."

Veers shook his head as he piloted the Jeep through traffic. "I hope we're doing the right thing."

Randall rolled down his window, stuck his cigarette out and flicked ash. "Don't go soft on me, Eric. Not now. We're at the five-yard line, man. In a few days, the world is going to be a very different place."

"You know I'm on board," Veers said. "Just promise me no more law enforcement. We're supposed to be the good guys, remember?"

"It's all over now," Randall told him. "The wheels are in motion."

"We still have a lot of cargo to move," Eric reminded him.

Randall shrugged. "The hard part is done."

CHAPTER FIFTEEN

JAQUELINE ARMSTRONG WAS IN THE BACK SEAT OF A black Lincoln Towncar headed west across the Potomac toward Langley. The rain had finally let up and the sun poked through banks of iron-grey clouds. Armstrong had her hair up and held in place by a plastic clip. A pencil-stripe skirt revealed a pair of toned thighs. She was somewhere over forty, under fifty, and looked younger than her age, but crow's feet were starting around her eyes.

She had just finished briefing the president on a possible defector inside the Iranian regime. The commander in chief was enthusiastic about the potential intelligence coup but hesitant to greenlight a crossing. In the end, they had decided to run the agent in place as long as possible, which wouldn't be too long. The radical factions running Iran were paranoid about security, but Armstrong had promised to do her best.

A stack of newspapers lay on the leather seat next to her. The head of her personal security detail, Duc Hwang, had picked them up while she was in the Oval Office. The *New York Times* was running a story about a Secret Service officer who had accidentally hanged himself. Armstrong tossed that aside. Underneath, she found an *Investor's Business Daily* with the headline, *"BILLIONAIRE INVESTMENT BANKER SHORTING THE US DOLLAR."* She folded the paper over and scanned the article.

"He must know something I don't," she muttered.

Duc glanced in the rearview. He was a squat Korean with jet-black hair and a beard that stuck out like a steel bristle brush. Massive shoulders strained the seams of his black suit jacket. A former Navy SEAL, Duc had made the leap to CIA and ended up on Armstrong's protective detail. He said, "What's that?"

Armstrong shook her head. "I was talking to myself."

Duc nodded and returned his attention to the road.

Armstrong made a mental note to have a talk with her investment advisor. The economy was roaring along and the dollar wasn't showing any signs of weakness, but economic realities can change faster than the weather. The likelihood the dollar would crash was slim, but stranger things had happened. Armstrong didn't want her retirement to evaporate if the US dollar tanked.

Ten minutes later, they passed through the security checkpoints at Langley and Duc piloted the Towncar down the ramp to the garage. He parked and Armstrong folded the IBD under her arm before riding her private elevator up to seven.

Her secretary, a legacy named Ginny Farnham, held out a stack of folders marked with a red slash and EYESONLY. Farnham's hair was pulled back in a strict bun and her mouth turned down in a perpetual frown. She greeted Armstrong with the barest of nods.

Armstrong accepted the stack without a word on her way past. Their relationship was one of polite hostility. Armstrong didn't like Farnham very much. Farnham liked Armstrong even less, but they were both professionals.

Armstrong pushed the door to her office open with her hip. The DCI's private space was lined with leather-bound books lit by track lighting. Double-paned windows looked out over the parking lot and a pair of sofas flanked a low table. A smoke-eater hummed in one corner. Armstrong dropped the pile of folders on her desk, kicked off her shoes, and started at the bottom of the stack. She had been doing this long enough to know Farnham would shuffle the most pressing business to the bottom just to make life difficult. Sure enough, she found two urgent communiqués from agents in North Korea and a sticky note about Cook and Witwicky.

Leaning back in her seat, she gazed up at the ceiling and tried to place the names. She had over five thousand employees under her command at Langley and twice that number overseas. Then it struck her—the Sacha Duval affair. Cook and Witwicky had blown the case wide open. They would both be up for intelligence commendation medals if they hadn't also broken into the CIA mainframe in the process.

Armstrong made a few calls and learned that Wizard had personally requested the analysts for an intelligence-gathering operation codenamed MOUSETRAP. She buzzed Dulles's interior line and waited for him to pick up. "Al? Can I see you a minute?"

He arrived in her office seconds later, a five-foot-seven smoking vulture in a black suit with stooped shoulders.

She didn't bother to mention the cigarette. Armstrong was a smoker and kept the machine running to clean the air. She waved him to a seat. "Got a notice from Moberly says you poached Cook and Witwicky for a new project?"

Wizard nodded. "He's got more than enough gnomes down there in the basement. They won't be missed. Besides, I should only need them another day or two at most."

"What's operation MOUSETRAP?"

He plucked the cigarette from his mouth. "You really want to know?"

She leaned back in her seat and crossed her arms. "This isn't the sixties, Al. You can't run unsanctioned operations without congressional oversight. Have you heard of the Church hearings?"

A lopsided grin turned up one side of his mouth. "Relax, Director. It's an intelligence-gathering operation."

"I hope so," Armstrong said. "If you're laying in a special operation without my knowledge, we'd be having a whole different conversation."

"Nothing like that," Wizard assured her. "I need a couple of computer cowboys to collect intel on a suspected terror group operating out of South Africa."

"Does the Chief of Station in South Africa know about this?"

Wizard inclined his head. "She gave me the tip that started the dominoes tumbling."

"Why do I get the feeling you're holding out on me?"

"Suspicion is built into the job description."

Armstrong fixed him with a hard stare. Wizard held her

gaze. A contest of wills was pointless. The man could stare a hole through a brick wall if he set his mind to it. Armstrong broke off and rearranged the papers on her desk. "This better not blow up in my face."

"Like I said, I'm just putting together information." He took a drag and asked, "What did the president decide about our friend in Iran?"

"He wants us to run her in place for now."

"That's a dangerous gambit," Wizard croaked. "China? Sure. Russia? No problem. But Iran? Easier said than done."

"Which is why I want you to lay in the plumbing for a defection," Armstrong told him. "I want the pipeline ready and waiting if this goes bad."

"I'll get right on it," Wizard said and cranked himself out of the chair.

She watched him go. Wizard liked to play things close to the vest. He was a veteran of the Cold War, a holdover from the days when the CIA had been infiltrated by Soviet spies. It had been a dark time. Top-secret information was finding its way back to the Kremlin and good agents wound up dead. Wizard had lived through the worst of it. He had lost friends to the Red Menace. It had ingrained certain habits into him that he couldn't let go of. Because of that, he never told the whole truth to anybody. He probably kept secrets from himself. And it was becoming a problem. Wizard liked to run his shop as if it were an independent organization from the rest of the CIA. But that was the old way of doing things. The new CIA was an interconnected organism When Wizard's shop refused to cooperate and share info, it hurt the organization as a whole. Armstrong considered the fact that Wizard might be past his sell-by date. It wasn't the first time the thought had crossed her mind. She briefly thought about walking down the hall to the situation room. It would be easy enough to poke her head in and ask Cook and Witwicky what they were working on, but part of her was afraid to know the answer. The phone rang, pushing the issue to the back of her mind.

CHAPTER SIXTEEN

EZRA AND GWEN WERE LESS THAN THRILLED TO BE working on an operation without congressional oversight, even if it was laid in by the DDO. Their varied careers with the Company thus far had taught them to keep their heads down, avoid notice, and not make waves. Other analysts considered the pair trouble on four legs. Of course, Gwen and Ezra didn't go looking for trouble; it just seemed to find them. Both had been surprised and a little anxious when the DDO tapped them for a special assignment. Apprehension had turned to dread when Jake Noble walked into the situation room. No good could come of any mission involving Jake Noble—even if he was on the other side of the globe.

"Did you see the look in his eyes?" Gwen asked.

"Did I see it?" Ezra shuddered. "I nearly crapped my pants when he walked through the door."

"He looked mad," Gwen said. "Like he wanted the whole world to burn."

"Guy like that probably does," Ezra commented.

Gwen agreed with the assessment.

They had spent most of the night combing through countless hours of footage from every major airport up and down the East Coast. They finally found what they were looking for at JFK. A brunette had flown into New York the day before Fellows was killed. An IMGINT tech made a positive ID. The assassin had entered the States on a Canadian passport under the name Elizabeth Michaels. From there, it was relatively easy to retrace her movements as she bounced around the globe.

They called Wizard just after seven in the morning to let him know they had picked up the assassin's trail. The wizened old operations officer appeared in the situation room moments later. A cigarette dangled from the corner of his mouth and a cloud of smoke trailed after him. "What have you got?"

"Our intel on South Africa was correct," Gwen said. "She flew out of Johannesburg under the name Elizabeth Krantz."

Ezra picked up the narrative. "In Paris, she was Erzabet Markowitz."

"And in Canada, she was Bethany Mitchel," Gwen finished. "And get this: Liza Krantz owns a house in a rural town north of Johannesburg which she rents out to an Elizabeth Michaels."

"So her real name is probably Elizabeth or something close," Wizard concluded.

Ezra and Gwen nodded.

It's common practice for field agents to assume fake identities with the same, or at least similar, first names as their real-life counterpart. A field officer who responds to the wrong name in a foreign country ends up in jail awaiting trial for espionage. To avoid that mistake, agents are given legends that closely match their true identity. A CIA officer named Jessica Burns might be sent to the Ukraine under the name Jenika Burkov.

"That's good work." Wizard shot smoke from both nostrils. "Noble's plan should be landing about now. He'll check in soon. Let him know what you found."

"Yes, sir," Ezra said.

"Um, sir," Gwen said and swiveled around in her chair to face the DDO. "Are we sure Jake Noble is the right man for this operation?"

Ezra shot her a warning look but Gwen ignored it. Her career had been sidetracked one too many times by Jake Noble. She didn't want to end up in hot water again when he went off the rails, which was only a matter of time in Gwen's estimation.

Wizard plucked the cigarette from his mouth and blew smoke up to the ceiling where it formed a lazy halo around the buzzing fluorescents. "What's on your mind, Ms. Witwicky?"

"Well sir," Gwen began, searching for the right words. "It's just that he looks a little ..."

"Unhinged," Ezra finished for her.

Wizard sized up the two analysts before saying, "Jake Noble was in love with Samantha Gunn."

Ezra and Gwen sat there in stunned silence, staring at the DDO.

Wizard said, "He was there the night she was killed. He watched her die."

They both knew Samantha Gunn was dead and they had heard rumors it was somehow tied to the affair that had put Gwen in the hospital, but they had never gotten the full story. The operation, and the events surrounding it, were classified. It was more than either of their jobs were worth to go digging.

Gwen said, "I'm sorry. I didn't know."

Wizard gazed off into the distance, like he was looking into the past, or maybe he was peering into the future. For a moment, he looked even older and more stooped, like the weight of the job was dragging him down. He abruptly straightened up and said, "Keep digging on Elizabeth Krantz and see what you can turn up on P. Arthur Fellows. Call me if anything breaks."

Then he was gone, leaving behind the overpowering stench of cigarettes.

Gwen turned to Ezra. "Did you know about Sam and Jake?"

"No, and I can hardly believe it. Sam with Noble? The guy is a walking time bomb." He turned to Gwen. "Can you think of any reason Sam Gunn would like Jake Noble?"

A resounding *no* started up from her chest but got lost somewhere along the way. Gwen turned back to her computer screen and pushed the glasses up the bridge of her nose. All girls say they want a nice guy who treats them with respect, but that's just talk. Ezra was a nice guy and women weren't exactly flocking to him. What girls really want is a guy who can protect them. Girls fall for the bad boy type, not because they're attracted to danger, but because the bad boy can take care of himself. Jake Noble might not be a conversationalist, but a girl could feel safe around him. He reminded Gwen of an untamed lion roaming the Serengeti. He wasn't looking for a fight, but if a jackal came calling, the lion would unleash hell. And the more she thought about it, the more that primal, untamed fury appealed to something deep inside her. She realized she was blushing and muttered, "Maybe a little."

CHAPTER SEVENTEEN

NOBLE TOOK A CAB FROM THE AIRPORT INTO THE HEART of Johannesburg, where he spent the next two hours running a surveillance detection route. It was just after two in the afternoon and the sun was a brilliant white eye overhead, banishing shadows and turning the streets to shimmering mirages. He squinted against the blinding light and sweat pasted his cotton polo to his back. He felt like a man trekking across the Sahara. He strolled the sidewalks, stopped in front of department store windows, turned down-trash strewn alleys, and doubled back to throw off pursuit. He had no reason to believe he was being followed, but he did the SDR out of habit. Better safe than sorry. Besides, it gave him a chance to familiarize himself with the city.

Johannesburg is one of the last great boomtowns of the late nineteenth century. Located more than five thousand feet above sea level, prospectors found gold here in 1885. Ten years later, the mining camp had swollen to a city of over one hundred thousand souls. The British took over after the Boer War and it's been a city characterized by race relations ever since. Whites had enforced strict segregation through apartheid until the early nineties, when blacks had risen to power and they had set about punishing whites through reparations. Turnabout, it would seem, was fair play.

The city's architecture reflected the turbulent history. Neighborhoods were clearly segregated. Glass and-concrete skyscrapers loomed over shanty towns where reeking piles of garbage filled the curbs.

When he was sure he hadn't been followed, Noble stopped in a sunglasses shop, bought a pair of Ray-Bans, and then made his way to the Legacy Guest Lodge on Fortesque Road. The place was in bad need of a facelift. The lobby was a mixture of opulent and shabby and told the story of a swank hotel past its prime. Pink marble pillars supported a whitewashed ceiling of cracked wainscoting. Thick cobwebs clung to a dusty chandelier. A bored desk clerk managed a half-hearted smile as Noble entered. He had skin so dark it was nearly blue and eyes tinged with yellow. "Checking in, sir?"

"You'll find the reservation under Jacob Goodman."

"Fifth floor okay?"

"Second floor would be better," Noble told him. "Preferably close to the stairs and away from the elevator."

The clerk ran Noble's credit card and handed him a room key.

"You should have a package for me," Noble said. "Some product samples."

The clerk disappeared into the storage room and

returned with a FedEx container roughly the same size and shape as a cereal box. He passed it to Noble and instructed him to enjoy his stay. Noble had been told to go to hell and die with more enthusiasm. He turned toward the elevator and spotted a stack of newspapers on the counter with the headline, DEADLY HIT AND RUN.

An unidentified driver behind the wheel of a Ford Explorer had plowed through a crowd of pedestrians near a busy shopping arcade, killing two people and injuring three more. There was a picture of the carnage and, below the fold, two headshots of the victims. One was a young black man who had been riding his bicycle. All of sixteen years old. The other was a blonde in her late twenties. The caption beneath the photo read, *Elizabeth Michaels was pronounced dead at the scene.*

"It's free," the clerk said.

Noble looked up, a frown fixed on his face. "What?"

"The paper," the clerk said. "It's free. You can take it."

"Thanks." Noble tucked the paper under one arm, rode the elevator up to the second floor, and let himself into a moldy room with a small balcony and a bed covered in stiff sheets. If the lobby need a facelift, the room needed a complete overhaul. Grime crusted the shower floor and the whole place smelled of mothballs. Noble tossed his carry-on and the FedEx box down on the bedspread and took out his phone. He waited through a dozen rings before Gwendolyn Witwicky's voice came on the line. "Goodman and Associates. How may I direct your call?"

"It's me," Noble told her. "I just landed."

"Oh hi, boss! What time is it there?" Gwen asked.

It was part of a prearranged call and response.

Noble consulted the Tag Heuer on his wrist. "It's four-thirty local time."

If Noble had been followed, or captured, he would have told Gwen he had forgotten to update his watch. The emergency code would let Langley know he had been arrested and was being played back, in which case they would cut off all communication.

With the call and response complete, Gwen said, "Glad you're safe. Going secure."

There was a series of clicks and she came back on the line. "Good news. We were able to pick up the assassin's trail and trace her all the way back to South Africa. We've got a name and an address."

"Let me guess," Noble said. "Elizabeth Michaels?"

"How did you know that?"

"I'm looking at a copy of the *Daily Sun*," Noble told her. "Elizabeth Michaels was killed early this morning in a hit-and-run accident."

There was silence on the other end of the phone while Gwen processed that information. Noble tucked the phone between his ear and shoulder, ripped open the FedEx box and emptied the contents onto the bed. Inside was a half dozen tiny microdot transmitters hidden inside a folder labeled "Inventory Management" and disguised as the quality-assurance stickies you find on garments in department stores. There was also a set of lock picks hidden inside the spine of a leather notepad, a ballpoint pen—the kind any executive might carry—with a titanium body, and a collection of milled aluminum parts inside a clear plastic bag labeled "Sample Products."

"How is that possible?" Gwen asked after a moment. "I mean ... what's the likelihood?"

"First rule of assassination," Noble told her. "Assassinate the assassin. Someone wants to make absolutely sure nobody ever finds out why P. Arthur Fellows was killed. Where are you on his case files?"

"Errr ... " Gwen said. "Wait one second."

She covered the phone and Noble could hear a muffled conversation on the other end.

He sorted the bag of parts. Useless metal widgets had been thrown in to disguise the real contents—Noble set those aside—and assembled a stainless-steel Kimber Ultra Carry chambered in 9mm, along with two full mags. A wire hanger from the closet and some masking tape would make a useable holster. Noble made a mental note to thank the South Africa Station Chief.

Gwen came back on. "We're working on accessing Fellows's case load now, but it's going to take time. The Secret Service isn't playing ball. Our only other choice is to hack into their database."

"Did you try calling?" Noble asked.

"Calling?" Gwen repeated the word like she had never heard it before.

"Yeah," Noble said. "Someone has to take over the dead guy's case load, right? Call the file clerk at Secret Service, claim you're the officer taking over the open cases, and have them fax the documents to your office."

"You want us to lie to the Secret Service?" she said. "We could get in major trouble."

"More trouble than hacking into their database and *stealing* government files?"

"Good point," Gwen said, but she didn't sound convinced.

"All the phone lines inside Langley are heavily encrypted," Noble told her, like a teacher explaining something simple to an especially slow student. "Even if the file clerk at the Secret Service realizes you're bluffing and tries to trace the call, he'll hit the Company firewall. You've got nothing to lose."

"That's a really good idea," Gwen said.

"Yeah, I have those every once in a while," Noble said. "Find out where the body of Elizabeth Michaels ended up."

"What do you have in mind?"

"My gut's telling me something's not right," Noble said. "Call it a hunch. This assassin, whatever her real name is, didn't survive this long by making mistakes. Can you track down the body?"

"Shouldn't be too hard," Gwen said and said to Ezra. "Find out what hospital they took Elizabeth Michaels to."

Noble waited, puzzling over the facts. Who would want to kill a Secret Service agent and why? What was Fellows working on? The assassin might be their only link to the person who ordered the hit. If she was dead, then the trail was cold. Noble opened the mini fridge and took out a small bottle of scotch. Ignoring the price tag, he tucked the phone between his ear and shoulder, twisted off the cap and drank. The liquor hit his system like a sledge hammer. His brain welcomed the alcohol even as his stomach recoiled.

Gwen came back on the phone after a few minutes. "Michaels is at the city morgue on Durston Avenue and get this: Next of kin has already claimed the body. It's scheduled for cremation."

"That's curious," Noble said. "Assassins don't usually have close family ties. Who claimed the body?"

"A James Naidoo. We checked: Those are two of the most common names in South Africa—the American equivalent of John Smith."

"Cute," Noble said. "I think I'll go have a look at the body."

"How do you plan on doing that?" Gwen asked.

"I'll think of something," Noble said and hung up.

He looked at himself in the mirror above the headboard. The face staring back at him was barely recognizable. He hadn't eaten in days and had barely slept. Maybe he could use that to his advantage? First, he opened the closet, took a wire coat hanger, and bent it into a makeshift holster for his weapon.

CHAPTER EIGHTEEN

Noble entered the city morgue a few minutes before closing time, his head down and shoulders slumped, looking like a man who had spent most of the day crying. His cheeks were flush and his eyes were puffy slits. The color around his nose and cheeks was courtesy of lipstick he had picked up from a drugstore down the block from his hotel. He had dabbed a little on and blended it with the tip of his pinkie finger. The puffy eyes were achieved by onions bought from a local grocer. Noble had chopped them in the hotel bathroom and rubbed the slices under his eyes. As an added benefit, his nose was now running freely and he was forced to keep sniffing.

Money is just one way a counterintelligence agent can illicit information, usually the least effective. People taking bribes are likely to hold back on pertinent details and prone to bouts of guilty conscience after the fact. The CIA often trades money for information, but the intel they get is considered unreliable and needs to be backed up by other sources. Appealing to a target's patriotism, morality or, in this case, emotions is usually far more effective than offering cold hard cash.

Noble stepped up to the counter, rubbing his nose and blinking. It was like looking at the world through a haze after swimming in a heavily chlorinated pool. Fluorescent lights bathed everything in a fuzzy glow. The morgue had a small waiting room with a few plastic chairs, a low table, and dog-eared magazines. A poster on the wall offered counseling services, along with a phone number. The place smelled like formaldehyde.

A pretty black girl with dreads stopped pecking at her cellphone and looked up.

"Uh ... I've come to see ..." Noble began. He swallowed like he was having trouble getting the words out and started over. "I've come to see my girlfriend. Elizabeth Michaels. Is this the right place?"

"One moment." She plugged the name into the computer. "Yes, we have an Elizabeth Michaels, but the brother has already claimed the remains."

Noble nodded. "I know. I just ... I need to see her one last time."

She started to shake her head. "I'm sorry, sir, there's really nothing—"

"Please," Noble choked out. He reached in his pocket and brought out a fake diamond on a ten dollar chain that he had picked up along with the lipstick. It looked real enough. Noble said, "This was hers. I want her to have it. Please. I just want to say goodbye."

The girl's eyes fixed on the necklace and her shoulders slumped. Noble knew he had her. She pressed her lips together, glanced at the computer screen and then at Noble. "Okay. But you can't tell anyone I let you back here."

"Thank you," Noble told her. "You're a good soul. Lizzy would have liked you."

She led the way through a pair of swinging doors and along the row of freezers until she found H-13. She popped open the door and rolled the gurney out to reveal a black rubber body bag.

"Are you sure you want to do this?" she said and added, "She was in a traffic accident."

Noble nodded.

The attendant looked like she was having second thoughts, but pulled the zipper enough to reveal the head and shoulders. The fetid smell of decomposing flesh wafted from the bag. Noble got just a hint. His clogged nostrils kept out the worst of it. Even if he had known Elizabeth Michaels, Noble wouldn't have recognized her. The face was a swollen mass of purple bruises.

"Take your time," the girl whispered.

He bent over the body like he was going to place the cheap cosmetic-store chain around her neck and took the opportunity to unzip the bag, exposing the corpse all the way down to her bare feet.

"Hey!" The attendant's eyes opened wide in alarm. "You can't do that."

"I need to see her tattoo," Noble said. He turned the corpse's left foot until he could see the ankle. The skin was cold beneath his fingers and the bones popped like celery. There was no tattoo. Just bloated purple skin.

The morgue attendant was demanding Noble leave before she called the cops.

"This isn't Elizabeth Michaels," Noble told her.

"What are you talking about?" she said. Most of the color had drained from her face.

Noble dropped the grieving boyfriend act. "I don't know who you have in this body bag, but it's not Elizabeth Michaels."

"How do you know that?"

"Elizabeth Michaels has a tattoo on her left ankle."

"Okay," the attendant said. She held up both hands and patted the air. "You're in shock. This can be a little confusing for some people."

"Do yourself a favor and run dental records before you incinerate her," Noble told her before walking out of the storage room. He let himself out of the dim coolness of the morgue and into the blazing-hot South African sunshine.

Elizabeth Michaels had taken pains to disappear, right down to a fake corpse. Noble didn't know how, but she had done it, and he was probably the only person who knew she was still alive. He made his way north along Durston, sticking to the shadows to avoid the worst of the heat, and dialed Gwen on his phone.

"Goodman and Associates. How may I direct your call?"

"Personnel," Noble said. "I need to track down an employee who's not at her desk."

"Going secure," Gwen said.

Noble waited to hear the tell-tale clicks and then said, "Elizabeth Michaels faked her own death."

"What? How did she manage that?"

"I'm not sure," Noble admitted. "But the corpse in the

morgue is not hers. Give me the street address you found for her."

Gwen read the number off and Noble committed it to memory. It was outside Johannesburg and, in this blinding sun, no way was Noble going to walk. He reached the end of the block and spotted a parking garage across from a towering high-rise. He said, "What about the Secret Service?"

"It worked!" Gwen's voice rose several octaves. "Ezra called and claimed to be the agent taking over Fellows's open cases. They close-copied the files to a dummy email. Only now we've got thirty-two case files to dig through."

"Start with the most recent and work your way back," Noble told her.

"We'll call if we find anything," Gwen said.

Noble hung up and crossed the street to the parking garage.

———

An hour later, Noble pulled to a stop along a dusty lane, behind the wheel of a dented pickup truck with one mismatched door and mud flaps emblazoned with Yosemite Sam brandishing twin revolvers and the words "Back Off." A pair of steel balls hung from the bumper and the cab smelled like dirty socks. When the brakes locked, the tires kicked up a cloud of dust that drifted apart on the wind. A large yellow sun blazed in a patchwork sky of blue and white. It was the type of sky Noble's father had always called 'God's canvas'.

Fifty meters up the road, just visible through a stand of

trees, Noble could make out the pitched roof of the farm-house. It was built on a slight rise overlooking Johannesburg and surrounded by low vegetation. There were no vehicles around and no fields to speak of, just a plot of untended land with empty rows of earth dotted by poison oak and scrub brush. Noble shifted into park and let the engine idle.

He took a moment to disable the dome lamp before getting out. The door cranked open with a loud squeal of rusting hinges and the sound carried on the quiet country-side. Noble stepped away from the truck, between a pair of stunted oaks and over hillocks of dead grass, then he waited, allowing his senses time to acclimate to nature. He doubted the assassin would risk coming back here after faking her own death, but he wasn't taking any chances. If she was smart enough to fake her own death, she was smart enough to leave a few surprises for anyone who foolish enough to come snooping around. And Noble didn't like surprises.

He high-stepped over grassy tussocks toward the corner of the farmhouse, eyes and ears alert for danger, listening to the cicadas and watching every shadow, wondering what sort of early warning systems the assassin might have in place. He hadn't gone far when he spotted movement. Noble hunkered next to a tree and his right hand crept toward the gun in his waistband.

A gray-and-white wolf dog appeared around the side of the house. The canine was nosing along, tail wagging. A long pink tongue lolled from the side of its open mouth. The dog went a few paces, stopped, lifted his head and sniffed at the air.

CHAPTER NINETEEN

THE BEAST'S TAIL STOPPED WAGGING. IT TOOK A FEW tentative steps in Noble's direction, nostrils flared and ears perked. Noble held still, not even daring to breath. His heart started to trot inside his chest. The skin around his mouth tightened. He had a soft spot for anything with fur, but the choice between killing a dog and getting mauled was no choice at all.

The animal took another step in Noble's direction before a sound in the underbrush caught its attention. Its head whipped around to the left and it let out a huffing half-bark from deep in its muscular chest, then bounded off through the trees.

Noble breathed through pursed lips.

The dog was distracted for the moment but, sooner or later, it would have to be dealt with. Noble wracked his brain. There was nothing in the pickup truck that might help. He circled the edge of the property, giving the house a wide birth. The sun continued its slow trek toward the horizon and shadows grew long as Noble crept through the trees. He came upon an old rusted-out tractor on flat tires near a scrap pile with grass growing up through it. The dog was busy chasing a critter. A single bark echoed across the wooded landscape. Noble sorted through a jumble of rotting lumber, twisted scraps of metal, and an old leather boot teeming with cockroaches. He pulled out a tangled coil of barbed wire, and it gave him an idea.

Wolf dogs make excellent security. They're strong, with a keen sense of smell and a nasty attitude—and when they bite, they don't let go. If a wolf dog gets hold of an arm or a leg, they clamp down and keep on jerking their head around, ripping skin and muscle, until you stop struggling. Noble hoped to take advantage of that trait.

He moved along the wood line in back of the house, not taking any particular care to stay quiet. He wanted the dog to hear him and come running. He gripped a bit of wood from the scrap pile in one hand and the length of barbed wire in the other. The rusty wire was knotted securely to one end of the board. Noble stepped between trees into a clearing with a view of the farmhouse. No lights were on inside.

Noble gave a high whistle and called out, "Here, pooch!"

The dog came bounding around the corner, ears flat against its skull. Powerful legs covered the open ground with terrifying speed. Noble hunkered like a linebacker bracing for impact. The muscles in his neck and back tensed. Sweat sprang out on his forearms. He planted his feet and held his breath. If this didn't work, he'd end up dead or maimed.

The dog let out a deep growl and launched himself. Noble thrust the length of wood out and the dog's jaws latched down with bone-crushing force. The impact slammed Noble right off his feet. He went down on his back and a hundred pounds of fur came down on top of him.

Slathering jaws clamped down on the old two-by-four. Wood splintered and cracked like a tree bending in a hurricane. Claws raked Noble's chest, shredding his shirt and savaging his unprotected skin. He quickly worked the barbed wire around the dog's neck. The beast growled and whipped its head side to side. Angry yellow eyes and slavering teeth filled Noble's vision. He looped the barbed wire several times around the length of lumber and the dog's neck, fixing the bit of wood in place, then shoved the dog off him and rolled clear.

The wolf dog scrambled to its feet and unhinged its jaws in an effort to let go of the wood. It took the animal a minute to realize that wasn't going to happen. Never let it be said wolf dogs are dumb. The beast lifted his front paw and batted at the two-by-four in an attempt to dislodge it. When that didn't work, it whipped his head back and forth some more, hoping to throw the wood clear. The dog turned baleful yellow eyes on Noble and let out a pitiful whine.

"Keep working on it," Noble told him.

His shirt was shredded and bloody. A patchwork of claw marks crisscrossed his chest and stomach. None of the cuts were deep, but they stung. Noble climbed to his feet and stumbled toward the house. The dog followed. At the backdoor, Noble took the lockpicks from his wallet, slipped the tension tool into the cylinder and used the rake to scrub the tumblers into place. The dog let out a deep and futile growl.

"Relax, will ya?" said Noble. "I'm not here to steal anything. Besides, she's not coming back."

The dog gave another furious shake and then whined.

Noble felt the last tumbler click into place and the lock turned.

The dog growled one last attempt to scare Noble off.

"You're dedicated. I'll give you that," Noble said as he let himself into the farmhouse. He held the door open. "You coming inside? Or you going to stand out there and thrash around all night?"

The beast padded into the house, looking dejected, plopped down on the rug and continued to work at the length of wood with its front paws. A puddle of saliva formed on the hardwood floor.

Noble left the dog in the living room while he searched the house. He went slow, looking for pressure plates or trip-wires, but the canine seemed to be the first and only line of defense. A dozen creepy marionettes hung from the roof beams. Noble found a CZ in an umbrella stand near the front door, another in the refrigerator, and a Glock 19 under a sofa cushion. The bedroom had perfumes and lotions, a stuffed rabbit perched next to a reading lamp, and more pillows than any one person could use. It was all there, everything you'd expected to find in a woman's bedroom. But it felt like set dressing to Noble. The bathroom and the living room were more of the same. The only thing missing were selfies stuck to the mirrors.

The spare bedroom was the only room that didn't fit. Noble found an array of wigs on Styrofoam heads, racks of clothing in all shapes and sizes, and enough shoes to outfit an entire modeling agency, along with expensive stage makeup. There were even a few prosthetics. This woman could transform at will. She could look like anybody. One of the Styrofoam heads was empty, a wig was missing, and Noble wondered what Elizabeth Michaels looked like now.

In the garage, he found a coil of rope and wire cutters. He carried the tools back to the kitchen, turned on the stove, and rummaged through the refrigerator until he found a steak. The dog was still trying to free itself when Noble dropped the steak into a pan. It landed with a sizzle and the smell of frying meat filled the old farmhouse. The dog stopped fussing with the bit of wood and let out a plaintive whine.

Noble said, "Smells good, huh?"

Matchbooks from an auto repair shop on Jonkershoek Road filled a small dish on the kitchen island. Noble examined one of the matchbooks and stuffed it in his pocket before turning the steak. He put the side of meat on a plate and placed it on the floor. The dog's eyes went to the steak and it sat back on its haunches.

"Think you can behave?" Noble asked.

The dog blinked at him with big doggie eyes.

He patted the beast's flanks and scratched behind its ears until the animal settled. Then used the wire cutters. The dog spit out the length of wood and set on the steak with slavering noises. Noble watched it eat and when it finished, Noble asked, "Feel better?"

The dog panted in response. A long wet tongue hung like a banner from one side of its mouth. Closer inspection told Noble it was male and not just a wolf dog—it was a

Czechoslovakian wolf dog. In the fifties, the Czechoslovakian military had crossbred German shepherds with Carpathian wolves. The resulting breed had the all trainability and temperament of a shepherd, combined with the ferocity of a wolf. Soviet Special Forces commandos had used the breed before the collapse of the Communist empire. Now they were mostly used as search-and-rescue dogs.

While he rummaged through the spare bedroom for medical supplies, Noble considered all the facts; CZ pistols, marionettes, and a Czechoslovakian wolf dog. Everything traced back to the Czech Republic.

Noble left his shredded shirt on the floor and used alcohol swabs from a makeup kit to disinfect the wounds on his chest. A few dabs of prosthetic glue closed the worst of the cuts. When that was done, Noble found a plain black shirt that fit him well enough and then secured the rope to the animal's collar. The dog didn't seem to mind. Noble scratched behind its ears and said, "I've got a few more errands to run. After that, we'll see about finding you a home."

CHAPTER TWENTY

ELIŠKA PROWLED THE NARROW LANES OF OLD TOWN, enjoying the sound of Czech in her ears. It was strange being back. She hadn't been home in years. Everything was familiar, yet different. The streets were now crowded with tourists armed with cameras. A wax museum had popped up just down the street from the Astronomical Clock—an uncanny resemblance of Bruce Willis stood in the window —and a museum dedicated to the horrors of Communism had been installed next door to a McDonald's.

The sun was going down, casting the streets in shadow and bathing the rooftops in a rich orange glow. Eliška stopped at the door of the Communism Museum for a peek. Through the glass, she spotted a satirical poster of a happy woman holding up a flag. The caption read, *You Couldn't Get Laundry Detergent but You Could Get Your BRAIN-WASHED.* There was a statue of Marx in the entryway and the words, *Dream, Reality, Nightmare.*

Eliška smiled, turned the collar of her leather jacket up

against the cold, and continued on her way. She had been born shortly after the Velvet Revolution and remembered the poverty left in the wake of Socialism. She had grown up hungry but hopeful. Decades of Marxist economics were hard to shrug off. As Eliška entered puberty, more and more people were opening their own businesses. Jobs were slowly returning. The price of goods fell and the quality of life improved as competition and better manufacturing fueled market growth. Eliška didn't have much in the way of formal education—schools were slow to be restructured after the revolution—and by the time she was old enough to work, military service had been her best bet. Her only bet. She was just seventeen when she enlisted. That seemed like a lifetime ago.

Now, more than a decade later, she made her way through the maze of narrow corridors that make up Stare Mestro to a small brewery on the corner of Karlova Street. The outside was dark wood wainscoting with a tall carved relief of a woman in a flimsy white gown. Inside, soft lighting revealed a dark wood bar with brass accents and a few tables covered in crisp white cloth. Eliška spotted Miklos through the glass. He was short and pudgy, with a big head and no neck. He reminded Eliška of a bullfrog. She slipped into the shadowy recess of a doorway across the street and watched him. A lively crowd packed the small space. Miklos occupied a stool at the bar, nursing a beer, and casting nervous glances over his shoulder. He worked for Czech Intelligence. They had met during Eliška's stint in the military.

Eliška checked her watch. It was half past six. She looked back at Miklos. He was eyeing the door. "Go on,"

Eliška muttered under her breath. "You know you want to make a run for it."

He sat there another minute, then shook his head and slipped off his bar stool.

Eliška smiled. *Some things never change.*

She ducked back into the shadows as Miklos exited the bar. He weaved through the stream of tourists, making his way toward the underground. Eliška kept her head down and used the sea of people to stay out of sight. She let him reach the bottom of the steps before hurrying down after him. She spotted him again as he joined a throng of bodies pushing onto a train bound for Vyšehrad. Eliška had to dash across the platform. She slipped through the doors just as they hissed shut.

The ripe scent of unwashed bodies filled the car. Eliška waited until the train lurched into motion, then pushed her way through the press of commuters to the next car. Miklos was hanging onto a pole and swaying to the rhythm of the carriage. She sidled up next to him and dropped her voice. *"Dobry den, Miklos."*

He recoiled like a man shying away from a hissing viper. His eyebrows walked up his forehead and his shoulders hunched. His eyes did a circuit of the underground car. He let out a breath and his expression changed from surprise to annoyance. "How did you find me?"

Eliška rolled her eyes. "Don't insult me. I knew you'd bail on our meeting."

Without looking directly at her, he asked, "Then why did you bother to contact me?"

"Because I need a favor," Eliška told him.

He stared out the window at the dark tunnel rushing past. "Last time I did you a favor, I nearly went to jail."

"Is that any way to greet an old friend?"

"*Friend*?" He snorted and shook his head. "More like a curse. I don't know where you've been all these years but you should have stayed gone. You know what they'll do if they find you?"

"They aren't going to find me," Eliška said. "Unless you tell them."

When Miklos didn't respond, she said, "Miklos, did you tell anyone I contacted you?"

He managed to act insulted. "No."

Eliška closed the distance between them and put her hand into her leather jacket. Her fingers wrapped around the hilt of a switchblade knife. "Don't lie to me, Miklos."

He edged away. "I didn't tell a soul. I swear."

Satisfied, Eliška produced a picture of the American sitting at Café Organica. She had been in the crowded shopping center less than fifty feet away—disguised as an overweight, middle-age brunette. She had watched Bob make a phone call, saw the escort's body disappear under the Ford Explorer, and then watched the American casually stroll away. Eliška had been close enough to kill him. She wanted to walk up and put a bullet in the back of his head, but Bob was just an errand boy. Eliška needed the man behind the American. The man pulling the strings. She passed the picture to Miklos.

He cast another nervous look around the train car before taking the photograph. "He's not my type."

"He tried to kill me," Eliška said. "I want to know who he is and, more importantly, who he works for."

Miklos stuffed the picture in his coat pocket. "That's a big ask."

Eliška leaned close. Her lips brushed his earlobe. She whispered, "I'll think of a way to repay you."

Miklos let out a trembling breath. "What if I get caught?"

"Don't be such a cold fish. Girls don't like that in a man."

He bristled. "Where do I start?"

"He's American."

"The world is, unfortunately, full of those. Got a name?"

Eliška scrunched her face up in an apologetic frown.

He gave another snort. "I'll see what I can do. No promises."

"One more thing," Eliška said.

"There's more?"

"Have you still got the cabin?"

Miklos was already shaking his head. "Out of the question."

"I need a place to lay low."

"I'd suggest Angola. It's nice this time of year."

She gave him a hard stare. "Someone is after my father, Miklos."

He softened. "Fine. You can have it day after tomorrow."

"Why not tonight?"

"Someone's in it," he explained.

"Who's in it?"

"A few years ago, I turned it into an Airbnb for extra

cash. I'll have to cancel a reservation. It's going to hurt my rating. You owe me."

She planted a kiss on his cheek. "You're the best."

The train was pulling into the station. The high-pitched scream of the hurtling missile dropped several octaves to a throaty rumble. Miklos looked out the glass at the station. "How do I contact you if I find anything?"

"You don't," Eliška said. "I'll contact you. Keep your phone handy."

The train slowed to a stop. There was a chuffing of air brakes and the doors opened with a pneumatic hiss. Eliška stepped onto the platform along with the crowd as it herded toward a set of escalators that led up to street level.

CHAPTER TWENTY-ONE

THE OLD PICKUP TRUCK STARTED TO RATTLE AND knock as Noble reached the outskirts of Johannesburg. Picturesque countryside gave way to shanty towns of corrugated steel and weathered boards. The temperature gauge edged steadily closer to the red line. The wolf dog sat in the passenger seat panting. He flashed his teeth at passing cars —Czechoslovakian wolf dogs rarely bark, one of the many reasons they make such great guard dogs—otherwise he seemed to enjoy the adventure. It was full dark by the time Noble reached the auto repair shop. He swung the hiccupping pickup into an empty spot and killed the engine. The truck farted a cloud of black smoke and cooled with a series of soft ticking sounds.

The bay door was up and a Crown Vic was parked in the garage. Fluorescents reflected on the automobile body. The biting rhythm of a Danzig tune blasted from the stereo. A large black man in coveralls was bent over the engine of the Ford, half hidden by the open hood.

Noble climbed out and the dog tried to follow. He held up a hand. "Stay."

The dog sat back with a whine.

Noble cracked the window, shut the door, and crossed the lot.

The black man straightened up, wiping his hands on a filthy shop rag. The yellow stitching on his shirt said, *Nelson.* "Closed," he announced in a baritone voice. "You want to leave the truck, I'll have a look at it in the morning. Otherwise you gonna have to come back tomorrow."

"That old heap isn't worth the effort," Noble said with a look over his shoulder at the pickup.

"Then what you want?"

"A friend sent me," Noble told him. "Said I could find someone here to help me with a little business problem I'm having."

Nelson shook his head. "Don't know nothin' about that. I fix cars."

"I know how it works," Noble said. "You just make the introductions."

Nelson's brow knotted together. He waved his dirty shop rag like he was shooing a bothersome fly. "You talking crazy, white boy. Go on, before I get angry."

"Listen, Nelson ... Can I call you Nelson? I got a real problem. I got a deputy district attorney back in Sydney digging through my business with a fine-tooth comb. He's a real Boy Scout. I've tried everything. He won't be bought or threatened. He's going to bring down my whole operation."

Nelson said, "What do you want me to do about it?"

"Please," Noble said. "I'm desperate. All I'm asking for is an introduction. Can you help me or not?"

"I told you once already," Nelson said. "I'm not going to tell you again. Get out of here."

"Not until I talk with her."

Nelson turned to a rolling cart and grabbed a wrench. The wolf dog loosed a series of explosive barks, clawing the window of the pickup with his front paws. Noble ducked and felt the wrench whistle overhead.

He came back up in a boxer's crouch and delivered a short uppercut, catching Nelson under the chin. His knuckles impacted with a solid *thock*. Nelson's head rocked back and his knees started to buckle, but he managed to stay on his feet. Noble lunged for the wrench. Two months of hard drinking had taken their toll. His moves were slow and sloppy. Noble felt like he was moving through thick soup stock. Both his muscles and his mind were out of shape and it might cost him. One hit from the wrench would mean lights out. He latched onto Nelson's wrist and used an armbar to force the big man down to the shop floor. It took twice the effort it should have. Noble felt the cuts on his chest reopen. With a savage twist, he yanked the wrench free of Nelson's grasping fingers and rapped him behind the ear with it. The solid steel made a meaty crunch and Nelson's eyes rolled up.

CHAPTER TWENTY-TWO

OTTO KEISER LISTENED WITH RAPT ATTENTION TO THE soprano playing Madame Butterfly as she lamented her forlorn love affair with the American officer. The singer, a pretty young Italian, wrung every last drop of emotion from the scene. She looked the part as well, in a green kimono with golden dragons and jet-black hair piled on top of her head in a bun. The beam from a center spot cast her in brilliant light while the rest of the stage was lost in shadow. The audience held its collective breath as she delivered her final, impassioned plea.

A tear tracked silently down Keiser's liver-spotted cheek. The despondent refrains pierced right to his heart, lifting him up and carrying him away from the prison of his wheelchair. The audience exploded with applause when she drove the knife into her belly.

"*Bravura!*" Otto clapped along with the crowd. "Bravura!"

Behind him, a security man stood with his shoulder

against the door of Keiser's private balcony. His name was Westley or Wexler—Keiser could never remember. He was towering pile of muscles with pale skin, flaming red hair and a puggish nose, flat and wide so you could see right up his nostrils. He looked like Opie on steroids, but he had Lucas's seal of approval and that was enough for Keiser.

Keiser levered himself out of the wheelchair for a standing ovation when the performers emerged and lined up on stage. Westley/Wexler stepped up behind him, ready to catch him if standing proved too difficult. It was an effort. Keiser's legs wobbled like a newborn colt, but he managed. He was breathing heavy when he lowered his corpulent frame back into the chair. Thunderous applause brought the cast out for a second bow and Keiser jerked a thumb over his shoulder at the door.

Westley/Wexler maneuvered the wheelchair up the ramp and through the door. The rest of Keiser's security detail fell in around him as steroid-Opie mashed the call button for the elevator. The opera was only the beginning of the evening's festivities. There was the after-party where Keiser was a guest of honor for his contributions to the Bern Theater. And the after-after-party.

The first stop was the ultra modern Hotel Allegro on Kornhausstrasse. The event hall looked like the inside of some super-sleek interstellar cruise ship with curving balconies and soft purple lighting. The women were clad in low-cut evening gowns. The men wore black-tie and clutched champagne flutes, smiles fixed on their faces. An aria played softly in the background and the crowd filled the room with a sound like squabbling geese.

Keiser made the rounds, shaking hands, remarking on

the performance and offering advice to men looking for the next hot stock tip. He cautioned against commodities and told them to put everything they could spare into a cyber security IPO. Most of them scribbled the name of the company on a cocktail napkin. Tomorrow they would start moving funds. Some of them simply smiled and nodded. They would sit on the information and regret it six months from now. There are two kinds of people in the world; those who take what they want out of life and those who spend all their time trying to hold on to what little they have. Keiser had no time for the second kind. He couldn't stand weak people. *Be ready when opportunity knocks*, that was his motto. You have to take risks if you want to change the world. And Otto Keiser planned to change the world. Governments and politicians could not be allowed to direct the fate of mankind. Keiser intended to do that himself.

He worked the room and finally found himself smiling up at the beautiful young soprano who had played the part of Madame Butterfly. She was even more stunning in an emerald green gown with a plunging neckline and a string of pearls around her delicate throat. The theater manager introduced them as Keiser clasped her dainty hand in both of his own.

"*Herr* Keiser, I would like you to meet our newest talent, *Frau* Theresa Sipriani," the theater manager said. He was a foppish man in a loud tuxedo with tails and a garish pink bowtie. He turned to Theresa. "*Herr* Keiser is a patron of the arts, my dear, and our top sponsor."

She flashed a set of white teeth. "A pleasure to meet you, *Signor* Keiser."

"Please, call me Otto, and the pleasure is all mine," he

told her. "Your performance was inspired, young lady. Tell me, where did you study?"

Theresa managed to look humble. "I studied under Marissa Tulva in Roma."

"Ah! I saw her perform *Don Giovani*," Keiser said. "She was magnificent."

Keiser impressed her with his knowledge of classic opera, proving he wasn't just another socialite with too much money, he actually appreciated the music. Within minutes they were chatting like two old friends. When Keiser causally insinuated that he could be influential in furthering her career, Theresa's smile never faltered. He was just about to invite her to a private gathering at his home in Tuscany when Westley/Wexler leaned over his shoulder and whispered, "Something's come up."

Keiser scowled. "What is it, man?"

He kept his voice down. "Somebody is making inquiries into Randall."

Keiser felt a block of lead drop into his stomach, but he smiled up at Theresa. "You must excuse me, my dear."

She offered her hand and Keiser kissed her knuckles before maneuvering his wheelchair around and making his way through the crowd. He steered past the theater manager, who was deep in conversation with an older gentleman, and Keiser crooked a finger. The theater manager bent down. Keiser said, "Send her up to my penthouse."

He glanced over his shoulder at Theresa and said, "She is engaged to be married, *Herr* Keiser. Her fiancé is—"

"I don't care if she's taken a vow of celibacy," Keiser

grumbled. "If she's not in my penthouse in thirty minutes, you should start looking for a new job."

The theater manager bowed in acquiescence and started to stammer his obedience, but Keiser was already pushing the wheelchair into a quiet corner. He got clear of the crowd and spun to face his security man. "Who's been asking about Randall?"

"A signals specialist in Czech military intelligence."

The assassin was Czech and now someone in Czech intel was looking into Randall? Lucas had screwed up. If someone traced the assassination of the Secret Service agent to Randall, they might link it back to Keiser. His liver-spotted hands knotted together in worry. He was so close now. The thought of anything going wrong at this late stage left a sick feeling deep in his belly. He had spent a lifetime putting his plan together, slowly maneuvering all the pieces into place, manipulating world markets so that conditions would be just right. He couldn't afford any mistakes. Not now. He said, "Get Lucas on the phone."

CHAPTER TWENTY-THREE

LUCAS RANDALL FLOATED ON THE WEIGHTLESS TIDES of the Adriatic Sea—what the locals called *Jadransko*—clad in a wetsuit and fins. A three-quarter moon hung in the sky, but beneath the waves was inky blackness stretching in every direction. A small dive lamp fixed to his goggles provided him with enough light to see a few scant meters. On his left, a massive sea turtle glided along above the ocean floor. The ancient sea creature cocked its head to the side and studied Lucas with one reptilian eyeball before moving off in search of food or maybe a mate.

Lucas used flippers to propel himself through the water. A yellow dive tank was strapped to his back. Bubbles gurgled up from the tank and raced to the surface. The sound of the ocean was incredibly loud in his ears. Through the wall of darkness, he spotted the first of six rotting concrete pylons thrusting up from the ocean. Time and the elements had eaten away at the concrete until barnacled rebar showed through.

The tide was trying to carry Lucas out to sea. Waves retreated from the shore, pulling him backward like some giant magnet exerting invisible pull. Then the ocean changed direction and threatened to slam him into the support. He was forced to hold on to the pillar with one hand while he reached inside his satchel. He brought out a small square of plastic explosive, no bigger than a deck of playing cards. He secured it to the pylon with a trigger cord. If anyone found the bomb and tried to remove it, the cord would set off the explosive. Next, Lucas attached a simple detonator and cellular receiver inside a waterproof Pelican case. He spent the next twenty minutes camouflaging the device with an old fishing net and seaweed from the ocean floor.

Lucas set five more devices on the other pylons. When that was done, he swam two hundred meters and surfaced in the shadow of a catamaran. Hearing returned. Hawser lines creaked and the moon reflected off the white fiberglass hull in dim flashes as it gently rode the waves. Lucas paddled over to the ladder and hauled himself up.

Eric was waiting for him on the stern with a towel in one hand and a phone in the other.

"Who is it?" Randall wanted to know. He seated himself on the gunwale, worked off his fins, pulled off the mask, and shrugged out of the harness. The tank settled on the deck with a gentle *clank*.

Eric covered the receiver with one hand. "It's the old man."

Lucas reached for the phone. "What is it?"

"I've been calling," Keiser said.

"I've been busy," Lucas fired back. "What so important?"

Keiser said, "I don't pay you to be smart."

"You pay me to do what you and all your money men can't," Lucas told him.

"Exactly," said Keiser. "And so far, you've failed to do it."

Lucas stood up and gazed out over the Adriatic to the dim shadow of the torpedo factory thrusting out over the black waters. The abandoned launch house was just visible in the light from the moon. The charges attached to the supports would bring the whole structure crashing down into the waves at the push of a button. Lucas's face worked into a frown. "What are you talking about?"

"Someone in Czech military intelligence has been asking questions about you. A man by the name of Miklos Dvorak. My sources tell me he served with the Cermáková woman. I thought she had been dealt with?"

"She was."

"Well, somebody's asking questions. If they connect you to Cermáková, they might tie it back to me. That would destroy everything we've been working toward."

"You're on an open line," Lucas warned.

Eric got Lucas's attention and questioned him with a look.

Lucas held up a finger. He said, "If someone is looking in to me, they've already started making connections. This might be a problem."

"I pay you to solve problems, Randall, not make them. This is your mess. Clean it up. And this time, I want proof the job is done."

"I'll take care of it."

"You'd better, or I'll find your replacement."

The line went dead.

Lucas turned back to Eric. "We've got a problem. Someone in Czech intel is asking questions."

Eric cursed. "What are we going to do?"

"Find out everything you can about a guy named Miklos Dvorak. Then round up half a dozen men and book transportation to Prague."

"I told you we never should have gone after Fellows," Eric said. "I'm beginning to think this whole thing was a mistake."

"Hey!" Lucas grabbed his lapel and gave him a hard shake. "It's too late to back out."

"This is getting out of hand," Eric said. "Now we're going to kill Czech intel officers? Did you ever stop to consider what happens after? What happens when it's done and Keiser has no more use for us?"

"Just get it done," Lucas told him.

Eric didn't look happy about ordering another murder but took out his phone and dialed.

CHAPTER TWENTY-FOUR

By the time Nelson woke up from his nap, Noble had him loaded into the front seat of the Crown Vic—no easy task—and a length of rubber hose fed in to the passenger window from to the tailpipe. He was using duct tape to seal the gaps when Nelson moaned and shifted in the seat. His face pinched. One hand went up to ward off an invisible blow. His lips moved, but an unintelligible jumble spilled out. The Crown Vic, meanwhile, was slowly filling with poisonous fumes.

Noble had disabled the starter and closed up the shop. The Czechoslovakian wolf dog sat on his haunches, rope leash still around his neck, panting. Nelson finally got his thoughts in order and his eyes sprang open. He looked around and spotted the hose wedged in the passenger side window. A choking cough wracked his chest. He went for the door, desperate to escape before inhaling any more deadly gas. The dog let out a deep growl and batted the driver's side door with both paws, leaving marks in the paint.

Nelson let go and lunged across the seat, meaning to pile out the other side, but the wolf dog scrabbled around the shop floor to intercept him. Nelson tried again for the driver's side. This time the dog bounded onto the hood of the Cadillac and growled at Nelson through the glass.

"Come on, man!" Nelson screamed. "Call off the dog! Let me out!"

"Not until you tell me what I want to know," Noble said. "And you'd better talk fast. You won't last long breathing in that exhaust."

"I just fix cars." Nelson turned on the air conditioning, switched it to outside air, and put his mouth to the vents. It would buy him more time. Not much, but he was grasping at straws.

Noble said, "You're the middleman for an assassin who spent the last several years operating out of South Africa. I want to know where to find her."

"I don't know what you're talking about." Nelson shook his head and coughed. The air in the Cadillac was getting hazy. "I'm just a mechanic. I swear."

"Sure you are," Noble said. "And I'm Liberace. What's her name? Where do I find her?"

"I don't know anything about any assassins."

Noble said, "Nelson, the fumes cause irreversible brain damage long before you pass out. A few more minutes and you'll start losing cognitive function. Want to spend the rest of your life pissing yourself?"

"Please!" he begged. "Let me out!"

"Start talking, Nelson."

"What do you want to know?"

"Where is she going?"

He shook his head. "She'll kill me."

"The fumes will get you first," Noble said. "Or should I open the door and let Cujo here do his thing?"

The dog stood on the hood, his teeth bared and his ears flat against his skull. He gave a deep growl, daring Nelson to get out of the car.

Noble said, "You're going to start getting sleepy, Nelson. That's the beginning of the end."

He was coughing so hard he could barely talk. "She's Czech! She's probably headed back there."

Noble leaned on the hood and crossed his arms over his chest. "I already know she's Czech. You're going to have to do better than that. Give me something I can work with."

Nelson hunched over and coughed up a line of yellow mucus. He wiped his mouth with the sleeve of his coveralls. Noble could tell he was doing some fast thinking. Finally he choked out, "Her father lives in Prague. She sends him money every month. That's all I know."

Noble took a tight hold on the leash before opening the driver's side door. Nelson spilled out onto the shop floor, vomited and rolled onto his back, gasping for air. The wolf dog strained against the rope, but Noble held fast.

"Got a name?" Noble asked.

"Just Lizabeth ..." Nelson had to stop and cough up more bile. He wiped his mouth and said, "That's all she ever went by. Call the dog off, please."

"Alright, Nelson." Noble patted the animal's head and

made shushing noises. "If it turns out you're lying—or Lizabeth finds out I'm coming—me and my dog are gonna come
back here. And next time, he'll be hungry. Understood?"

Nelson nodded and palmed tears from his eyes.

Noble hauled the bay door up, yanked the dog outside
and coaxed the beast back into the pickup. He had to pump
the gas a few times but the engine finally turned over.
Noble took out his phone and dialed as he backed out of the
parking space. The wolf dog licked his chops a few times,
then lay down on the seat with his head in Noble's lap.

Gwen picked up after two rings.

Noble said, "Go secure."

There was a series of clicks and Gwen came back on the
line. "Is everything alright?"

"Our assassin is Czech." Noble glanced at the dog.
"And probably ex-military. She's got a father who lives in
Prague. Tap into Czech military records, pull up anyone
with the name of Elizabeth or Lizabeth and any permuta-
tion on that first name."

"That's likely to be a long list," Gwen said.

"Eliminate anybody with known whereabouts," Noble
said. "It's a start."

"Okay," Gwen said. "We're on it."

"Any luck on P. Arthur Fellows?"

"Nothing yet," said Gwen. "But he was investigating
everything from tax fraud to money laundering and we
haven't even been though all the files yet."

Noble said, "I'm going to need a flight to Prague.
Nothing commercial. I'm carrying hardware."

"I'm on it."

"One more thing," Noble said.

"What's that?"

"Pull up a list of reputable kennels in Joburg."

CHAPTER TWENTY-FIVE

Ezra and Gwen were running on Red Bull and ramen. Being the only two analysts on the operation meant working round the clock and sleeping in shifts. They had smuggled a sofa in from an empty office down the hall and wedged it into a corner of the situation room. Neither analyst knew it, but it was the same ratty sofa Matthew Burke had used to sneak naps on. All they knew was that it smelled like armpit and was comfortable despite the fact that it sagged in the middle.

Gwen was at her computer, scrolling through lists of Czech Army personnel who had first names that started with E or L. She narrowed the pool down to anyone born between '80 and '90 with fathers still living in the Czech Republic, which left over seventeen hundred names. After that, she worked on eliminating anyone with a known address. It was slow, tedious work. The Czech Republic is part of the European Union and EU citizens cross borders like Americans change socks. It makes keeping tabs on individuals difficult if not impossible. Many of the soldiers who serve in the Czech military leave when their tour of duty is up and move to other EU nations with better prospects and job opportunities. Others disappear into the vast criminal underworld that ranges across Europe, the Middle East, and Asia, all of which made looking for the assassin like searching for the proverbial needle in a haystack.

Gwen took off her glasses and rubbed her eyes with thumb and forefinger.

Ezra was stretched out on the sofa, breathing deeply in his sleep. It wasn't quite snoring, but it would be when he got a little older and a little heavier. A packet of papers was balanced on his chest. More were stacked on the floor. Notes were scribbled in the margins. Ezra had been going through P. Arthur Fellows's case files, looking for anything that might be worth killing over. So far he had found a whole lot of nothing.

Gwen watched him sleep. She was conflicted. She owed him big time and she knew he wanted more—she had always known—but she hadn't been able to admit it until Coughlin tried to run her off the highway and kill her. Ezra had saved her life that day and he was there for her while she recovered. He had barely left her bedside. He smuggled in burgers when she got sick of hospital food and even ripped a copy of the latest Marvel movie. One night shortly after the premier, Ezra had arrived with his laptop and a tub of popcorn. They had watched it together, crammed side by side on her little hospital bed. It was sweet and heroic and Gwen had started to see Ezra in a whole new light. She had been confined to a hospital bed and Ezra had been her whole world. For a little while, she thought she was falling for him.

Once she got back to work, those feelings quickly fizzled. Ezra was her best friend but, no matter how hard she tired, Gwen couldn't summon up any romantic feelings for him. And she did try. The problem was, Gwen felt like she owed him. She felt Ezra expected some kind of return on his investment—which put a lot of pressure on the situation and made everything awkward.

The worse part was, Gwen knew she should be happy with Ezra. He was a good guy with a good job. And it's not like she had many options. The guys she usually fell for didn't spare a second glance at nerdy girls in Coke-bottle glasses. Guys like Jake Noble went for girls like Samantha Gunn. Sometimes Gwen told herself to just settle, but that wasn't fair to either of them.

She sighed and went back to work. The list of potentials didn't seem to be getting any shorter. She reached for a can of warm Red Bull and had it halfway to her mouth when a notation next to one of the names caught her attention. Gwen clicked the file and read.

"I found her!"

Ezra grunted in his sleep. "Five more minutes."

"Ezra, wake up," Gwen said. "I found her."

He came awake with a snort. The sheaf of papers slid off his chest and onto the floor with a *flop*. "Whazzat?"

"I found the assassin," Gwen told him.

He pushed himself off the couch and rubbed sleep from his eyes. "How'd you go through all those files so fast?"

"We aren't the only ones looking for her," Gwen said. "She's wanted for *murder* in the Czech Republic."

Ezra looked fully awake now. He said, "We should have singled out anyone with a criminal record. We'd have been done ages ago."

Gwen agreed with a nod.

"Should we tell Wizard?"

Gwen didn't know if it was day or night. Without windows, her circadian rhythm was thrown completely off. She had to check her computer for the time. It was 3.15 a.m. Wizard was home in bed. "No sense waking him up," Gwen said. "We still don't know why someone would want P. Arthur Fellows dead or who paid to have him killed."

Some quick mental calculations told her it was just after nine in the morning Prague time. She said, "Noble's plane should have landed."

She reached for the phone. Noble picked up after two rings.

"Goodman speaking."

"Good news, boss. You know that specialist you were looking for? Well, I found her."

"Go secure," Noble said.

Gwen mashed the button on the phone and had to wait while the Company computers encrypted the line and ran a feedback loop to detect anyone listening in. A moment later she said, "We found her. At least, I'm pretty sure it's her. We haven't finished going through the list of possibles. It will take another couple of hours to eliminate people with known addresses and we still haven't—"

"What have you got?" Noble cut her off.

"Oh, right, uh ..." Gwen pushed the glasses up the bridge of her nose. "Name: Eliška Cermákova. Born 1986. Only child. Mother deceased. Father disabled. Eliška joined the Czech military at the age of seventeen. She did four years as a weapons specialist before being recruited into the *vojenské zpravodajství*. That's Czech for—"

"Military intelligence," Noble finished for her. "What makes you think this is our girl?"

"She's wanted in connection with the murder of a Russian diplomat," Gwen said. "She had spent three years with the VZ, where she specialized in covert operations, then disappeared while on assignment. The vojenské zpravodajství thought she was dead. Six months later, her DNA turned up on the murdered Russian. Looks like she went into business for herself. That's got to be our assassin. What do you think?"

"It walks like a duck and quacks like a duck."

Gwen's face pinched. "I'm not sure I follow."

"It's something my mother always says," Noble explained. "If it walks like a duck and it quacks like a duck, it must be a duck."

"Oh." Gwen smiled. "I get it now."

"You said the father is disabled?"

Gwen consulted the file. "That's right."

"Got an address?"

"Hold on." She rapped keys and read off an address in the heart of Prague.

"Thanks," Noble said and hung up.

Gwen put the receiver back on the cradle. "He's not much for small talk."

"Did I hear something about ducks?" Ezra asked. He had been leaning over her shoulder and caught most of the conversation.

Gwen said, "It's something his mother says. Ducks

waddle and quack, so if something waddles and quacks, it must be a duck."

Ezra only looked confused. "What does that have to do with anything?"

Gwen waved it off. "Never mind. We ID'd the assassin. Now we just need to figure out why someone would pay to have Fellows killed."

"Why bother?" Ezra said. "Noble will probably beat it out of her."

Gwen gave him a flat look. "Wizard will be here in a couple of hours. Wouldn't it be nice to have this all wrapped up in a neat little bow?"

"If it means I can go home and go to bed," Ezra said.

She pointed to the thickest case file. It was two and a half inches of single-spaced type. "Pass me that one."

"Feeling lucky?" Ezra asked.

"Finding the assassin got my adrenaline pumping," she told him. It was true, uncovering the identity of the assassin had given her a shot of energy. She felt fully awake for the first time in forty-eight hours but she knew the excitement wouldn't last. She flipped to the first page of the report and said, "Might as well put that extra energy to good use."

CHAPTER TWENTY-SIX

Noble was behind the wheel of a dark blue *Škoda*, watching a crumbling six-floor walkup built in the bleak Soviet style. Piotr Cermákova lived in a rundown neighborhood south of Wenceslas Square. The residents were mostly retirees and blue-collar workers. If the assassin was in Prague, she'd show up at Daddy's sooner or later. Noble had parked three doors down with his bumper facing away from the grim concrete pillbox and he used the rearview to keep an eye on the front of the building.

Prague is an old-world city straddling the banks of the Vltava River. Called the City of a Hundred Spires, it has survived both World Wars and communism. Medieval stone houses rub elbows with some of the most inspired modern architecture in the world and, in the middle of it all, squat decrepit reminders of the former Soviet bloc. It's a thriving country where tourism is emerging as one of the biggest industries. People from all over the world come to the Czech Republic to see castles and experience the culture.

Noble reached for a cup of coffee on the dash and sipped. He tried to stay focused, but his mind kept wandering. Noble had been on his share of sneak and peeks. Normally he was pretty good at it. The Green Berets had taught him the value of patience. He once spent a week lying in a crevice on the side of a mountain in Afghanistan, but just lately he found waiting next to impossible. Sitting still gave him time to think, and thinking was dangerous.

He watched the front of the building but his mind drifted to Paris—and Sam. Noble found himself back on the deck of the ship, feeling the icy spray and the pitch of the river barge beneath his feet. He heard the *whipcrack* of the pistol, saw Sam jerk, and watched her tumble over the side of the ship into the dark waters. Tears doubled his vision. He gave himself a shake to clear his thoughts and took a few deep breaths.

Get your head back in the game, soldier.

Noble pushed a thumb and forefinger into his eye sockets in an effort to bully his mind back on point. It was just after three and the afternoon sun was slanting on the buildings. Winter still clung to the city, reluctant to surrender to the forces of spring. Bare trees clawed at a clear blue sky, and wisps of smoke drifted up from the chimneys of Prague. Noble was dressed in a navy-blue windbreaker and denims. His toes felt like chips of ice. He could have used the heater, but the cold was helping to keep him awake.

A pair of schoolboys came up the street, passing a soccer ball back and forth. Their feet made soft punting sounds against the scuffed ball. One made a joke. The other chuck-led. Noble didn't speak Czech and couldn't tell if it was funny or not. Ten minutes later a beat-up old land cruiser backed into a spot on the street. A bent and wizened old woman was behind the wheel. Noble watched as she wres-tled the big car into the space with a lot of jerky moves. The wheels humped onto the sidewalk and the back fender crunched against a parked Citroen. The old woman climbed out and limped to the front of building, relying heavily on her cane. She had a shopping bag clutched in one arm and her hand trembled as she tried to slot her key. Noble thought about getting out to help, but couldn't risk exposing himself.

As he watched, the old woman dropped the keys. They landed on the step with a metallic *clack*. She muttered to herself, bent down slowly to retrieve them and a melon tumbled out of her shopping bag. It bounced next to the keys and started to roll. She caught the wayward fruit before it could go bounding down the steps, stuffed it back in the paper sack and then groped for the keys, looking right at the Škoda as she did.

Noble slouched down in the seat and tried to look disin-terested. The old woman straightened up and this time she managed to insert the house key. The front door swung open on tired hinge. The woman threw one last curious glance at the Škoda before swinging the door shut with a rattling *bang*.

Noble sat staring at the scarred wood, replaying the scene in his mind. Had there been something about the woman? Or was he just being paranoid? How's the old saw go? *Just because you're paranoid, doesn't mean you aren't being followed.* In the field of covert intelligence, paranoia came with the job description. Matthew Burke had drilled that into him. Noble decided to snoop the car. He gulped the last of his coffee before climbing out into the chilly air. His heels raked the uneven cobble stones. He passed the old beater, with its passenger-side tires on the curb, for a peek. Nothing unusual, but if the assassin was smart enough to fake her own death, she was smart enough not to leave evidence in the back seat of a car. On the other hand, the old woman might be exactly what she appeared to be.

CHAPTER TWENTY-SEVEN

Eliška Cermáková tucked the cane under one arm and mounted creaking steps two at a time. She had spotted the rangy looking customer in the dark blue SUV earlier in the day. He might be a jealous lover stalking an ex or maybe just a fella waiting on a friend, but Eliška doubted that. More likely he was a hitter waiting for her.

She stopped on the fourth-floor landing, pulled off the silver wig and shook out her short blonde hair. The hallway smelled like molding wood and stale urine. Eliška could hear the television through the door. She raised a fist to knock and hesitated. She considered turning around and going right back down the stairs. It wasn't too late. The world thought she was dead. She could go out the back door and disappear. But she wasn't going to do that, and she knew it. She was just delaying the inevitable. Coming here was an unnecessary risk, but she had to make sure the old man was safe.

Get it over with, Eliška told herself.

She rapped her knuckles against the flimsy wood. The sound was barely audible over the TV. Eliška waited. She was about to knock again when she heard floorboards creak. She slipped a hand inside the floral-print blouse and her fingers curled around the hilt of a 9mm Kahr in a shoulder holster.

The chain rattled and the lock clicked. Eliška heard clumsy fingers wrestling with the knob and relaxed her grip on the pistol. The door finally opened and an old man's face appeared in the gap. For a moment, she was afraid he wouldn't recognize her.

"Been a long time," Piotr Cermákova said. He turned and shuffled to a tattered recliner in the center of the living room.

Eliška set the groceries on the kitchen counter, propped the cane in the corner, closed the door and put the chain back on. "Papa, never take the chain off the door until you see who's on the other side."

He waved away her concern with one mangled claw. Only the ring and pinkie fingers remained on his right hand. The left had three digits and a thumb, but the appendage was withered and mostly useless. He gripped the arm of the recliner with his ruined hand and lowered himself down. He was older than she remembered. His eyes were milky white orbs and wisps of white hair clung to a bald scalp.

"Have any strangers come here, Papa?"

He shook his head. "Nobody. Why?"

On the television, a news anchor was talking about the migrant crisis in Europe and Italy's decision to deport thousands of Muslim refugees. Eliška found the remote and turned the sound down.

"I was watching that," he said.

She sat across from him on a dusty sofa that smelled of mothballs. "The same report will be on again at five and at six."

He shrugged boney shoulders. It was an impatient gesture that Eliška knew all too well. It meant he didn't agree but wasn't going to argue the point. He said, "Where have you been all these years?"

"Working," she told him. "I've been working, Papa."

She looked around at the shabby apartment. There were cracks in the plaster walls and water stains on the ceiling. A thick layer of dust clung to every surface. "Have you been getting the checks?"

The money was coming out of her account. Somebody was cashing the checks.

He nodded. "Got the checks."

"What are you doing with the money?"

He offered another shrug. "Saving it."

"Saving it," Eliška said. "For what?"

"An emergency," he told her and reached for the oxygen mask hanging on a tank next to his recliner. He twisted the valve and took a deep hit.

"Papa ..." Eliška shook her head. "Use the money, Papa. I can always get more. Buy yourself a hearing aid so you don't have to turn the television up so loud. Or move to a new apartment and buy a big screen TV."

"What do you care?" He took the mask away from his face. "How are you getting all that money? That's what I'd like to know. What have you been doing, Ellie?"

She swallowed a hard knot in her throat. "What does it matter?"

"Blood money," he said. "That's what it is. Plain and simple."

"I do what I have to do," Eliška told him. "You certainly have no problems cashing the checks."

He shook his head. "Don't use me as an excuse."

"You always did the right thing." Eliška waved a hand at the crummy apartment. "And look where it got you. You gave your fingers for Czechia and the only thing you got in return is a one room flat in a rundown tenement built by the Communists." After a beat, she added, "The same Communists you fought."

He gripped the arm of the chair and pushed himself up a little straighter. "I fought for freedom. I gave up my fingers to free Czechia from tyranny. I'd do it again."

"Lot of good it did." She rubbed her forehead. "Now we have crooked politicians who line their pockets while pensioners survive on crumbs."

"It's not a perfect system, but it's better than what we had before. You don't know. You weren't there. You never laid awake at night fearing a knock at the door." He settled himself back into the recliner and pointed to the shabby surroundings with the two remaining fingers on his right hand. "Change takes time. Rome wasn't built in a day. What we did, we did for a better tomorrow. We did it for the next generation. I don't know why you chose the path you did. You could have had a future in the military. You could have been running military intelligence by now. Instead you chose the easy money." He gave another of those impatient shrugs and his tone softened. "I blame myself. Your mother died before you were grown and I was never much of a father."

"Sorry I was such a disappointment." Eliška sat there, feeling hot with shame. She dashed a tear from her eye.

He said nothing.

She thought about walking out and leaving the old man to his fate. She took a minute to collect herself and said, "Papa, we need to go."

He scowled and cranked himself around in his seat for a look at her. "Go? Go where?"

"You remember Miklos? He's got a cabin in the foothills south of the city. It's a nice place in the woods with no distractions," Eliška said. She was trying to make fleeing for their lives sound like a pleasant surprise.

He sniffed and waved away that idea with one mangled claw.

"Won't it be nice to get out of this dusty old apartment?" Eliška asked. "Some fresh mountain air will do you good."

"I don't need mountain air. I need oxygen." He held up the mask as evidence. "You expect me to lug this tank up a mountainside?"

"I've got a car, Papa. We can take the tanks with us."

Eliška stood up and went to the window. Her brow wrinkled. The dark blue SUV was still parked at the end of the street. Whoever he was, he was watching the front of Papa's building. She needed to get rid of the surveillance before she could move the old man. She said, "I've got to take care of few things first. Pack a suitcase while I'm gone and be ready to go when I get back."

"I'm not going anywhere," he said.

Her patience reached the breaking point and she grabbed him by the lapels. His cloudy eyes opened wide.

Sour breath washed over her. Eliška spoke through clenched teeth, "Listen to me, you stupid old fool! I'm trying to save your life. There are some very bad people after me and they'll use you to get to me. Now, pack a bag. We're leaving as soon as I get back."

His unshaven chin trembled. A small sound worked up from his sunken chest. Eliška let him go, grabbed the wig off the counter and went to the door.

CHAPTER TWENTY-EIGHT

Noble was back on the Seine, feeling the freezing spray and the deck rolling beneath him. He saw Sam step around the pilothouse. He heard her final words but they were muffled and indistinct, like they were coming through a badly tuned radio. The pistol cracked and Noble watched her fall.

"Why her?" He asked the empty car.

The scene played inside his head on a continuous loop until Noble thought it would drive him mad. He lost sight of the street and the rental car and the crumbling Eastern bloc architecture. All he saw was Sam dying, over and over and over again. And every time she plunged over the railing, the warmth of his heart dimmed until a deep depression took hold.

Tears were building behind his eyes, threatening to break free, when a door closed with a soft *clump*. The sound jerked Noble back to the present. He blinked and passed a hand over his face. The elderly woman had emerged from the bleak Soviet pillbox. She hobbled down the steps and turned north.

Noble sat up a little straighter. His eyes narrowed. There was something different about her, but Noble couldn't put his finger on it. He watched her for a minute, wondering what had caught his attention. Then it clicked. Noble said, "You forgot your cane."

A grim smile turned up one side of his face. He had to respect her tradecraft. She was good. Not many thirty-somethings could transform themselves into a doddering grandmother at will. The change was so complete, if she hadn't slipped up and left the cane behind, Noble never would have spotted her.

He started to turn the key in the ignition, but he couldn't follow her in the car. She was moving too slow. He would have to tail her on foot. That gave her the advantage. She was from Prague and knew these streets. Noble had only been here a handful of times. Most of his knowledge came from studying maps on the flight over.

He waited until she reached the end of the block before climbing out and following at a leisurely stroll. Apartment buildings gradually gave way to corner stores, restaurants, and fashion boutiques. Noble was moving at a crawl. He imagined snails passing him on the sidewalk. Even plodding along, it was hard to keep her in front of him. Noble stepped inside a corner market and pretended to browse the fruit selection while he watched the old woman make her way up the sidewalk. She stopped at the intersection, glanced once over her shoulder and then disappeared around the corner so fast it was like watching a magic trick.

Pretty spry for an old gal.

She was headed for Wenceslas Square, where she could lose him in the crowd. It was the smart play and exactly what Noble would have done in her situation. He stepped outside, jogged to the end of the block and turned the corner into a sea of people.

Originally a horse market, Wenceslas Square is now one long shopping arcade that ends at the National Museum. A large stone fountain commands the center of the busy pedestrian area and stately oaks line the boulevard. Vendors sell everything from cheap T-shirts and knock-off designer handbags to *trdelnick* pastries and chocolates, which aren't as good as Belgium chocolates, but close.

A thousand voices filled Noble's ears and the warm smell of the sugar-coated pastries made his stomach rumble. Pigeons waddled beneath the feet of gawking tourists while a pair of street performers played "Paint It Black" on cellos. Noble shouldered his way through the masses and craned to see over the crowd. For a moment he thought he had lost her, but halfway across the Square he spotted gray hair moving at a trot. Noble dodged around a fat man and set off at a run. He had closed half the distance when the silver-haired grandmother darted inside a joint called Hot Peppers.

Suggestive silhouettes flanked the entrance and flashing neon announced, *VIP Lounge*. Noble pushed through the door into a thick wall of smoke and pulsing sound. The inside was all plush red leather, dim lighting, and mirrors. On stage, a dancer in a small square of black lace twisted around a polished brass pole. Noble worked his way along the bar, scanning the crowd for little old ladies on the move.

A bottled ginger in an impossibly short skirt sidled up next to him with a smile.

Noble waved her off. "I looking for something older."

He searched the tables around the stage but the assassin had vanished. Noble stood there a moment, taking in the room. The adrenaline rush that comes with a chase was wearing off and failure crowded around him like a cloak. His gut had twisted up in knots during the chase and now it started to let go. He was just about to double back toward the entrance when he glimpsed a head of gray hair headed for the back of the club. Noble set off in that direction. He passed a slim blonde with a boyish cut. She was dressed in a halter top and shorts. He didn't think anything of her until he saw the silver wig lying on an empty bar stool. By the time he realized his mistake, it was too late. A hand came down on his shoulder and he felt a knifepoint in the small of his back.

CHAPTER TWENTY-NINE

WIZARD SAT IN A CORNER BOOTH AT THE OCCIDENTAL with his back to the wall. A plate of wagyu beef and two martini glasses stood on the table in front of him. It wasn't yet lunchtime. The crowd was thin. The Occidental is a regular haunt for DC's movers and shakers. A trio of senators had a table near the window and the head of the State Department was at the bar along with the new AG, deep in conversation. Dean Martin was on the sound system asking how lucky a guy could be. *Very lucky if you happen to be a member of the Rat Pack*, thought Dulles.

Across from him sat Ron Hinson, a senior investigator with the Secret Service. He wasn't what most people thought of when they pictured a Secret Service agent. Ron was middle-age and middle-class, with no distinguishing features. He could walk through a room and nobody would spare him a second glance. What most people didn't know was that Ron Hinson's everyman appearance was a carefully cultivated cover. It allowed him to do his job more efficiently. Wizard always thought Hinson had missed a brilliant career in intelligence work.

Hinson picked up a seltzer water and said, "To what do I owe the pleasure?"

"Been a while." Wizard cut off a slice of beef. "Thought we should catch up. How's the wife and kids?"

Ron laughed and speared his steak tartare with his fork. "They're just fine, thanks for asking. But even my wife knows Albert Dulles doesn't call up old friends for a three-martini lunch unless he's got an angle."

Wizard favored the younger man with a rare smile. It was a small movement that twitched at the corners of his lips, but it was there—for those who knew what to look for.

Ron glanced around the dining room before leaning in and lowering his voice. "Spill it, Al. What are you working on?"

Wizard coughed, massaged his chest and said, "I suppose you heard about P. Arthur Fellows?"

A frown worked its way onto Ron's face. "I heard. Hell of a way to go. Fellows was a good enough sort. Never would have pegged him for a pervert. I suppose you're going to tell me it wasn't an accident?"

Wizard shook his head. Like his smile, it was a small movement.

Ron leaned in more. "Murder?"

Wizard nodded once.

Hinson whistled and leaned back in his seat. "How do you know?"

Wizard hunched forward and propped both elbows on the table. "Something he was working on got him killed."

"Well, you've lost me there, Al. Fellows was a strictly

midlevel investigator. He wasn't snooping anything worth killing over."

Wizard just waited.

Hinson explored a molar with his tongue. "What have you got in exchange, Al?"

"Just the identity of Fellows's killer."

Hinson's eyebrows went up. "Okay. I'll bite."

"Her name is Eliška Cermáková. She's a Czech assassin wanted for half a dozen murders."

"Have you got people on her?"

"I have a man in place," Wizard said.

"One man?"

"One of my best," Wizard told him. "What was Fellows working on?"

"He was investigating a series of supernotes."

"What's a supernote?" Wizard asked.

"A counterfeit bill so good it's indistinguishable from the real thing."

"If it's indistinguishable, how did he tumble to it?"

"A genuine US banknote will have slight imperfections," Hinson told him. "The money you have in your wallet isn't perfect. Plates get old, ink tars up in the channels, paper shifts as it moves through the press. It all adds up to tiny inconsistences.

"The bills we found are perfect, and I mean *perfect*." Hinson said. "No runs, no blurs, no ragged lines."

"So this counterfeiter is making bills better than the ones the US government prints and that's how you got onto it?"

Hinson inclined his head. "We've found three so far. We have no idea who's printing them or how many more might be floating around the system. But Fellows wasn't working the case anymore. He spotted the forgery and kicked it up the chain of command just two days before he turned up dead."

"And you didn't find that odd?" Wizard rasped.

"Of course we did." Hinson waved a hand in the air. "We knew whoever killed Fellows was trying to cover their tracks. We want them to think they threw us off the trail. It's easier to investigate if they don't know we're looking for them. Counterfeits as good as the ones we're talking about get the full resources of the Secret Service."

"What have you found out so far?"

Hinson shrugged his shoulders. "Talking to the wrong guy. I'm not on the task force."

"Come on, Ron. I don't believe that for a second. Even if you're not, you keep your ear to the ground."

Hinson turned his glass in clockwise circles, making damp rings on the tablecloth. "Not much, and that, in and of itself, is saying something. In order to print a bill of this quality, you need an intaglio press. They're rare—only a few in existence—and we thought we knew where all of them were located."

Wizard nodded. "Okay. What else?"

"You also need rag paper and specialized ink," Hinson told him. "Neither is cheap and there are only a few manufactures in the whole world. Sale of the materials is highly regulated."

"So you would have known if someone bought a large quantity of paper and ink?" Wizard asked.

"Without doubt," said Hinson. "Besides that, you need printing plates. Whoever minted these bills knew what they were doing. They have access to materials and they've got an intaglio press—which tells us this is not some teenage anarchist working out of his parents' basement. This is a full-scale operation, probably located somewhere in southern Europe judging by forensics."

"Forensics?" Wizard questioned.

Hinson nodded. "Traces of saltwater on all three bills we've recovered came from the Adriatic Sea."

Wizard scratched an eyebrow with one nicotine-stained fingertip. "So it's possible there are more of these in circulation?"

"Not only is it possible," said Hinson, "it's probable. You don't go to this kind of effort to print up a few Benjamins."

"What's the fallout from something like this?"

Hinson rocked his head side to side. "Depends on the depth of market penetration. A flood of indistinguishable counterfeit bills could, in theory, crash the dollar. But it would take billions in supernotes. That's not to say it doesn't have an impact. Counterfeiting is a serious problem, don't get me wrong. It devalues the currency, disrupting markets and ..."

Wizard was only half listening. He had stuck on the idea of crashing the dollar. Something inside his brain clicked. Hinson kept talking, but Wizard was twenty miles away, back in his office at Langley. He had spent countless hours staring at the wall, trying to fit the pieces together, looking for the missing link, searching for the piece that would finally complete the puzzle. Was this it? After all these years?

CHAPTER THIRTY

NOBLE'S BREATH FROZE IN HIS LUNGS. THE MUSCLES IN his back turned to spring steel. He stood rooted to the spot, waiting for the knife to drive home. The assassin had him dead to rights, but instead of jamming the blade up under his ribs, she leaned in close and spoke German: "One wrong move and I'll cut your liver in two."

She pressed up against him, shielding the knife with her body, and steered Noble past a sea of gawking men—eyes glued to the stage—to the private rooms. She said, "Keep a smile on your face."

Noble moved on autopilot. His arms were pinned to his sides and his knees didn't want to bend. It's tough to look natural with a knife in your back. He kept expecting someone to see the blade and shout, but they pushed through a beaded curtain without anyone noticing and into a dimly lit hall with cubbies on either side shielded by privacy curtains.

"All the way to the end," the assassin ordered.

Noble allowed himself to be herded along on legs that felt like wooden oars. They reached the end of the hall. The assassin kicked the curtain aside to be sure the cubby was empty before shoving Noble inside. A small sofa crammed up the space. The only other furnishing was a blacklight poster of a nude woman in the throes of ecstasy. The assassin crowded in behind him and Noble made his move.

He used his forearm to bat the knife aside and tried to lock up her wrist. They struggled for control of the weapon. The assassin drove an elbow into the side of Noble's head and fairy lights exploded in his vision. She followed up with a knee. She was going for his groin, but Noble turned at the last second and took the blow on his hip instead. A grunt of pain ripped from his throat. The tight space didn't give him any room to maneuver and the assassin was a bobcat. Noble was playing nice because she was a girl and the part of him raised in Western culture still believed there was never any reason to hit a woman. But if he was going to walk away from this without getting carved up, he had to fight dirty.

He got both hands around her wrist and then used a headbutt. It was a desperate gamble, but it worked. It rocked her head back on her neck. She let out a startled gasp that was more surprise than pain. Noble swept her feet out from under her with a kick and used his weight to wrestle her to the sofa. She went down kicking and thrashing. Noble pinned her, jammed a knee in her stomach, and pressed down until her face turned red. A vein throbbed in her forehead.

Even struggling for breath, she still wasn't ready to give up. She tried to force the switchblade up to Noble's throat. He had the weight advantage and slowly bent her wrist until the knifepoint was under her chin. It was no easy feat. Even on top and with forty extra pounds on her, the assassin made him work for it. He was breathing heavy by the time he got the knife pressed under her chin, the point dimpling her pale white flesh. He spoke through clenched teeth. "Let it go."

There was a long moment when Noble thought she would go on struggling and he'd have to ram the knife home. She finally ran out of oxygen. Her eyes rolled up in her head and her muscles relaxed. Her fingers slowly uncurled. Noble didn't dare let go of her wrists. Instead he used his teeth to pluck the switchblade from her open palm. He turned his head to the side and spat the weapon onto the floor before relaxing some of the pressure on her abdomen.

She sucked air and gasped out, "You're American?"

"That's right," Noble told her. He adjusted his hold, got both of her wrists clasped in his right hand, and took out his phone with his left hand. "Say cheese."

She shot a bird as Noble snapped a picture.

"Now let's talk about who hired you to kill a Secret Service agent and why," Noble said.

Before she could answer, they heard voices in the hall.

CHAPTER THIRTY-ONE

THE DANCER LED HER CUSTOMER BY THE HAND ALONG the dimly lit hall. He was a grossly overweight Russian with wiry hairs growing from his nose. He smelled like cabbage, but he was a regular and he had money to burn. The girls called him Hippo—never to his face, of course. To his face he was always Sweetie or Honey. After dropping a couple grand in the club, Hippo would take one of the girls to a nearby hotel where he would fork over another grand for what usually amounted to fifteen minutes of work. The lucky girl—or *unlucky* depending on your point of view— got to keep half. The other half went to management. Most of the girls didn't mind. It paid their rent for the month. Tonight, it seemed Celeste was going to be the lucky girl. She pushed aside the curtain and was surprised to find someone in her booth.

A blonde girl in skimpy shorts was straddling a customer. Her hips moved to the steady beat of the pounding bassline. The customer had one hand around the back of her neck. The other hand was lost from view. Celeste had never seen the girl before. She must be new. Girls came and went all the time. Some of them found a rich businessman eager to save them from the life. Others just vanished after a while and new girls showed up to take their place. There were always more girls ready to try their luck at dancing. It was easier than working and generally paid better. What they didn't know was that dancing eventually led to prostitution, and if they didn't have a drug problem before they started dancing, they would have one after they started turning tricks. It was only a matter of time.

"This is *my* booth," Celeste said in Czech.

Without stopping, the blonde looked over her shoulder and said, "Do you mind?"

Celeste huffed, threw the curtain closed and led Hippo to another stall.

————

Noble sat on the couch with the switchblade knife tucked under Cermáková's chin. His left hand cupped the back of her neck. He could slit her throat with a flick of his wrist. She straddled his lap and went on grinding even after the curtain fell shut.

"We haven't got long," she said in English. "She'll complain to management that someone else is in her booth."

"Then you'd better start talking," Noble said, ignoring the way her hips pressed up against him. "Who hired you to kill Fellows and why?"

"That's what I'd like to know," Eliška told him. "First they threatened me and then they tried to have me killed."

"Who was your contact?" Noble said. It was an effort to keep his mind on the questions and off her body. She was trying to distract him and doing a good job. Noble said, "Who paid you the money?"

"An American. I don't know his name, but I managed to get a picture of him. A friend in military intelligence tracked him down."

"This friend have a name?" Noble asked.

"Miklos," she said. "I'm supposed to meet him this afternoon at the train station. I want the man who hired me just as much as you. When I find him, I'll find out who is pulling his strings. Let me go and I'll share the information with you."

Noble managed a humorless laugh. "Nice try. We'll go together."

She stopped grinding and climbed off him. "Okay, American, we'll do it your way. What do I call you?"

"Jake."

"Jake," she said, testing the word in her mouth. "Short for Jakob."

She gave the name a Czech inflection. It came out sounding like *Yakob*.

"Close enough."

"Eliška Cermákova," she said. "Nice to meet you, Jakob."

"Forgive me if I don't shake hands," Noble said.

She motioned to her skimpy outfit. "How do you propose we get out of here?"

"Walk out like we own the place," Noble told her. He took her by the elbow, tucked the switchblade knife against her ribcage and led her out through the busy club, ignoring curious looks from the rest of the men gathered around the stage.

CHAPTER THIRTY-TWO

By noon Gwen and Ezra were both fast asleep. It was Gwen's turn on the sofa. She was stretched out with a stack of papers on her lap. Ezra was on the floor with his back against the sofa and his head resting against Gwen's thigh. A file lay open on his lap. The only sounds were buzzing fluorescents, the hum from the air vent, and Ezra's snores. Empty food cartons littered the tables and the computer screens glowed in silence.

Ezra would have gone right on sleeping but an electronic chirp cut through the fog of dreams. He snorted, smacked his lips, and peered stupidly at the monitor. It was another minute before his mind made sense of what he was seeing. He pushed a hand through his hair in an effort to clear out the cobwebs and elbowed Gwen. "Hey, take a look at this."

"Am I late for class?" She sat up, rubbing sleep from her eyes.

"Check it out." Ezra pointed to the computer screen.

"Were you asleep?" Gwen asked.

"No," Ezra lied, trying to banish the sleep from his voice. "Course not. Don't be silly."

She gave him a skeptical look, swung her legs off the sofa and lurched over to her station. On the screen was a picture of Eliška Cermáková. The assassin was flicking off the camera. Gwen pinged the location of the text. "Looks like Noble found her. They're in Wenceslas Square."

Ezra said, "She looks dangerous."

A cold hatred burned in Cermáková's eyes. It was easy to see why they called her the Angel of Death. She was both Beauty and the Beast: a deadly woman with an angel's face. Gwen wouldn't want to be on the receiving end of that stare. It made her shiver. She said, "Should I call him?"

"No," said Ezra. "Let him call us."

It was hard to make out much from the picture. The assassin's head and shoulders filled most of the frame. They could see her bare shoulders and her hand, middle finger extended, but that was all.

Ezra cocked his head to the side and narrowed his eyes. "Is she wearing clothes?"

Gwen squinted. "I don't think so."

Ezra made a curious sound at the back of his throat.

"Guys are such perverts," Gwen said shook her head. She wondered why it bothered her so much. She wasn't interested in a relationship with Ezra. So what if he ogled other women? *What if he met someone?* Gwen thought. *Started a relationship?* The idea left her confused and anxious. She decided to focus on work instead. She said, "He's made contact. We can only assume he has her in custody."

"Or she has him," Ezra quipped.

Gwen ignored the wisecrack. "We need to organize an extraction. Find out what personnel we have in the area capable of smuggling a person out of the country."

Ezra used his computer to bring up a list of assets in Prague and the area around the Czech Republic. He shook his head. "Surprisingly little. We have assets in Hungary with military experience and field agents in Germany skilled in extraction, but no one close."

Gwen pinched her bottom lip between thumb and fore-finger. "Think Noble can extract her on his own?"

"I wouldn't put it past him."

They were busy discussing the details when Wizard came through the door. He was dressed in his usual dark suit and polished wingtips. His gray was hair combed straight back. He snatched the cigarette from his mouth and breathed smoke. "What's the latest?"

"Noble made contact," Gwen told him and motioned to the picture on screen. "But we're having trouble putting together an extraction team. Quite frankly, sir, it's going to be difficult—if not impossible—to get her out of the country."

Wizard blew smoke. "That may not be necessary."

"Sir?" Gwen asked.

Wizard frowned, rubbed two fingers against his chest and then reached in his jacket for a bottle of pills. He shook a pair into his open palm, tossed them back, and dry-swallowed. Ezra and Gwen waited. Wizard cleared his throat and rubbed at his chest, like he was waiting to see if his heart would stop. When it was clear he wasn't going into cardiac arrest, Wizard said, "Noble's capable of a field interrogation."

"What about after?" Gwen said. "She's wanted for murder. We can't just turn her loose."

Wizard held her gaze without comment. A cold weight settled over the room. Ezra and Gwen exchanged a look. What Wizard was suggesting amounted to murder. Despite their best efforts to keep their heads down and fly under the radar, they had found themselves in another operation without congressional oversight. These type missions eventually came in to the light. When they did, people lost their jobs.

The phone rang and Gwen snatched it up. "Goodman and Associates. How may I direct your call?"

"It's me," Noble's voice came on the line. "Go secure."

Gwen pushed the switch and then put the phone on speaker. "Secure."

Wizard said, "Jake, Albert Dulles here, give us a sit rep."

"I'm with Eliška now," Noble told them. "She's our assassin, all right. Tried to use me as a pin cushion."

"You and the assassin are on a first name basis?" Wizard asked.

"We're not Facebook buddies, if that makes you feel any better," Noble said.

That information did not appear to make Wizard feel any better. He said, "Does she know who hired her?"

"No, but we've got a lead."

Gwen frowned at that turn of phrase.

Wizard took the cigarette from his mouth. "Did you say *we?*"

"Long story," Noble said. "Any luck figuring out what Fellows was working on?"

Wizard relayed about his meeting with Ron Hinson and about the counterfeits. He said, "But it got kicked up the chain of command. That's why we didn't find it sooner. He was no longer assigned to it when he died."

Noble said, "So Fellows got killed over a case he wasn't even working on?"

"Looks that way," said Wizard. "Has Cermáková got anything that will lead us to her employer?"

"We're on our way to meet a contact that might have more information for us," Noble told them. "I'll let you know when I have something to share."

He hung up before they could ask any more questions. Wizard stood there smoking. After a long silence, he remarked, "War makes strange bed fellows."

CHAPTER THIRTY-THREE

"Where is this friend of yours?" Noble wanted to know.

They were at a newsstand in the main concourse of Prague Central Station, pretending to read magazines. A large LED board showed arrivals and departures. A loud speaker announced the train to Budapest, first in Czech, then English and German. A burger joint next to the news-stand was twisting Noble's stomach in knots. The tempting aroma of beef and simmering onions beckoned to him. A Jimmy Buffet song popped into his head. Prague was a long way from paradise, but the smell was close. He was seriously debating dinner when a pair of security guards in blue and yellow vests ambled past.

Eliška buried her face in a newspaper. "He'll be here."

She was dressed in a Rolling Stones T-shirt and a short leather jacket. A pub cap covered her short blonde locks. None of it matched, but at least she wasn't walking around in bra and underwear.

They had piecemealed the outfit together as they passed through Wenceslas Square. Noble had swiped a pair of denims while Eliška distracted the woman running the stall. They worked well together, taking cues from each other without having to exchange a word. Eliška lived on the fringes—thieving was second nature to her—and sleight of hand had been part of Noble's counterintelligence training at the Farm. Eliška had swiped the jacket from the back of a chair at an outdoor café and Noble haggled for a knock-off handbag while Eliška lifted the shoes. Once she was dressed, they had taken the underground to the train station and spent the next hour and a half waiting on her contact.

Noble put down a copy of *Prague Times* and picked up a celebrity gossip magazine. The fat man behind the counter watched them with open hostility. His expression said, *"Buy something or get lost."* Noble ignored him and muttered, "I don't like this. He's late."

In the world of covert intelligence, when in doubt, walk away. An informant showing up late could be as simple as traffic, but it could mean your cover is blown. Better to err on the side of caution. Noble stood there, eyes staring at the gossip rag without really seeing, fighting the urge to walk out. His training told him to abort, but he might not get another crack at Eliška's informant.

The same pair of security guards happened past less than five minutes later. Noble flipped the magazine closed, stuffed it back on the rack, and took Eliška by the elbow. "Let's go."

She tossed her newspaper on the counter and allowed Noble to drag her away. He led her along a tiled hall and up a flight of stairs to the number 4 platform where a train was just pulling into the station. Noble shot a quick glance over his shoulder. The security guards were twenty meters back. They had just reached the top of the steps. Noble cursed under his breath.

"Are they still behind us?" Eliška asked.

"Yep."

She echoed his curse.

The train slowed to a stop with a chuffing of air brakes. Passengers spilled onto the platform. Noble and Eliška mixed with the crowd waiting to board. He had to bend his knees to keep his head level with the crowd. While they waited, Eliška rested a hand on his shoulder and leaned in close, like a lover whispering in his ear. She used the motion to watch the station cops over his shoulder.

Noble asked, "Did they spot us?"

"Yes."

"Coming this way?"

"Do you even need to ask?"

The last passenger stepped off the train and the crowd surged forward. Noble and Eliška climbed aboard and made their way along the line of cars. They shouldered past a knot of people stowing luggage and jockeying for seats, passing the two cops hurrying in the opposite direction. They went forward three cars, exited the train, and went right back down the same flight of stairs they had come up.

In two minutes, they were back at the main concourse. Eliška swiped a prepaid burner from a phone booth as they passed. They left the station and made their way through a wooded park with a statue dedicated to American president Woodrow Wilson, then along Opletalova Boulevard.

Eliška tore the phone out of the clear plastic shell and

powered it on. She dialed a number. When there was no answer, she dialed again. There was no answer the second time and Noble said, "I think your informant is compromised."

"He's not compromised," Eliška said. "He's a coward."

She keyed in a text message that said, *I'm just going to keep calling.*

Thirty seconds later the phone vibrated.

Noble reached over and put it on speaker, a not-so-subtle way of letting Eliška know he didn't trust her. She shot him a nasty look but spoke into to the phone. "Did you forget about our meeting, Miklos?"

"I didn't forget," he said. "I've been picking up a lot of chatter. I think someone is onto me."

"You're paranoid," she told him. "What did you find out?"

"Get another source," he said. "I've got better things to do than get killed."

"Did you find the American or not?"

He hesitated before saying, "I did. He's nobody you want to tangle with. I suggest you let this one go."

"You know I'm not going to do that," Eliška said. "What did you find out?"

"*Not over the phone,*" Miklos said.

"When and where?"

There was another long pause. Miklos said, "Be at the top of Charles Bridge Tower in one hour."

The line went dead. Eliška pocketed the stolen burner. "I told you. He's just scared."

"Something's not right," Noble said.

"You think it's a setup?"

"I'm not sure what to think," Noble told her. "But my gut's telling me something's not right."

"I'd feel a lot better with a gun," Eliška said.

Noble snorted. "I wouldn't trust you with a squirt gun."

"What is a squirt gun?"

"Shoots water," Noble explained.

"What good is that?" she wanted to know.

"Never mind," Noble said. "Let's go. It's a long walk to the bridge."

CHAPTER THIRTY-FOUR

"YOU DID REAL GOOD, MIKLOS." LUCAS RANDALL SAT with his chair tipped back on two legs and a Marlboro stuck in one corner of his mouth. He had a Sig Sauer P226 handgun resting on his thigh. Navy SEALs had used the Sig as their sidearm of choice for over two decades. It was eventually replaced by the Glock 19, but Lucas preferred his Sig. This particular model had a skeletal frog etched into the slide. The hammer was back and Lucas's finger rested along the side of the weapon. He snatched the cigarette from his mouth and trailed smoke from both nostrils. "Keep playing your cards right. You might make it out of this alive."

Miklos was a scared little man, with a big head perched atop a round body and no neck. His hand shook as he placed the phone down on the kitchen table. Lucas had seen the type before. They want the respect that comes with the uniform but none of the danger. They take jobs in communications or supply logistics. They work in an office and tell everybody they meet that they're a soldier. Most of them use the uniform to get laid. In a word, *pathetic*.

The Czech Intelligence specialist lived in a first-floor apartment in the Nové Malešice district near Radio Free Europe. His place was small but well-furnished and obviously belonged to a bachelor. The focal point was a state-of-the-art video-game system connected to a flat-screen TV. The fridge was empty, except for a bottle of spicy mustard and a carton of curdled milk.

Tracking Miklos down had proven easy enough. Second-rate intel officers rarely remembered to cover their own tracks. They're used to collecting info on others. They didn't stop to think about who might be collecting info on *them*.

Eric pressed a Makarov pistol against the back of Miklos's pudgy neck. The rest of his crew was in the living room, playing video games and drinking beer. They were a collection of German hardcases. Some of them were former soldiers. All of them were ex-cons. They were in it for the money and had no qualms against killing. Veers thumbed back the hammer on the Makarov and said, "He is of no more use to us. Perhaps we should kill him now."

A terrified breath escaped Miklos. Eric wasn't going to waste him, but Miklos didn't know that. Eric was just trying to scare the little man. It worked. Miklos sat in the chair hyperventilating. His eyes rolled in their sockets and large beads of sweat trailed down the sides of his massive head.

Lucas watched him sweat. When he didn't think Miklos could take the pressure anymore, he shook his head. "We won't kill him unless we have to."

"As you wish, *Herr* Randall." Eric let the hammer down

with a gentle *click*. He was good. He played the part to perfection.

"Besides." Lucas reached over and chucked Miklos on the shoulder. The impact threatened to knock the little man right off his seat. "Miklos here is going to the meet. Isn't that right, Miklos?"

He licked his lips. His eyes darted from Lucas to Eric and back. "You said all I had to do was set it up."

Lucas took a long drag on his cigarette. The end flared bright and then dimmed. He fixed Miklos with a hard stare. "Help us nail Cermákova, and you can go back to analyzing photographs for the military. Refuse ..." Lucas shrugged and thrust his chin at the German. "Eric will drill a hole through your neck. Ever seen someone shot in the neck?"

Miklos shook his head side to side.

"Real nasty," Lucas told him. "Bullet severs the spine, paralyzing you instantly, and blows out your vocal chords so you can't even scream, but it doesn't kill you. Not right away. You lay there and choke to death on your own blood."

Lucas let that sink in before saying, "You going to play ball, Miklos?"

He hesitated only a second before nodding.

"See, I knew you were a smart boy," Lucas said. He turned to Eric. "Tell those idiots to turn off the video game and get in the van. We got work to do."

CHAPTER THIRTY-FIVE

JAQUELINE ARMSTRONG SPENT MOST OF THE DAY IN A meeting with the DNI, then had to climb the Hill to justify her budget to the House Select Committee. A budget crisis was looming and Armstrong wanted to get her shop funded before Congress stalled out over partisan issues. It didn't help that most of the senators on the committee were loyal to the opposition party. They had made it their unofficial mission to oppose the White House in every way possible. That meant stonewalling the new CIA director as well. Convincing them to green light covert action was impossible. A successful operation by the CIA would go down as a win for the president. Congress wasn't going to let that happen, which meant Armstrong's hands were tied. She could collect intel, but mounting any kind of operation was out of the question. It was unfortunate too; the information she was getting out of Iran could help defuse their nuclear ambitions. Certain politicians would rather see America nuked than allow a victory for the current president.

On top of that, Armstrong's daughter had been calling every fifteen minutes like clockwork. Nickie was dealing with her first real crush. He was, according to Nickie, a 'cool guy' who didn't even know she existed. The teenage hormone-fueled melodrama was too much for Armstrong, but she listened anyway. Or tried to. This was one thing Dad couldn't help with and Nickie had turned to Mom for advice. Armstrong was okay with Mr. Cool giving Nickie the cold shoulder—in fact she preferred it that way—but she wasn't about to tell her daughter that.

No one ever said being the Director of Central Intelligence was easy.

Armstrong made her case to the committee. The members were seated on a raised platform. Fifteen men and women stared down at her with openly hostile expressions fixed on stony faces. Armstrong felt like she was on trial. She had been hoping for professional courtesy from the women at the very least. If anything, they were worse than the men. When it was over, Armstrong packed away her documents, thanked the elected officials and made her way out of the soundproof room.

Duc Hwang was waiting for her. The big Navy SEAL looked out of place in his ill-fitting suit and his wild tangles of black beard. Well-dressed staffers gave him a wide berth as they passed him in the hall. He said, "I found something I think you'll be interested in."

Armstrong cast a quick glance over her shoulder at the door before leading Duc down the marbled hall toward the restrooms. Government buildings have ears; Armstrong had found that out the hard way. She lowered her voice and asked, "What have you got?"

"While you were arguing budgets, the DDO was having a luncheon with a top-ranking investigator for the Secret Service Department."

"What? How did you ... ?" Armstrong shook her head. "Never mind."

As head of her personal security, Duc had developed his own intelligence network. Nothing happened in Langley without him knowing. She said, "What did they talk about?"

"I don't know." Duc shrugged his cannonball shoulders. "But there's something else."

"More good news?" Armstrong said in a perfect deadpan.

"Jake Noble is no longer on his boat," Duc said. "I got curious and checked the logs. He used his security clearance at the front gate day before yesterday."

Armstrong blinked. She felt like Duc had just sucker punched her in the belly. Noble wasn't cleared for duty. He was still on bereavement, pending a full psych eval. What would he be doing at Langley? It came together for her in a flash. Wizard's request for analysts and Jake Noble in DC—it couldn't be coincidence.

"I need to get back to Langley."

Duc said, "I thought you might."

CHAPTER THIRTY-SIX

CHARLES BRIDGE SPANS THE WIDE AND WINDING BANKS of the Vltava River. The stonework balustrade is guarded by statues of martyred saints. Pigeons roost in their ancient crooks. Their droppings cover age-blackened stone like white frosting on chocolate cake. Every day, hundreds of tourists swarm the smooth cobblestones, stopping in the center of the span for selfies, and clogging up foot traffic. Groups of musicians armed with cellos and violins play classical renditions of modern hits on the eastern side of the bridge. Prague is famous for its symphony, and you can listen to some of the finest musicians in the city for free at Charles Bridge. Today, a small knot of players sawed their way through *God's Gonna Cut You Down* by Johnny Cash.

Stone towers flank either end of the bridge. In Medieval times, they guarded against invading armies—defending the road to Prague Castle—and formed a part of the coronation route for Czech kings. Now they serve only as a tourist trap. For a hundred Czech crowns, you can climb to the top and take in a view of the city. Noble counted out the bills for a tired-eyed attendant and she passed him a pair of ticket stubs.

Eliška motioned for him to go first.

Noble put a hand in the small of her back and gave her a push. "Ladies first. I insist."

The door was a collection of petrified wood held together by rusting iron. Noble had to duck. He gripped the Kimber hidden in his waistband and followed Eliška up a set of winding stairs. She took the steps two at a time. It was easy to see how P. Arthur Fellows had been caught flat-footed. She had the kind of hypnotic sway that keeps a guy up half the night just imagining the possibilities.

At the top of the steps, Noble found a stone statue of a leering old man with his robes hiked up, irreverently displaying his backside. They passed the statue into a vaulted chamber. Aging timbers held aloft a shingled roof and a cold wind whistled around the sloping eaves. A shifting, shadow-laden twilight spilled in from a pair of doors leading to a balcony that wrapped around the top of the fortification. The small space under the roof was empty and quiet, except for the wind.

Noble whispered, "Where is he?"

Eliška shook her head. "Outside maybe?"

He followed her to one of the doors and stepped onto the balcony. Wind whipped his hair into a cloud around his head. He could see the entire city from up here. The red-tiled roofs and ancient spires of Prague marched away into the rich red dusk of the setting sun. A defensive stonework of fleur-de-lis wrapped around the balcony, forming windows through which archers could rain down arrows on approaching enemies. It also made an excellent privacy screen for clandestine meetings. They circled the tower and found Miklos staring out over the bridge toward the opposite tower. His eyes opened wide at the sight of Noble.

"Who is this?" Miklos said. "You didn't tell me anyone else was coming."

"Relax," Eliška said. "His name is—"

"Doghouse Reilly," Noble interrupted. He didn't want Miklos having his real name and Doghouse Reilly was the first thing that popped into his head. It came from one of his favorite films starring Humphrey Bogart. "You've got some information for us?"

Miklos shook his head and started to backtrack toward the door. "Not for you. I don't know you."

Eliška caught his sleeve. "Miklos, I need your help."

Miklos stared at Noble. "He could be a cop!"

She gave his windbreaker a tug to get his attention. "Never mind him. What did you find out?"

Miklos shot a nervous glance at Noble and said, "I found out this American is no one you want to mess with. He works for some very unpleasant people. You want my advice? *Walk away.*"

"It's too late for that," Eliška told him. "He tried to kill me."

Miklos jerked his arm free. "Consider yourself lucky."

Eliška grabbed his lapels and pinned him against the balustrade. "What's his name?"

"His name isn't important," Miklos said. "It's the people he works for that you should be concerned with."

"Who's he working for?" Noble asked.

"A terrorist organization called the United Front."

"Never heard of 'em," Noble said.

"Neither had I, until yesterday," said Miklos. "And I wish I hadn't gone snooping around."

"What did you find?" Eliška asked.

"Enough to scare me," Miklos commented.

"Who are they?" Noble asked. "What do they want?"

"That's just it," Miklos told him. "Nobody knows. They're well-connected and well-financed. Anyone who runs afoul of them ends up dead. I'm telling you, Eliška, you need to get out of here. Go now. Before it's too late."

Miklos grabbed Eliška's hands in an attempt to pry her fingers loose from his lapels and Noble noticed several of his fingernails were missing. The wounds were swollen and angry.

Noble said, "What happened to your hand?"

Miklos jammed his fist back into his pocket like a child trying to hide a cookie. "Nothing. Nothing. I hurt myself working on the house."

"Looked more like someone yanked out your fingernails to me," Noble said.

Eliška grasped his cuff and pulled his hand from his pocket. She saw the bloody nail beds and her nostrils flared. "What did you do, Miklos?"

When he didn't answer, she gave him a shake. "What did you tell them?"

"I had no choice, Ellie." His face melted and his chins trembled. "They came to my house. They know all about—"

There was a loud *hiss*, followed by a *snap*. The top of Miklos's head disappeared in a shower of gore. His knees buckled. His body sank like a trapdoor had opened beneath his feet.

CHAPTER THIRTY-SEVEN

Noble dropped to his belly as a second bullet tore a chunk from the age-blackened stone. A third shot whistled overhead and a roof shingle exploded. Noble clawed the gun from his waistband. The smell of blood filled his lungs. His heart crowded up into his throat. Eliška was hunkered down with her back to the wall. Miklos lay on the ground at her feet with half his skull missing and dark-red blood forming a puddle. Eliška stared at the body with shock written on her features.

"The shots came from the west," Noble said more to himself.

Eliška tore her eyes away from the body. "Probably from the other tower."

Noble hadn't heard the report, only the impacts. Elevation and wind helped, but the shooter must have been using a sound suppressor. Noble wondered if anyone on the bridge knew bullets were zipping overhead. A quick peek through the gap in the stonework showed him crowds milling about unconcerned. The shooter could plink at them all day without anyone noticing. Noble said, "We have to get out of here."

Eliška gave a jerky nod.

They scrambled around the corner, staying low to avoid any more bullets. Noble slipped through the opening in a crouch as another shot blasted chips of stone from the door frame. Eliška was right behind him. The top floor was empty, but Noble's ears pricked up the sound of feet on the steps.

Eliška held out a hand. "Give me the gun."

"Not a chance."

"Then the knife," Eliška said.

He shook his head. "No way."

She motioned to the head of the stairs. "They'll be here any second."

He didn't know how many hitters were coming up—it sounded like more than one—and he didn't know what kind of hardware they were sporting. He had the Kimber, but shooting it out on a spiral stair was suicide. He cast about for anything that might tip the scales in his favor. The only thing he found was an old fire extinguisher collecting dust in the corner. It probably should have been replaced twenty years ago.

Noble snatched it off the hook, and Eliška said, "What are you going to do with that?"

"Try to even the odds," Noble told her and pulled the safety ring. "Stay behind me."

Eliška crowded so close he could feel the points of her breasts against his back. With his heart ping-ponging around inside his chest and sweat soaking through his shirt, he moved to the top of the steps, aimed the nozzle and squeezed. The extinguisher belched a blinding white cloud down the winding staircase. Noble went down the first few risers and triggered another blast. He was rewarded with a surprised grunt from below.

He shot two more long bursts and then plunged into the blinding fog. The air was full of choking white powder. Noble put his shoulder against the wall, using it to steady himself, and screwed his eyes down to slits. He went slow. He was afraid of missing a step. It would only take one to end up at the bottom with a broken neck. Eliška was behind him, her hands clutching his coattail. He stopped every few feet to trigger the extinguisher. He could hear the hitters choking on the fire retardant. They were just around the next turn. Noble aimed the nozzle and loosed one long blast before switching the heavy extinguisher to his right hand. Tears welled up in his eyes, rolled down his cheeks and doubled his vision. Noble spotted the barrel of a gun through a wall of white and he swung the extinguisher.

The metal tube impacted with a solid *thump*. Noble heard a grunt. There was a clatter as the pistol went tumbling down the steps and the heavy sound of a body collapsing. Noble kept moving, putting one foot in front of the other, hoping he didn't take a header. He stepped over the body of the first man and tangled with a second shooter coming up the steps.

Noble shoulder-checked the goon. The man staggered backward into the wall. A pistol barked. The bullet impacted the stone inches from Noble's head. Eliška let out a high-pitched curse. Noble swung the extinguisher over-hand like a man breaking rocks with a sledgehammer. The first swing missed and bounced off the steps. The goon fired twice more. Noble felt the wind from a slug as it passed between his legs. His stomach twisted into a tight knot and his manhood tried to crawl up inside his pelvis. He swung again. This time he felt the crunch of metal on bone.

The goon went tumbling down the steps. He crashed into a third man coming up—Noble heard them collide. There was a surprised curse, the sound of a struggle, then five ear-splitting blasts.

The last man had gotten confused and shot his partner dead. Noble used the mistake to his advantage. He surged around the turn and swung the extinguisher, catching the man in the stomach. The goon doubled over in pain. Noble followed up with a kick. He managed to connect and sent the man tumbling.

Eliška had stopped and was hunkered down on the steps.

Noble said, "Are you hit?"

When she didn't answer, he went back to check on her. She wasn't injured. She was patting one of the fallen thugs in search of a weapon. Noble grabbed her arm and gave her a tug. "No time!"

Tears doubled his vision and his lungs were on fire. He felt like he would choke to death before he reached the bottom. He buried his face in the crook of one elbow and focused on not missing any steps. He passed the crumpled body of the third man and then stumbled as his feet found the ground floor. He did a clumsy double step to stay upright, dropped the extinguisher and herded Eliška through the door.

She coughed and beat at her chest. She looked like she'd been caught in an explosion at a dumpling factory.

Noble flapped his arms like a bird trying to lift off in an effort to get the last of the smoke out of his clothes. He had been gassed in basic training at Fort Benning, Georgia. All of eighteen years old, Jake, along with the other new recruits, had filed into a large olive drab tent flooded with tear gas. The point of the exercise was twofold: It taught soldiers to trust their gas masks—Noble clearly recalled standing in the dark and breathing through his mask, the sound incredibly loud in his own ears as the tent filled with thick white smoke—and it taught soldiers to fight through nauseating pain. Just when the recruits started feeling comfortable, drill sergeants had ordered them to remove the masks. Before they could leave the tent, every soldier was forced to clearly state name, rank, and military number. Once outside, another drill sergeant had ordered the recruits to flap their arms and spit. That's just what Noble did now. He worked up a throat full of bile, turned his head to the side, and blew snot all over the cobblestones.

They were under the arch, near the foot of the bridge. White smoke billowed from the open door behind them. A crowd was gathering. Several people had cellphones out. A few were calling the fire department. The rest were taking video. One man asked if they were alright. The shooter was on Noble's left, atop the western tower. On his right was Old Town. The labyrinth of narrow streets would be the perfect place to disappear. Noble started pushing his way through the throng and spotted a black van parked at the corner. Two men, hands buried in the pockets of their overcoats, climbed out.

CHAPTER THIRTY-EIGHT

EZRA AND GWEN HAD OBTAINED SHIPPING RECORDS from all the textile firms producing currency-quality rag paper, along with the sales records from ink manufacturers. They even had the locations of nineteen intaglio presses scattered around the globe, including one in Pyongyang. Kim Jong Un had bought the machine on the black market and thought it was a secret. The North Korean dictator used the print to counterfeit US currency. Langley knew about it and used the shipments of counterfeit bills to pinpoint North Korean intelligence operations around the globe.

They had crossed North Korea off their list of suspects after inspecting one of the confiscated bills from the Office of Technical Services—it was good, but it wasn't a supernote—but the investigation into Korea got Gwen thinking about parts. Six months ago, North Korea had ordered a full set of replacement springs under the guise of using them in a newspaper press. Gwen had theorized it was possible to assemble an intaglio from spare parts and they had set to work pulling up a list of anyone who had ordered parts over the last five years.

"What did you find?" Wizard asked. He stood with his boney hips against one of the desks. Smoke curled up from the stub of a cigarette. The air in the situation room had gone from stale coffee and molding carpet to an overpowering mixture of ripe bodies and cigarette ash. Fortunately, as neither analyst had left in hours, they no longer noticed the smell. Ezra was in bad need of a shave and Gwen longed for a shower, but they were both too excited by their progress to worry about little things like personal hygiene.

Gwen pushed the glasses up the bridge of her nose. "Well, sir, we compiled a list of any company who ordered parts that could be used in an intaglio press. We found an unusually high number of parts ordered by a company in South East Asia called GenNext Infratech."

Ezra added, "They specialize in infrastructure—mostly water-purification plants and sewage."

"Why would they need intaglio parts?" Wizard asked.

"They wouldn't," Gwen said. "That's what caught our eye."

Wizard breathed smoke. "Have they got enough to assemble a working machine?"

"No," Ezra shook his head. "But we found a half dozen other companies, scattered across Asia and the Middle East, who also ordered parts."

"And you think they're working together?"

"We know they are," Gwen told him. "They're all owned by an umbrella corporation called Regency International based out of Bern, Switzerland."

"I'll be damned," Wizard rasped. "Who owns Regency International?"

"That's where we hit a brick wall," Gwen admitted. "Regency is a conglomerate and the controlling members are a collection of law firms."

Wizard straightened up. His wiry salt-and-pepper brows pinched. "It's *him*."

"Him?" Ezra asked. "Him who?"

"*Him*," Wizard said, as if that explained it. "He's the only man I know with this kind of reach. It's got to be him."

Gwen and Ezra shared a look. Gwen said, "We're still looking into the fact that it might be controlled by Saudi Arabia or China."

Wizard shook his head. "It's him. I know it is. I recognize his handiwork. Keep digging. Find out everything you can about the law firms running Regency International."

Before they had even turned back to their computers, the door flew open and Director Armstrong materialized in the frame. She asked, "What in the hell is going on here, Al?"

"Just tracking down some counterfeit bills, Director."

"Yesterday, you told me you were putting together a profile on a South African terror group. Today, I learn Jake Noble flew out of DC on a jet bound for Johannesburg. Don't tell me that's a coincidence."

Wizard put the cigarette to his lips and took a drag while he studied the Director, like he was deciding exactly how much he wanted to tell her.

Armstrong crossed her arms under her breasts and nodded at the pair of analysts. "Do I get it from them or from you?"

Wizard told her about the dead Secret Service agent, the assassin, and the counterfeits. He laid out the whole operation from beginning to end, but left out the part about his shadowy adversary.

Armstrong shook her head. "So you sent Jake Noble to track down an assassin. He's not cleared for field duty. Three days ago, he was a pass-out drunk!"

"Kid's done alright so far." Wizard lit one cigarette off the end of another.

Armstrong rubbed the tips of her fingers against her forehead. "I just came from a budget meeting on the Hill where I assured Congress we weren't running any covert ops."

"That's why I didn't tell you," Wizard said. "I wanted you to have plausible deniability. If it blows back on us, I'll take the heat."

"In the current political climate, you'll go to jail," Armstrong countered.

Wizard didn't seem phased by the threat. He went on smoking as if the Director had informed him he might need to push his lunch break back an hour.

Armstrong turned to Cook and Witwicky. "What have you learned about this counterfeiting operation?"

Gwen told the director about the intaglio press and Regency International. She wanted to justify her part in the operation and tried to make it clear that she and Ezra were following orders. She ended with, "Wiz ... I mean Deputy Director Dulles believes that a hitherto unknown criminal element is behind the plot."

Wizard shifted his weight. His head moved side to side. It was a subtle gesture, nothing out of the ordinary, but it spoke volumes. He let Gwen know she had said too much without saying a word.

A disbelieving smile crept onto Armstrong's face. "Is that what this is all about? Your illusive mystery man? Another wild goose chase in search of your arch nemesis?"

"He's real," Wizard insisted.

"Do you have any evidence?"

Wizard waved an arthritic claw at the pair of analysts. "The evidence is right here. You heard them. Someone built an intaglio press from spare parts and they're using it to forge supernotes. Who else would have that kind of reach?"

Armstrong threw her hands in the air. "Oh, I don't know ... the Russians, Iran, China. Just to name a few."

"It's not the Russians," Ezra said. "We looked into them firs—"

Armstrong silenced him with a withering look and turned back to Wizard. "There is no super villain pulling strings from the shadows, Albert. You don't have any evidence that these spare parts have been used to make a working press, and if it turns out to be true, I promise you it won't be some sinister figure working behind the scenes to manipulate world affairs. It's just another pathetic attempt by an unfriendly nation to upset the reserve currency. Now, I'm shutting this operation down."

"What about the dead agent?" Wizard asked. "What about the supernotes?"

Armstrong held up a hand. "We'll continue to look into the parts and follow it wherever it leads, but this Big Foot expedition is officially over. I'm not going to have Jake Noble running around out there causing an international incident." She pivoted back to Ezra and Gwen. "I want you two to pull Noble in immediately."

Ezra said, "He's in the middle of—"

"I don't care if he's at tea with the Queen. Pull him in."

Gwen picked up the phone and dialed. She waited through a dozen rings, hung up and tried again. "He's not answering."

"Keep trying until you get him."

Gwen did as she was told. She dialed the number a third time and got and out of service message. Her brows inched up her forehead. She said, "That's odd. The number is not currently in service."

Armstrong turned back to Wizard. Her voice was frosted glass. "Can I see you in my office?"

CHAPTER THIRTY-NINE

Noble felt like a rat in a cage. He was pinned in. The pair of hoods were less than twenty meters away, pushing and shoving through the crowd. Eliška, still mopping tears from her eyes, was moving right toward them. Noble caught her arm and managed to choke out, "Not that way. Two more."

"Where?" she asked through a hacking cough.

Noble didn't bother to answer. Instead, he wheeled her around toward the bridge.

"What about the sniper?" she asked.

"He won't be able to pick us out of the crowd," Noble said. After a moment, he added, "I hope."

They joined the throng. Noble kept his knees bent and his head down. It was a long way to the other side, but the bridge was his only option.

"They probably have people on the other side," Eliška said, plucking the thoughts right out of Noble's head.

He nodded but kept moving. There were definitely men

behind them. He chanced a peek over his shoulder and saw the two bricks. One was tall enough to see over the crowd. He was a big man with blond hair down past his shoulders and a lantern jaw. His eyes locked on Noble, and he spoke into a lapel mic.

Noble cursed and crouched down just as an angry wasp buzzed past. The lead hornet stung flesh with a meaty *thawk*! A blood-curdling shriek split the air. It sounded like a woman, but it could have been a man. The sniper had missed and hit an innocent bystander instead—a tourist out enjoying Prague.

Another shot sizzled overhead. This one tore up a chunk of cobblestone. There was a moment of confusion as the crowd looked to see who was screaming. Someone yelled, "She's been shot!" and confusion gave way to panic. People ran in every direction—some of them turning east, others surging west. Noble moved in a crouch and checked on the heavies. They were less than fifteen meters back with their guns drawn, shoving aside shrieking tourists in their effort to get a clear shot.

Eliška hunkered next to him. Her eyes were wide. She shouted, "What are we going to do?"

Noble edged to the stone railing and poked his head over. He saw the dark, swirling waters of the Vltava and asked, "How deep is this river?"

"Not that deep," she said.

————

Lucas knelt atop Mala Strana Tower on the western end of Charles Bridge with the butt of a sniper rifle nestled in his shoulder. The barrel of the 7.62 Dragunov was supported on the crumbling stonework. White smoke billowed up from the opposite tower. Lucas watched the crowd milling about while he looked for the assassin and her new friend. *What a mess*, Lucas silently berated himself. He knew he had screwed up. He should have killed the Cermákova woman first and dealt with the intelligence officer later, but the newcomer had changed the equation. Lucas had decided to kill Miklos before he could talk. There was always a chance Cermákova and her friend might escape the trap. Lucas didn't want them leaving with sensitive information. It was a tactical decision made on the spur of the moment. Lucas exhaled through pursed lips as he scanned the mob of pedestrians on the bridge.

Cermákova had narrowly avoided death twice now. Lucas promised himself it wouldn't happen again. He swept the mass of bodies and spotted a head of short blond hair, but it was a skinny boy of twelve or thirteen.

Stanz was talking in his ear, trying to zero Lucas in on the fleeing targets.

"They're directly in front of us," Stanz was saying over the closed circuit. "They're moving your way."

Lucas ignored that information. There were a hundred people, maybe more, moving in his direction. He passed his scope over the sea of people, hoping to get lucky, and sighted Cermákova. He instinctively pulled the trigger, but he had only caught a glimpse and she was moving fast. The rifle bucked and the suppressor muffled the shot. The sound of the weapon cycling was louder than the bullet leaving the barrel. The shot missed. A middle-age woman in parka doubled over in pain. Lucas couldn't hear her scream, but he saw her mouth open wide. He tried to zero back in on Cermákova, but now the crowd was a stampede. People were just colorful blurs his scope. He raised his head for a look over the rifle, sighted a slim blonde crouching amid the chaos and adjusted his aim. Cermákova moved at the last second. It saved her life. Lucas tried to track her and his crosshairs settled on her companion. His finger was tightening on the trigger when the blood in his veins turned to ice.

He was staring at Jake Noble.

How could it be? Lucas felt like someone had just caught him with an uppercut. His mind reeled. He had lost touch with the SF community after going to work for Keiser, but last he heard, Jake Noble was babysitting celebrities. How had he ended up in Prague?

Never mind the how, Lucas told himself. *He's a part of it now, and he needs to be dealt with.*

Lucas settled his finger back on the trigger, but he couldn't bring himself to take the shot. He and Jake had spilled blood together in some of the same sand. Killing a meddlesome Czech intel specialist was one thing—Lucas didn't know the man and had never served with him. Killing the assassin was just good business. But killing Jake Noble was something altogether different.

While Lucas wrestled with his emotions, Noble caught hold of Cermákova's sleeve and they both lunged toward the short stone wall. It was a smart move. They had a better chance of surviving a fall than a sniper's bullet. Lucas shook off the surprise and took up the slack on the trigger. The action cycled and the suppressor coughed out a bullet.

CHAPTER FORTY

Another wasp went buzzing past Noble's ear. The sniper had spotted them and wouldn't miss again. Noble had fractions of a second to make his move or die in the middle of the bridge. He grabbed Eliška's hand and shouted, "Come on!"

They threw themselves over as a bullet winged off the balustrade, spitting chips of rock, and the river leapt up to claim them.

Noble hit with a *splash* and went under. Numbing cold enveloped his body and a rushing torrent filled his ears. For a brief moment, he felt Eliška thrashing in the water next to him. Then he was alone. He swam for what he thought was the surface, but the water only got colder and darker. Panic started to claw at the edges of his thoughts. He wheeled around, searching for light refracting on the surface, but all he saw was more blackness. His heart was beating painfully hard inside his chest. His lungs were on fire. He couldn't figure up from down. Noble held his breath as long as he could, but the air finally escaped in a burst. His arms and legs felt like lead. His brain begged for oxygen. He was going to drown and he couldn't even scream. His world narrowed to a pinprick of consciousness. Then he spotted bubbles racing toward the surface and, with the last of his fading strength, Noble followed.

He exploded from the water, gasping for air and shaking his head. Droplets flung from his shaggy hair. The current had pulled him under the bridge. He turned and spotted Eliška clinging to one of the pillars.

"Are you alright?" she called to him.

"Never better," Noble managed to say. He had lost the Kimber. It was somewhere at the bottom of the Vltava, but he didn't tell that to Eliška. He concentrated on treading water and fighting the current at the same time. They hid under the span until they heard sirens. With the police on their way, the sniper would be forced to abandon his perch. At least, that's what Noble was hoping. As the sirens closed in, Noble let the current take him. They passed under the bridge, emerging on the southern side, and paddled for the east bank. Noble kept expecting to hear bullets impact the water, but they made it to shore and slogged up a slippery embankment under the curious gaze of several onlookers.

"Let's get out of here," Eliška muttered.

Noble agreed and followed her up the slope. They had to scramble over a waist-high storm wall of roughhewn stone. Eliška took a narrow alley between buildings, leading Noble away from the river and the chaos on Charles Bridge, then along Anenská Road.

"We need to get off the street," Noble told her. His fingers and toes were blocks of ice and his teeth chattered in his skull. "Find someplace warm where we can get out of these wet clothes."

She kept walking, eating up the sidewalk with long, determined strides.

"Hey!" Noble reached for her, but she jerked away from him. Noble said, "Whoever killed your friend Miklos is still out there."

"Exactly," Eliška told him without slowing down.

Noble grabbed her and pinned her against the wall. "You're not going anywhere."

She tried to throw him off, but Noble outweighed her by forty pounds. He held her against the bricks. She said, "They know about my father!"

Noble relaxed his grip some. "They know where he lives?

Eliška nodded. "They threatened to kill him if I didn't take the contract on Fellows. That's why I had to fake my own death."

She gave him another shove. This time Noble allowed himself to be pushed. He thought about what he would do if a pack of trained killers were on their way to the Wyndham Arms. He'd move heaven and earth to protect Mom. He softened his tone and said, "If they know about your father, they've probably got people sitting on his apartment. They'll use him to get to you. You can't go in guns blazing. They'll be expecting that."

"He's my father." She turned on her heel and stalked away.

Lucas watched as Cermákova and Noble went over the side of the bridge and disappeared into the water. He trained his scope on the other side of the bridge and waited for them to emerge, but they never came up. The distant wail of sirens climbed above the whipping sound of the wind and Lucas knew it was a lost cause. He put the rifle down, took a small can of aerosol bleach from his coat pocket and sprayed the weapon. When that was done, he pulled the watch cap off his head and made his way down the tower. A dead Czech military intelligence specialist on one tower and a Russian sniper rifle on the other should keep investigators busy for a while. Lucas reached the bottom of the steps and mixed with the hurrying mass of people fleeing the bridge.

Cermákova was proving hard to kill. And now she had help. Lucas turned a corner off Mala Strana and made his way south, through a twisting maze of passageways. He had gone two blocks when a Jeep pulled up beside him. Lucas opened the passenger-side door and climbed in next to Veers. The German said, "She'll run straight to Daddy."

"Get us there first," Lucas said.

Eric nodded.

"What happened to the men in the tower?"

"Two are dead," Veers said. "The other is banged up pretty bad."

"Will he talk?" Lucas wanted to know. The hardcases in the tower had been Eric's men. Lucas didn't know how reliable they were.

"I'll make sure that doesn't happen," Eric assured him.

From the back seat, Stanz asked, "Anyone know who the newcomer is?"

"His name is Jake Noble," Lucas said. He lit a cigarette

and filled the Jeep with smoke. How had Noble gotten mixed up with Cermáková? Was he back working for the CIA? Or was he freelancing? The questions crowded Lucas's mind. The answers could completely change the mission.

"You know him?" Stanz asked.

"He's former Special Forces," Lucas told them. "United States Army."

Stanz cursed.

What Lucas didn't tell them was that the CIA had sheep dipped Noble for a Special Operations Group and that he might, even now, be working for the United States government. The less they knew, the better. Jake Noble showing up in the middle of an operation was a bad sign. Lucas reached into his waistband, pulled out a Sig pistol, and did a press check to be sure a round lay in the chamber. He glimpsed brass and said, "We need to find the girl and kill her."

"What about Noble?" Eric asked.

Lucas hesitated less than a second before saying, "If he gets in our way, then he dies too."

Eric took the first left, headed for Wenceslas Square. The two men in the back seat checked the action on their weapons. They were both former soldiers in the West German Baader-Mienhof Group, better known as the Red Army Faction. They had fought for the cause and done time in Germany's notorious Plötzensee Prison. They were no pushovers, but they had no idea what they were walking into. Lucas said, "Everybody, listen up. Noble's no punk. Don't screw around with this guy. If you get a shot, take it."

CHAPTER FORTY-ONE

"WHAT THE HELL WERE YOU THINKING?" ARMSTRONG asked. She paced back and forth behind her desk. Her face was a carefully constructed mask devoid of emotion. A storm was brewing below the surface. Wizard sat across from her with an unlit cigarette clamped between his lips. Armstrong stopped, gripped the back of her chair, and eyed him. "You laid in a covert operation without congressional approval and you lied to me about it. And for what? A counterfeiting operation with a hired killer on their payroll? This is the type of cowboy antics I was hired to put an end to. If this ever came to light, those fools up on the Hill would rake us both over the coals. What's worse, you put Jake Noble in the field. He hasn't even passed his psych evals, and you've got him chasing down assassins."

Wizard took the unlit cigarette from his mouth and tapped it on the arm of his chair. "This is just what Jake needed to get his head back in the game."

Armstrong stopped him with an upraised hand. "I'm not going to argue that. Hopefully you're right, but has it occurred to you what happens if he fails? We'll be cutting another star into that wall."

"Is that what you're worried about?" Wizard rasped.

"That's the least of my worries." A vein throbbed in Armstrong's forehead. She dropped into her chair. "Al, you're probably the best damn Operations Director this agency has seen in decades, but this obsession of yours for this criminal 'mastermind' has gone too far. You don't have any evidence that this guy even exists. You have no proof at all."

She waved an arm in the direction of his office. "There is no villainous intellect behind all those reports and news clippings tacked to your wall. There's just a bunch of randomness. You see connections where you want to see them."

"He exists," Wizard insisted. "And if you let me keep pulling at this thread, I can prove it."

Armstrong clicked her tongue. "I've got a lot of respect for you, Al, but you're chasing ghosts. I'm not going to let you waste anymore of my time—or tax-payer dollars—looking for the boogeyman." She drew her chair up to her desk and woke up her computer with a nudge of the mouse. "Furthermore, I'm recommending you speak with a Company therapist."

A humorless smile turned up one side of his face. He studied the unlit cigarette in his hand. "I may be losing a step in my old age, but I'm not crazy."

"Are you sure?" Armstrong asked. "Because you sent a

grief-stricken drunk halfway around the globe to track down a hired killer in the *hopes* he would lead you back to some criminal mastermind directing world affairs from the shadows."

Wizard sat in stony silence.

"You know what I think this is?" Armstrong said. She leaned back and crossed her arms but spoke in a friendly tone. "I think this is one last hoorah. I think you're getting old, and you miss the glory days when it was America versus the spymasters in the Kremlin. I think you're pinning for one last victory against a worthy opponent before you hang up the spurs, cowboy."

Wizard had been down this road before and knew what Armstrong wanted to hear. Insisting he was right would only convince her that he was crazy. Because crazy people don't know they're crazy, do they? That idea nagged at Wizard on long sleepless nights when he had too much time to think. But he wasn't crazy. He pushed those doubts out of reach and forced a smile on to his face. "Maybe you're right. Maybe I am pinning for the glory days."

"The Cold War is over," Armstrong said. "It's not America against the evil Soviet empire anymore. Our enemies are just a collection of nations with different goals. There are no good guys or bad guys—just a bunch of countries with opposing world views."

"That's all it ever was," said Wizard. "Different people with opposing world views. But some of those world views are morally right. Others are morally wrong."

Armstrong reached for a box of cigars on her desk. "I never took you for a philosopher."

"I believed in American exceptionalism," Wizard told her. "Still do."

She snipped the end from a cigar, clamped it between her teeth, and flicked a lighter. Wizard took the opportunity to light up as well. Armstrong leaned her head back and blew smoke at the ceiling. "Yeah, me too." She paused a beat and then added, "But I still want you to speak to a therapist."

He nodded. "Fine. I'll make an appointment the beginning of next week."

"Make it first thing tomorrow," Armstrong said.

"I'd have to cancel my UFO meeting," he said with a perfectly straight face.

Armstrong didn't bother to hide her smile. "Don't crack up on me, Al."

He stood to leave. "Don't worry about me, Director. My head is still in the game. Do me one favor?"

She nodded.

"Stay on top of the supernotes," Wizard said. "My gut says this is more than just a counterfeiting operation."

"Counterfeiting is a Secret Service problem, but I'll have them keep me in the loop," Armstrong said. "If they ask for our help, you'll be the first to know."

Wizard let himself out of her office and crossed the hall to his own sanctum sanctorum. He closed the door, leaned his hips against his cluttered desk, and stared at the wall while smoke drifted up in lazy curlicues that gathered around the fluorescent lights in the ceiling. Was Armstrong right? Had he been chasing a phantom all these years? Wizard traced the lines of string on the wall, moving from incident to incident. He went over each and every piece in his mind, connecting all the dots. The man, whoever he was, existed. He was real, and Wizard was going to prove it. He was going to find him and expose him.

Too close to give up now, Wizard told himself.

CHAPTER FORTY-TWO

Noble hurried after Eliška. She strode along the sidewalk with her head down and her hands stuffed deep in her pockets, leaving a trail of damp shoeprints on the cobblestones. Noble chewed the inside of one cheek and considered his options. If Noble wanted to stop her, he would have to hog-tie her and carry her over his shoulder like a sack of potatoes. Her father was in danger. Eliška was determined to save him. She might be a remorseless killer, but every girl loves her daddy. That was pop psychology 101. His other option was to help.

He checked his cellphone and found it was dead. The dunk in the river had killed it. He wanted to contact Langley and find out what they knew about the United Front. That would have to wait. He pocketed the useless device and said, "Alright, I'll help, but we're going to do this my way."

"I didn't ask for your help," Eliška said without slowing down.

"You don't have a choice," Noble told her. "It's my way or the highway."

She stopped and turned to him. "What does this mean? 'My way or highway'?"

"It's something my mother says," Noble explained. "It means we can do this my way or not at all."

She sized him up and nodded. "Okay, Jakob. What is your plan?"

"We're going to need hardware," Noble said and clarified, "Guns."

"You are in luck," Eliška told him. "Czechia makes the world's best guns."

"Agree to disagree," Noble said.

She led the way through the crowded streets of Old Town to a crumbling building tucked away on a side street off Malá Štepánská. The brick façade looked like it was ready to come down any second. Noble imagined the front of the building calving like the side of a glacier into the street. A simple placard had the name in Czech and a picture of barbell underneath.

Noble said, "Is this a gym?"

"Praha CrossFit." Eliška pulled open the door and motioned him inside.

He stepped into a spartan gymnasium of bare concrete floors covered in dusty mats. The equipment consisted mostly of Olympic bars and kettlebells. A few pull-up stations were bolted to the walls. The place smelled like armpit and chalk. A powerfully built woman in spandex clean-and-jerked a 150-pound barbell to her chest. Her face turned beet red. Veins stood out on her neck. She pressed the weight overhead, then let the bar slam to the ground—it impacted with a heavy *clang*. The woman transitioned directly to a pull-up bar and cranked out a dozen reps while Noble watched.

"Impressive, yes?" Eliška asked.

Noble nodded.

There was a young man thumbing through his phone behind the front desk. He looked up when they entered and asked if they were members, first in Czech, then English.

"I'm need to speak with the manager," Eliška told him.

He motioned to a door marked, "PRIVATE."

Eliška motioned for Noble to follow. They crossed the gym, passed the locker rooms, to the manager's office. Eliška opened the door without knocking. The room was small and lit by green-tinged fluorescents. A very fit man in a red tracksuit sat with his feet stacked on the desk and a magazine open on his lap. A glass of red wine stood on the desk, along with the remains of his dinner. He sat up when the door opened, recognized Eliška and spoke in Czech.

Her response was short. It didn't sound pleasant to Noble, but then Czech wasn't a pleasant language. It had none of the beauty of the romance languages and all the gruffness of the eastern Slavic tongue.

The manager stood up and left without a word. Noble waited until he was gone and closed the door, shutting out the grunts and clanging barbells. "How do you happen to know the owner of a CrossFit gym?"

"He's just the manager," Eliška explained. "I'm the owner. He works for me."

"Does he know what you do for a living?"

"He knows better than to ask questions."

"You use this place to launder your earnings," Noble said. It was more statement than question.

"I suppose I'll have to sell now," she said.

There was an electrical panel on one wall. Eliška pulled it open to reveal a hollowed-out space filled with a large olive-green duffle bag. She extricated it with some effort, blew off the dust, and pulled the zipper. Inside was half a dozen pistols, two submachine guns, loaded magazines, flashlights, knives, cleaning supplies, bandages, several passports, and stacks of Euros.

Noble hooked the bag with his toe and dragged it away from her. "I'll take over from here," he told her. "You watch the door."

Her lips pressed together in a tight line.

Noble said, "You didn't think I was actually going to trust you with a gun?"

Her nostrils flared. "Grab what we need and make it quick."

He checked the action on a CZ pistol, gathered three spare magazines, along with a few stacks of Euros and a SpyderCo knife, while Eliška kept watch at the door. She had enough hardware in the duffle to wage a small war. Noble wondered how many more stashes she had hidden around the globe. A Qual-A-Tec sound suppressor on a .22 pistol caught his eye.

"You know how this works?" Eliška asked. She circled around behind the desk and dropped into the office chair. "The suppressor locks up the action. It's single-shot. You have to cycle the pistol every round."

"I've used one before," Noble assured her.

"The .22 is a small round," she said. "Hardly any knock-down power."

"It's not the size of the boat," Noble told her as he removed the can. He put the suppressor in one pocket and the small .22 caliber in the other. "It's the motion of the ocean."

Her face pinched in confusion. "This is another of your mother's sayings?"

Noble chuckled. "No, it's an innuendo."

"What does it mean?"

"Never mind." He stuffed a collection of bandages, gauze, and medical tape into his pockets.

Eliška said, "Do you think we'll need it?"

"Better safe than sorry."

"This expression, I know," Eliška said.

Noble stuffed the bag back into the hiding place. He shut the fake electrical panel and gave it a tug to be sure it was closed, then crooked a finger at Eliška. She stood like a schoolgirl summoned by the headmaster. Noble took her by the elbow and steered her out of the CrossFit gym.

Stars winked in the night sky and a cold wind cut right through Noble's wet clothes. Eliška pointed him toward the nearest subway entrance. They took the stairs to the underground and Eliška walked right past the electronic ticket reader without slowing down. There were no turnstiles, just a machine with a slot for validating stubs.

Noble said, "Don't we need tickets?"

She shook her head.

The underground in Prague works on the honor system. Passengers are supposed to validate tickets as they enter the station, but meeting transit authorities is rare and the penalty for riding without a validated stub is a few hundred Czech crowns. More often than not, the fine can be paid directly to the corrupt transit cops. Noble followed Eliška onto the platform as a shuttle hissed to a stop and they joined the crowd of people pushing onto the train. Eliška said, "So what is your plan?"

"First, we get to your father's apartment and scope out the situation," Noble told her. "Then we'll come up with a plan."

CHAPTER FORTY-THREE

PIOTR CERMÁKOVA SAT IN HIS THREADBARE RECLINER. His ruined hands lay in his lap and his eyelids drooped. The sound from the television washed over him, lulling him into a fitful doze. He rarely slept in his bed anymore. Shuffling to the bedroom seemed like too much work. Instead, Piotr simply cranked back his recliner and let the television put him to sleep. It was more like lucid dreaming. He laid in his chair, eyes closed and lips slightly parted, reliving the dark days of Socialist rule.

Piotr Cermákova had been a Colonel working at uncovering dissidents in the Czechoslovakian military during the Cold War. A decorated soldier and a respected member of the Communist Party, he had served Moscow faithfully the first few years. In the beginning, he had been an energetic supporter of Socialism. The philosophy had appealed to the idealistic young officer. No more bourgeois aristocracy wielding their land and titles over penniless workers.

Socialism was going be the great equalizer. Young Piotr had envisioned a classless society where no one went hungry. The reality, however, had turned out very different. Instead of an age of plenty, Socialism had ushered in unparalleled poverty and starvation.

At first, Colonel Cermákova had performed his duties with religious zeal. He arrested hundreds of traitors, sentencing them to death and sending their families to forced labor camps. But as the arrests and executions tallied up, Piotr's belief in the ideology eventually collapsed under the weight of all those dead bodies. When he could no longer deny the horror of what was happening under Socialist rule, Piotr had started feeding information to dissident groups—the very groups he was tasked to uncover. By the end, Piotr Cermákova was actively working for the resistance as a double agent. It was only a matter of time before the Soviets discovered his betrayal.

He remembered the night they came for him. October 28, 1989. He remembered the knock at the door and the cold hand of dread that had gripped him. A pair of Soviet KGB officers had dragged Piotr from his home while little Eliška wept. Piotr spent the next month in a cold concrete cell. They tortured him for information. He held out as long as he could and was saved from death by the Velvet Revolution in November of that year.

These memories were playing through Piotr's head when he heard a stealthy tread on the creaking floorboards outside his front door. His eyes snapped open. His heart thundered beneath his sunken chest. He could feel the blood pounding in his ears. For a moment, he was convinced it was still 1989 and the KGB had come for him. He shook off the sleep. He wasn't sure if the sound was a dream that had spilled over into wakefulness, or if there was someone outside his door. The old soldier's instincts took over and his crippled hand went to his hip, but there was no gun there, not anymore.

Lucas Randall winced at the creak of rotting wood beneath his feet. Shoddy Soviet architecture made stealth all but impossible. He didn't let it worry him too much. Their target was an ageing pensioner, probably had bad eyes and poor hearing. Lucas put his shoulder to the jamb and checked the action on his Sig P229.

Gregor, Muller, and Stanz stacked up on the other side of the door, pistols held tight to their sides. Lucas counted down on his fingers and then gave the signal. Stanz stepped up and kicked the door just below the knob. The flimsy wood crashed open, taking a large part of the frame with it. One of the hinges tore away from the wall with a shriek of wood and twisting metal.

Gregor went first. He stepped inside with his gun up, looking for targets, and saw the old man coming at him with an oxygen tank. He couldn't fire or risk rupturing the tank and killing them all. Instead he threw an arm up to block and tried to backtrack. He ran into Muller coming through the door behind him and they bottlenecked in the doorframe.

The old man swung the tank with a grunt of effort. The

metal tube crashed down on Gregor's forearm. Pain lanced up his arm and into his brain. It felt like the bones in his arm had turned into bits of broken glass. He choked out a scream but managed to hang on to his weapon. The old man tried for another swing, but his spindly arms gave out. His strength was gone. He lost his grip and the oxygen tank clattered to the floor.

Gregor recovered and cracked the old man with the butt of his pistol. He caught Piotr in the mouth. There was a sickening *crunch*. The pensioner stumbled back, spitting blood and teeth. Stanz hit the old man twice more. The first blow rocked Piotr's head back on his scrawny neck. The second put him on the floor in a senseless heap.

The Germans would have killed the old-timer if Lucas hadn't intervened. "Don't kill him," he ordered. "We need him."

He produced a yellow plastic zip tie, knelt down, and secured Piotr's hands. He gave the zip a sharp yank. The plastic bit into paper-thin flesh.

Gregor cradled his injured arm in one hand. "I think he broke it."

"Soldier through," Lucas told him. "When this is over, we'll get you to a hospital."

Gregor nodded but stared daggers at the prostrate figure.

Lucas gave the old man a few light taps on the face to bring him around. Piotr's eyelids fluttered open. Lucas said, "Where's your daughter?"

When he didn't answer, Lucas tried German.

"I speak English," Piotr said. He turned his head to the side and spat a mouthful of blood on the dusty floor. "KGB thugs tried and failed to break me. I'm certainly not going to talk to the likes of you."

Lucas smiled. Even maimed and crimpled, the tough old goat had proven dangerous. "That's okay," he said. "You don't have to talk. She'll be along soon enough, and we'll be waiting for her."

CHAPTER FORTY-FOUR

Noble watched the front of the Soviet-era pillbox. He and Eliška were sheltered in a narrow alleyway across the street. The Škoda was still parked right where Noble had left it. That seemed like ages ago. The sky was a black dome littered with pinpricks of light. A cold wind worked under Noble's wet clothes and into his bones.

Cermákova, teeth chattering, said, "I'm freezing."

"We need to get out of these wet clothes," Noble said by way of agreement. It's possible to die in temperatures as low as forty degrees Fahrenheit. It had to be ten degrees colder than that now. Noble's breath steamed up in silver clouds that broke apart on the wind. He wasn't terribly worried about freezing, but the cold would slow him down, cause him to shake. If things got loud, he didn't want to waste bullets because his hands were shaking too badly to hit a target. He cupped his paws together in front of his face and blew into his palms. It wasn't much but it brought a little life back into his fingers.

He spent ten minutes looking for any sign of movement on the fourth floor. The lights were out and the windows were dark. There was nothing more to be gained by waiting. It was likely a trap, but one they had to walk into if they were going to save Eliška's father. Noble was just about to suggest they make their move when he heard a noise behind him. The small hairs on his arms stood up. His heart leapt. His scrotum tried to crawl up inside his pelvis. He wheeled around and clawed the .22 from his pocket.

A stray cat streaked from an overturned trash can and went speeding off down the alley.

Eliška let out a shaking breath.

They looked at each other and shared a quiet laugh. The situation had them both on edge. Noble shook his head and threaded the suppressor onto the barrel while he waited for his heart to settle back into his chest. "Let's go see if anybody's home."

He held the gun down against his thigh and crossed the street. Eliška was close behind him. They mounted the steps and Noble murmured, "Get the door."

She reached for the knob.

Noble entered with the gun up. The small entryway was silent and deserted. A row of mailboxes were built into one wall. A flight of sagging steps led to the upper floors. Noble went first. Eliška followed. Every riser groaned under their combined weight. They made it to the fourth floor and Eliška motioned silently to her father's door.

Noble already knew which apartment, but didn't bother to tell her. He had been here once before. Shortly after landing in Prague, he had parked the Škoda and climbed the stairs to the old man's apartement. Piotr Cermákova had answered the door. Noble pretended to have the wrong address, figuring the old-timer would forget all about it. He did it to get a look at Piotr Cermákova and, more importantly, a peek inside the apartment. What he had seen told him Piotr and Eliška were estranged and that the elder Cermákova probably wasn't hiding his daughter.

Now the door was open. Someone had kicked it in and left it swinging on twisted hinges. The living room—what Noble could see from the hall—was empty. He nudged the door with his toe and slipped inside. The place smelled like an old man who sits in front of the television day after day without bathing. A timid yellow light from the street filtered through moth-eaten curtains and a tattered armchair was parked in front of an aging television set. Noble made a quick sweep of the apartment and came back to the living room. Cermákova was staring down at a mobile phone on the recliner cushion.

She reached for it and Noble caught her hand.

"Could be a trap." He dropped down on his belly and searched underneath the recliner for wires or explosives and then gently probed the seat. When he was relatively certain there were no bombs, he carefully lifted the phone. He had barely picked up the device when it started to ring. A video call was coming through. The ringtone was *Dirty Deeds* by AC/DC. Noble wondered if the song was meant for Cermákova or him. In the end, he decided it didn't really matter. He thumbed the green button and Lucas Randall's face filled the screen.

Lucas said, "Hello, Jake."

Noble's brows pinched. "Lucas?"

"Been a long time," Lucas said.

Eliška gave Noble a withering look. "Friend of yours?"

He held up a hand for her to wait. "What the hell is going on, Lucas?"

"You're screwing up a mission I spent the last year and a half planning," Lucas said. "That's what's going on."

CHAPTER FORTY-FIVE

NOBLE FELT HIS REALITY GRINDING TO A HALT, LIKE the planet would stop spinning and break apart. Lucas was supposed to be one of the good guys, a Navy SEAL—a Tier One operator. They had fought together, shed blood together. Lucas had been there on Noble's last mission for the CIA when a Qatar politician walked into their op and got himself killed. Noble shook his head, unwilling or unable to believe his own eyes. He said, "Tell me you aren't part of this? The dead Secret Service agent? The counterfeits?"

"You know about the counterfeits, huh?"

Noble only nodded.

"I wish I could take the credit," Lucas said. "Somebody much smarter than me is driving the bus."

"So you're just a hired thug?" Noble asked. "You sold out for money?"

"Please, don't insult me, Jake," Lucas said. "This isn't about money. It isn't even about power. It's about a corrupt

system that needs to be overhauled. America has failed. Capitalism is a tool of oppression, Jake. You of all people should know what I'm talking about. You fought for your country. What did it get you? You got fired. Hung out to dry. They should have pinned a medal on your chest. Instead, you live all alone on that boat of yours, trying to scrape together enough money to keep your mom in a nursing home. Meanwhile, the politicians who sent us out to fight are busy lining their pockets with tax payer money. The free market is a lie. Democratic Socialism is the only way forward."

While Lucas was talking, Cermákova moved to the windows and parted the moth-eaten curtains for a peek at the street.

"You used to fight for freedom," Noble said, still trying to make sense of it all.

"I still am," Lucas told him. "The United States is the only thing standing in the way of a one-world democratic government. It took me a long time, but I've finally realized America is the problem, not the solution. Well, in a few days, all of that is going to change. We're going to hit the reset button. When the dollar collapses, America will be forced to join a coalition of nations directed by a global government. Think of it, Jake: no more countries, no more borders, no more wars. Just one government. One world."

"With you at the helm?" Jake guessed.

Lucas shook his head. "Not me. Somebody much smarter than me. He showed me the way."

"He sold you a bill of goods," Noble fired back. "I've heard this idea before. Hitler tried to sell Germany on the same thing. That didn't turn out so well."

"Don't lump us in with the Fascists," Lucas said. "They thought some people were better than others by way of birth. We believe all people are equal. It's the politicians who are the problem. We want to put the power back in the hands of the individual."

"You killed a Secret Service agent for God's sake. An innocent man."

Lucas frowned. "Regrettable but necessary. The world can't go on like this, Jake. Nation against nation, every country trying to get rich at the expense of all the others. You've got trade wars. Race riots. Migrant crises all over Europe. Famine. Disease. The world is coming apart at the seams. We have to do something before it all goes to hell."

"And you think a Socialist regime is the answer?" Noble asked. "Crack a history book, Luke. The Socialists killed a hundred and fifty million of their own people."

Lucas dismissed that with a snort. "They got it wrong. They allowed the bureaucrats to run the politburo. It was doomed from the start. We aren't going to make the same mistake. We're going to do it right this time. In a few days, the American economy is going to crumble and we're going to reshape the world from the ashes."

"You're causing an international crisis so you can rebuild the world you think is best for everybody?" Noble said. "Nobody else gets a vote? And you think you're the hero?"

"I know I am. A hundred years from now, people will say the United Front saved the world from ruin. That we ushered in unparalleled peace and prosperity."

"A hundred years from now no one will even remember

your name," Noble told him. "I'm going to make sure of that."

Lucas shook his head. "You know I thought about bringing you on board? But you were always so damned righteous. I knew you'd never see the big picture."

"You want the big picture?" Noble asked. "I'm going to find you and I'm going to stop you. That's the only picture I see."

"I don't think so," Lucas said. He panned the camera so they could see over his shoulder. Eliška's father was sitting on the floor with one hand chained to a radiator. The old man didn't look good. Both of his eyes were swollen shut and his mouth was a bloody gash. One of Lucas's men stood over him with a Makarov pistol pressed to the back of his head. Lucas said, "I've got Papa Cermákova here. He's got a lot of grit. They don't build 'em like that anymore."

Eliška spit a stream of curses in Czech. "I'm going to rip your guts out! You hear me?"

Noble pushed her back and said, "Let him go, Luke. He's not a part of this."

"Not until I finish what I started," said Lucas. "We're here at your friend Miklos's cabin. Eliška knows the address. It's a nice place. Secluded. Plenty of privacy. You and Eliška are going to come here—unarmed—and turn yourself over to my men. I promise we'll treat you with respect. We'll hold all three of you until our mission is complete. We'll even bandage up the old man and make him comfortable. When this is all over, we'll let you go."

"And if we don't?"

"Eric here will put a bullet in the back of Daddy's head," Lucas said.

Noble said, "Don't do this, Luke."

The call ended. Noble felt like hurling the phone across the room. He said, "Is that your contact?"

Eliška nodded. "That's him. You know him?"

"He's a former frogman," Noble told her. "United States Special Forces."

Eliška paced the small apartment like a caged lion. She said, "What are we going to do?"

"We can't turn ourselves over," Noble said. "That's for sure. Lucas will kill us ..."

Eliška snagged the CZ pistol from his belt and pressed the barrel against his neck.

"Don't try anything, Jakob. I like you, but I'll kill you where you stand."

Noble froze, one hand still gripping the cellphone. "I can help you save your father, but you have to trust me."

"I don't need your help," Eliška told him. "And I'm not going to end up at CIA black site either."

She put her free hand over his shoulder. "Keys."

Noble dug the keys from his pocket and dropped them into her open palm.

"Now the pistol."

Once she had all the guns, there was nothing to stop her from executing him. He hesitated and Eliška pressed the muzzle hard into his neck.

"Don't force my hand."

He could hold on to the gun and get shot in the back of the neck, or give it up and hope she didn't kill him anyway. It was an effort to keep his hands from shaking. She had killed P. Arthur Fellows in cold blood. Noble had to believe she would kill him too. Either way was a gamble. He passed the weapon butt-first over his shoulder.

She snagged it out of his grip and moved backward to the open door of the apartment, never taking the pistol off him. "Goodbye, Jakob. It was nice to make your acquaintance. If I see you again, I'll kill you."

CHAPTER FORTY-SIX

IT WAS NEARLY SIX O'CLOCK IN THE EVENING. EZRA AND Gwen hadn't been idle. The mission was scrubbed, but neither analyst could go home until Noble was located and the assassin delivered to the nearest CIA station chief in Berlin. While they waited for Noble to make contact, they continued their investigation into the intaglio parts. They calculated a rough total of counterfeit currency possibly in circulation. The sums they came up with were astronomical. Assuming the print had been completed and in operation for five months, they estimated just over 1.1 trillion dollars. They had each fantasied about what they would do with that kind of money. Gwen was going to solve the world's hunger problem, while Ezra was going to beat SpaceX to Mars. When that conversation ran its course, they talked about what they planned to do as soon as Noble was on a plane back to the United States.

"I'm going to take a long, hot bath," Gwen said, leaning back in her chair and closing her eyes. She had a smile on her face as if she could already feel the luxurious warmth of the water enveloping her body.

Ezra turned pink at the thought and, worried Gwen might somehow intuit what he was picturing, he filled the silence with, "I'm going to order pizza."

"Pepperoni?"

"Hawaiian," Ezra told her. "I'm going to get an extra-large pie and eat the whole thing by myself. Unless, of course, you want to come over and share."

Gwen was caught completely off guard. She tried to rationalize it by telling herself it wasn't a date, not really—just two friends having pizza. But Ezra would read into it. That was the real danger. Gwen tried to think of an excuse and was saved by a telephone call coming through on the secure line. She snatched up the receiver and answered with the cover line about Goodman Associates.

"It's me," Noble told her. "I had to pick up a new phone. Mine got wet."

"Going secure."

She waited to hear the clicks. The encryption wouldn't do anything to Noble's end, but it would scramble Gwen's side of the conversation. Anyone listening in would only hear Noble's voice. Halfway secure was better than nothing at all. Gwen said, "Are you okay?"

"A little cold, but I'm alright," Noble told her. "What do you know about an organization called the United Front."

"Hang on a second." Gwen plugged the information into her computer.

"The United Front," she read from her screen. "They're a small, well-organized outfit that popped up a few years ago. They've pulled off a dozen high-profile terror attacks on seemingly random targets. They bombed a bank in Switzerland, kidnapped a French politician in Lyon, and poisoned a water supply in the Sudan. They don't even claim responsibility for their actions, which is odd for a terror group. Everything we have comes from third-party sources."

"What about their leader?" Noble asked. "Anything on him?"

"Nothing on the top guy," said Gwen. "You think they're involved?"

"The United Front hired Cermáková to kill Fellows," Noble said. "They're behind the counterfeiting operation as well."

Gwen was busy feeding this new information into the computer. "What else can you tell me?"

"See what you can dig up on a guy named Lucas Randall. He's a former Frogman. He did some work for the Company back when I was running a Special Operations Group."

Gwen turned to Ezra and whispered, "Frogman?"

"Navy SEAL," Ezra said. He picked up a set of headphones and spoke into the mic. "Are you suggesting one of our own might be involved?"

"I'm not suggesting it."

Gwen brought up his Company profile. "Lucas Randall left the agency shortly after you were ..."

"Fired," Noble filled in for her.

"He spent less than a year working for an outfit called Global Security Solutions headquartered in Bern, Switzerland. After that, he dropped off the radar. No one has heard from him since."

"He's working for the United Front," Noble said.

She scrolled through information on her screen. "Nothing in his file to indicate ties with a terror organization. You think he's working with the United Front? Why?"

"I know he is," Noble said. "He told me so. I've got good intel on his location. I need you to look up an address for me. A Czech military intelligence specialist was found dead on top of Charles Bridge Tower this afternoon. His first name is Miklos. I don't have the last name. He owns a cabin in the mountains outside Prague. Work some magic and find me an address."

"Er ... " Gwen said. "There's been a slight change in plans."

"Meaning?"

"Armstrong is pulling the plug," Gwen told him.

"Say again?"

"Armstrong found out about Wizard's op. She's shutting us down," Gwen said.

"What about the counterfeits?"

"She's turning our information over to the Secret Service. She says it's their bailiwick."

"And Cermáková?" Noble asked.

"We laid-in the pipeline for an extraction. Your orders are to deliver Cermáková to the Chief of Station in Berlin."

"Yeah, well, that's going to be a bit of a problem," Noble told her.

"Why's that?"

"Cermáková's in the wind."

"How did that happen?"

"Long story," Noble told her. "Get me the address for Miklos and I'll call you back when I have her in custody."

Gwen hesitated.

"Problem?" Noble asked.

Gwen said, "Armstrong is breathing fire. She wants this tied off."

Noble was quiet for several seconds and then said, "What time is it there?"

Gwen checked her watch. "Six thirty-five in the p.m."

"Is Armstrong still in her office?"

"No, but—"

"Then we've got all night."

"Noble, I can't authorize this."

"I'm not asking you," Noble said. "I'm telling you. Get me the address on Miklos."

"Noble, this mission is over. You're disobeying a direct order. You could get fired."

"I've been fired before."

"*I* could get fired," Gwen said. It came out a plaintive whine.

"Give me until morning," Noble said. "If I haven't got the assassin by then, we'll pull the plug."

"Okay but, just for the record, I was against this."

"Duly noted."

Gwen and Ezra spent the next hour combing through Czech law enforcement systems and collating reports from Charles Bridge. They finally found the last name of the victim. Five minutes later, they had two addresses—one in Prague, the other in the countryside. Gwen called Noble back and read them both off. She by asking, "What do we tell Armstrong if she calls?"

"Tell her you haven't heard from me. For all she knows, I still don't have a phone."

"So you want us to add lying on top of insubordination."

"Let me worry about Armstrong," Noble told her.

Gwen said, "Fine, but call me as soon as you've got the assassin."

Noble had already hung up.

Gwen blew out her cheeks.

Ezra gave an exasperated sigh. "Every time with this guy."

CHAPTER FORTY-SEVEN

Eliška steered the Škoda along gravel roads that switch backed up the mountainside. Headlamps picked out the slender bodies of towering pines. Everything else was blackness. She glanced in the rearview every few minutes, checking for a tail. It was a long shot, but a healthy dose of paranoia had saved her life in South Africa. She piloted the SUV through hairpin turns up the side of the mountain and parked a mile out. The engine died and an oppressive silence crowded Eliška. She checked the CZ pistol and then got out and climbed the hillside, going the rest of the way on foot. The sound of a car engine can carry a long way in the quiet of the mountains. She crept up the wooded incline, going slow, using thick evergreens for cover. She was thinking of Papa. Every step filled her with regret. He might be dead, and the last words she had spoken to him were in anger. She didn't want to think about her father dying. It was too big of an idea to wrap her head around. No matter how bad her life had been, no matter the mistakes she had made, Papa was the one constant in her world. The one thing that never changed. All these years, he had been her anchor, something she could hold on to. It didn't matter if he was halfway around the globe or that they hadn't spoken in years. He was there, and that was enough.

Now he might be gone and it was her fault.

A crisp wind blew down from the north. Eliška's breath steamed up in front of her face. She shivered against the last vestiges of winter. The leather jacket and Rolling Stones T-shirt had mostly dried out during the drive, but did little to protect her from the cold. She scrambled through the dark, taking care not to twist an ankle, until she spotted a log cabin perched on a rocky outcropping. A Jeep parked out front. All the lights were on and smoke piped up from the chimney, filling the air with the pleasant aroma of burning pine.

Eliška flitted from tree to tree until she was crouched behind the rear bumper of the Jeep. She watched the front of the cabin for several minutes. Nobody came or went. Her heart was drumming gently inside her chest, like a thoroughbred nervously prancing before a race. She knew it was a trap. She knew they were waiting for her, but love for her father compelled her forward. She circled the cabin to the back porch, put her shoulder to the door jamb, and slowly turned the knob. It was unlocked. Her heart pounded beneath her breast and her hands shook. She entered with the pistol up.

The American—Noble had called him Lucas—sat in a leather recliner. A cigarette was clamped in his lips. He had a Sig pistol in one hand and the TV remote in the other. On the television, a pack of lions were ripping apart a gazelle.

Lucas said, "Come on in, Ms. Cermáková. We've been waiting for you."

Anger welled up at the sight of him. Eliška raised the weapon in both hands and sighted on his chest.

"Wouldn't do that if I were you," Lucas said. He used the TV remote to motion over his shoulder. "Shoot me, and Daddy gets a bullet to the head."

Eliška edged to her left until she could see deeper into the spacious living room. Her father was chained to the radiator with a piece of duct tape over his mouth. His eyes were swollen shut and blood caked the front of his shirt. One of Lucas's henchmen stood over him with a gun.

"Drop the gun and come on inside," Lucas said.

"And if I refuse?"

"Then you'll die where you stand," he told her.

Eliška heard the porch creak and, before she could turn around, felt the cold steel of a gun barrel press against the back of her head.

"Put it down," Lucas told her.

An icy fist gripped her guts. Eliška felt like she would vomit. She was used to being in charge of a situation. Now she was completely at the mercy of Lucas and his men. She handed the CZ over her shoulder. The blond goon from Charles Bridge snatched it from her and then patted her down. Rough hands rammed into her armpits, under her breasts, and between her legs. He found the silenced .22, took that as well, and gave her a hard shove.

"You should have stayed dead." Lucas said.

Her nostrils flared. "I should have killed you outside Café Organica. I was there. I saw you walking away. I could have put a bullet in you."

"Hindsight is twenty-twenty." Lucas stood up and said, "Where is Noble?"

"He couldn't make it," Eliška said.

Lucas actually laughed. "We can force it out of you."

She made a show of not talking.

"Fine," said Lucas and produced a roll of duct tape from an end table near the sofa. "We'll do it the hard way. Müller has been looking forward to some *hands-on* time with you."

The blond thug strong-armed Eliška into the leather recliner. Lucas passed him the roll of tape and said, "Find out where Noble is and how much he knows, then make sure he doesn't talk."

"And her?" Müller asked as he duct taped Eliška's into the chair.

"No witnesses," Lucas told him.

Fear turned to stark, unreasoning terror. She had been a fool to come up here all alone. She had let her love for Papa and her hatred of Lucas cloud her judgement. She had operated from emotions rather than intellect. Now she was going to die. It was too late to put up a fight and her mind was too numb with dread to do anything but watch. She suddenly realized how badly she needed to pee. She didn't want to wet herself in her final moments. It was a crazy thought, but it's what was going through her head.

Lucas said, "Eric and I have to get back and oversee the last of the shipment. Can you handle things here?"

"*Da,*" Müller said. "I have more than enough men to handle one American agent. No offense, *Herr* Randall."

"Don't underestimate Noble," Lucas warned. He turned to Eliška. "You have been a giant pain in my butt, you know that? All you had to do was kill Fellows, take the

225

money, and go on your merry way. But you and your stupid rules. You forced my hand. If you had just killed Fellows without making a fuss, none of this would have happened."

Eliška wanted to make a smart come back but she was too scared for words. She was still stuck on the idea that she was going to pee herself before she died.

"Well, it's over now." Lucas held his cigarette between thumb and forefinger as he scratched at one eyebrow. He gave Eliška one last look, like a disappointed father, then shook his head and turned to leave. The one called Eric followed him.

The door shut behind them and Müller said, "It is far from over, *fräulein*. In fact, for you, it is only just beginning."

CHAPTER FORTY-EIGHT

ELIŠKA'S HANDS WERE NUMB. HER FINGERS FELT LIKE sausages ready to burst. Müller had started with a few hard slaps to the face. Her cheeks stung from the blows, but the German was just warming up. He had obviously done this before and was good at it. He waved a pair of pliers under her nose. "The American CIA agent? Where is he? What does he know of our operation?"

"He knows everything," Eliška lied. It was better than the truth. Admitting Noble knew next to nothing wouldn't buy Eliška an extra minute. She was hoping for a miracle, but knew this was the end. She had played all her cards. Her life could now be measured in minutes.

Müller jammed the pliers against her breast and squeezed. Every nerve ending in Eliška's body exploded in pain. The shockwave narrowed her vision to a pinprick. She arched her back and opened her mouth. It took the scream a second to make the trip from her lungs to her vocal chords.

Müller clapped a hand over her mouth while he twisted the pliers.

The sound of her muffled shrieks brought her father out of his stupor. He lifted his head and tried to see with eyes swollen almost completely shut. "Ellie? Is that you? What's going on?"

"Shut up, old man," Müller grumbled.

Piotr Cermákova pulled weakly at the cuffs chaining him to the heater. He tried to get his feet under him but couldn't. He wheezed out, "Leave my daughter alone."

Müller let go with the pliers and crossed the room to plant a boot in Piotr's stomach. Eliška let out a sob as her father doubled up and spit blood. Papa had been through enough. There was no more fight left in him. His face was swollen and crusted with blood. When Müller threatened him with another kick, Piotr cringed.

Eliška knew she needed to get Papa to a hospital. Seeing him like this put a cold hunk of hate in her belly. She forgot about her own pain. The fear took a backseat to outrage. She leveled a string of curses at the German. She didn't know how, but she was going get Papa out of here alive. She just had to keep her head in the game.

Müller came back with the pliers and gave her breast another savage twist. This time Eliška clamped her lips together and fought through the pain. Müller grinned. A dangerous light danced behind his eyes. He was enjoying this. He gave Eliška two more savage pinches and spots of bright-red blood blossomed on her shirt. She gasped for breath. Sweat lathered her skin. She didn't know how much more she could take and feared her breast was permanently mutilated.

Müller looked delighted, like a small boy with his nose pressed against a candy store window.

"Getting off on this?" Eliška spoke through clenched teeth. "You sick freak."

"As a boy, I used to catch cats and dogs," he said. "I liked to pull them apart and see what was inside. I learned to keep them alive for hours while I slowly disassembled their tiny carcasses. I'll do the same to you if you do not tell me what I wish to know. Where is Jake Noble?"

"You don't have to find him," Eliška said. She was lying, of course. She hadn't told Jakob the address. She had been a fool to come without him. She was just hoping to buy a little more time for her and Papa when she said, "He's going to find you."

———

Noble had parked the old beater at the base of the mountain and crept three and a half miles through the woods with nothing but the SpyderCo knife clutched in his fist. He passed the Škoda and, a mile later, finally spotted the cabin He slipped quietly across the yard to the corner of the house and stopped. He knew there would be at least one man walking the perimeter, because he knew the way Lucas's mind worked. Noble stood there a quarter of an hour before he finally spotted the patrol. The man strolled the edge of the property with his hands hidden in the folds of his overcoat. He ambled along, keeping mostly to the shadows.

Noble cast about, looking for something to use as a weapon. He didn't like the idea of going up against a hired gun with nothing but a knife. A man with his neck sliced open can still draw his gun and empty the mag before he bled out. Noble's eyes fell on an old rubber hose.

The guard went to the front porch for a peek through the window before continued on his rounds. His heels scuffing on loose gravel. He came within ten feet of the corner and stopped to take a leak. Noble waited with his back pressed against the wall. The sound of his own heartbeat was incredibly loud in his ears. He heard the purr of a zipper and the patter of the stream. The hardcase shook off and zipped up. Noble adjusted his grip on the garden hose. If this went bad, it would be the shortest rescue attempt of all time.

The guard turned the corner, eyes scanning the tree line on his left. Noble stepped up behind him, looped the hose around his neck and jerked it tight, choking off a scream. The man's face turned bright red. His eyes bulged from their sockets. His hand stabbed inside his overcoat and dragged a pistol from a shoulder holster. Noble, gripping the hose with white knuckles, gave the hardcase a savage twist. The goon managed to hang on to his weapon. He racked the slide and pointed the pistol over his shoulder.

For one awful second, Noble was staring down the barrel. The dark aperture looked like the yawning mouth of a train tunnel. Noble turned and threw the hardcase over his shoulder. The man's feet shot up in the air. His eyes got big and the pistol slipped from his fingers. Noble went down with him, landing on top. The impact knocked the last of the air from the guard's lungs in a loud *whoop*. Noble jammed a knee into the man's back. The veins in Noble's neck and forearms stood out in sharp relief as he pulled up on the hose. Large beads of sweat sprang out on his forehead. The muscles in his arms shook with the effort. The hardcase made a series of gasping noises and reached for the fallen pistol. The gun lay mere inches from his grasping fingertips. His nails cut trenches in the dirt. Noble held on until the man's eyes rolled up in his skull. The hardcase finally stopped struggling and lay still. Noble held him a few more seconds to be safe, then sat back, breathing heavy.

———

"You are bluffing." Müller chuckled and shook his head. "You only delay the inevitable."

"Am I?" Eliška asked. "How long since any of your goons checked in?"

A hint of doubt flashed across Müller's face but was replaced by a lazy smile. He put down the pliers and picked up a radio. "All stations report in."

The radio crackled and a voice came over the speaker. "Earnst reporting in ..."

"Gerhard reporting ..."

The rest was static.

The grin ran away from the Müller's face. He mashed the talk button. "Hans, report!"

He was met by dead air. His brow wrinkled. He pressed the transmit button again. "Earnst, Gerhard, keep your eyes open. We may have company."

A shot rang out. Müller flinched and reached instinctively for a pistol laying on the table. He pressed back the slide to be sure there was a round in the chamber and then went to the nearest window.

CHAPTER FORTY-NINE

A QUICK EXCHANGE OF GUNFIRE SPLIT THE AIR LIKE
Chinese firecrackers. The shots shattered the quiet and
rolled away across the mountains like distant thunder—and
Eliška knew Noble was close. She didn't know how, but
found Miklos's address and armed himself. Had he followed
her? If so, he had waited long enough to make his move. If
he had come an hour earlier, he might have been in time to
catch Lucas. None of that mattered now of course. Eliška
was just happy he was here. She felt a great swelling hope
beneath her chest that helped mute some of the mind-
numbing pain. She just had to survive the next few minutes.
Stay alive, she told herself. She needed to stay alive if she
was going to save Papa. She didn't want the old man to pay
for her mistakes. She wanted Papa safe and sound back in
his crummy little apartment near Wenceslas Square.

Müller pulled his shoulders up around his ears at the
bullwhip crack of pistols and mashed the talk button on his
radio. "Earnst, Gerhard, do you read me?"

When they didn't answer, he shouted into the radio, "Earnst! Gerhard! Report!"

Eliška said, "What's the matter, Müller? Not so tough without your backup?"

His Adam's apple bobbed up and down beneath his lantern jaw. He leveled the pistol at her face. "Shut up!"

The front door shook under a crushing blow. The timbers trembled and dust rained from the hinges. Müller spun and triggered his weapon. The pistol leapt and kicked. Hot brass rained down on Eliška. One of the empty shells found its way inside the collar of her T-shirt. She hissed at the white-hot finger against her flesh. Müller's shots blasted chunks from the door and a heavy weight settled against the wood.

There was no mistaking that sound. Eliška had heard it plenty of times before. It was the sound of a lifeless body slumping against the door. The implication left Eliška cold. She tried to breathe, but an iron glove was closing around her throat, choking off her air.

Müller, flush with excitement, leapt across the room and wrenched the door open. One of the Germans sprawled out on the cabin floor. Half of his head had been shot off. Sticky red brain matter spilled over the polished hardwood.

At the same time, Noble materialized at the back door with a gun in his hands. He moved in a crouch, a deadly panther emerging from the blackness of the jungle, and fired two quick shots before Müller even knew he was there. The handgun spit fire. Empty shell casings leapt from the breech, trailing smoke.

Both shots hit Müller between the shoulder blades,

driving him against the wall. Pain and surprise twisted his face into an ugly mask. He let out a groan, staggered backward and landed flat on his back.

Eliška closed her eyes. Air escaped her chest in a long, shuddering breath. Fear slowly ebbed away, leaving her weak and trembling. Her left breast would be permanently scarred by the German's pliers, but she was alive. She opened her eyes and said, "What took you so long?"

"Had to make a phone call." Noble stuffed the pistol in his waistband, wincing as the hot barrel touched his skin, and started pulling duct tape off her.

"Him first." Eliška thrust her chin at Papa.

The old man was slumped over, laboring for every breath. His face was a swollen, lumpy mass, like a bag of bruised oranges.

Noble turned to the table and searched for the handcuff key. It wasn't there, but he found a flathead screwdriver, which was just as good. The locking mechanism on most cuffs, even the civilian models, are pretty solid. The hinge is weak. The rivet is usually made of copper or other soft metals. Noble wedged the blade of the screwdriver between the double arms and levered his weight against the cuffs. The rivet let go with a small pop.

Piotr Cermákova slumped to the floor.

Noble checked for a pulse. His lips pressed together in a hard line. Eliška watched him and knew it was bad. Her heart squeezed painfully hard inside her chest. Noble came back and quickly ripped away the duct tape. "He needs a hospital."

As soon as she was free, Eliška staggered over and

collapsed on the floor next to her father. Her knees banged against the hardwood, but she barely noticed the pain. She bent over her father and whispered, "Papa?"

Piotr Cermákova drew in some air at the sound of her voice. One swollen eyelid peeled open. His good hand came up in search of her. Eliška took the mangled claw and gave it a squeeze. "Hang on, Papa. We're going to get you to a hospital."

A grin hitched at the corners of his mouth. He shook his head. "Too late for that."

"Don't say that, Papa. You're going to be alright."

"I'm sorry, Ellie."

"You've got nothing to be sorry for, Papa."

He coughed and a pink bubble formed at the corner of his busted lips. "I should have ... been there ... for you," he managed to say. His voice was a whisper. Eliška had to lean close to catch his words. He gasped out, "I wanted a better ... life ... for you."

"It's not your fault." She spoke through a tangle of emotions that stripped her voice of any modesty. Tears streaked her cheeks and a snot bubble formed in her nose. She said, "It's my fault, Papa. All of this is my fault. I'm so sorry."

He stroked her cheek with the knuckles of his ruined hand. His lips moved, but no words came out. Eliška put her ear to his mouth. All she heard was a long, rattling sigh and then his hand dropped into his lap.

"Papa?" Eliška gave him a shake. "Papa, please don't go."

A moan worked its way up from her chest. She scooped

her father up and cradled him in her arms as tears trailed down her cheeks. She was too late. She had done all she could, but it wasn't enough. She hadn't even told him she loved him. She sat on the floor, cradling her father's body, while her heart went to pieces like broken glass.

CHAPTER FIFTY

NOBLE BACKED OFF, GIVING ELIŠKA SOME PRIVACY. He had known it was too late even before taking Piotr's pulse. The old man's body couldn't take the beating Lucas and his goons had dished out. Piotr Cermákova had stood up to the Communists of Czechoslovakia—he had given most of his fingers to free his country—and should have died a hero. Instead, he had been kicked to death by hired thugs in a lonely cabin on a mountainside, south of Prague.

Noble turned his face away. It felt like he had an anvil sitting on his chest. He took a few deep breaths, hoping to relieve the pressure. He had lost Torres, lost Alejandra, lost Sam. Now Eliška's father lay dead on the floor. Noble couldn't shake a gut-level feeling that it was because of him. Death seemed to stalk him and the people closest to Noble paid the price.

It took a while, but Eliška finally cried herself out. She laid her father's body down gently and folded his deformed hands across his sunken chest. Without looking up, she said, "I hope you kept one alive."

Noble nodded.

Eliška took the pliers from the table and Noble led the way outside. The guard lay on his belly with his bare feet sticking up in the air. Noble had hogtied him with the garden hose and then stuffed his own socks in his mouth. It might have been funny under different circumstances. The guard looked up at the sound of footsteps, saw them, and closed his eyes. A moan worked its way past the gag.

Noble gave him a kick to the ribs, rolling him over onto his side, then bent down and tugged the dirty socks from his mouth. They came out soaked through with saliva. Noble tossed the socks and wiped his fingers on his pants. "You were hoping it would be someone else?"

The hardcase told Noble to do something anatomically impossible.

Eliška shouldered Noble out of the way, rammed the pliers into the man's crotch and squeezed with both hands. An ear-splitting shriek rent the air. Noble didn't try to stop her. He let Eliška work on him for several seconds. Sweat beaded on the man's forehead. His eyes started to roll up before Noble intervened. He took Eliška by the arm and pulled her back.

She rounded on him. Her face was a mask of rage. For one second, Noble thought she would turn the pliers on him.

Noble held up both hands. "We need information from him."

It was a minute before she calmed down enough to nod.

Noble knelt down. The hardcase was trying to curl into

a fetal position to protect his groin, but the rubber hose had no slack. All he managed to do was hunch forward a little. A dark stain seeped through the crotch of his of trousers.

"The old man you kidnapped?" Noble said. "That was her father. He's dead and you bastards killed him. Now you can talk to me, or you can talk to her. What's it going to be?"

His lips trembled. "You promise not to kill me?"

"Scout's honor." Noble said. "Who are you working for?"

"I work for Lucas."

"He recruited you?"

Another nod.

"How many more men does Lucas have?"

"I don't know," he said and shook his head.

"Where's the printing press?" Noble asked.

He hesitated and Noble game him a slap. "Hey! Where is the press?"

"A warehouse in Rijeka."

"I need more than that," Noble told him. "I need an address."

"It's in an abandoned torpedo factory. It juts out over the water. You can't miss it."

"How many men guard the warehouse?"

The hardcase shook his head. "I don't know."

Noble waved Eliška forward.

His eyes went to the pliers and he said, "Three men run the press. Six more arc on the loading crew. That's it."

"How is Lucas planning to move the money?"

He shook his head. "I don't know that. It's all compart-mentalized. Each man knows his job, and we don't share information."

"Who does Lucas work for?" Noble asked. "He hasn't got the funds to bankroll an operation this size. Who's funding the United Front?"

"I don't know."

Eliška held up the pliers.

"I don't know!" The hardcase was weeping now. "I swear to God, I don't know. Lucas is the only one I've ever had any contact with. I swear."

Noble asked, "Where is Lucas now?"

"Probably on his way to Rijeka. The cash ships tomorrow evening."

"Where? How?"

"I don't know that part." He laid his head down in the dirt. "I told you: It's compartmentalized. You'll have to ask Lucas. He's in charge."

"I'll do that."

Noble stepped aside. Eliška crouched down in front of the man with the pliers in her hand. Panic filled his eyes. His chin trembled. "You promised not to kill me!"

"I promised *I* wouldn't kill you," Noble told him and walked away.

The hired gun was going to die badly, but he had it coming. Besides, Eliška needed to vent all that rage and frustration. She needed to get it out of her system. Two months ago, Noble had spared Grey's life and spent every single night since then imagining all the things he could have—*should* have—done to the man who had killed Sam.

Maybe revenge is good for the soul, thought Noble.

Noble made his way down the road to the Škoda. The countryside lay still and quiet. Stars glittered in the velvet blackness. He started the engine and turned on the heat. He didn't want the support people at Langley hearing the screams of a dying man in the background. The analysts wouldn't understand. They didn't know what it was like in the field. To them, safe behind their computer screens, everything was a simple algorithm that fit within the parameters of a mission outline. Any questions could be easily answered by consulting a large ringed binder.

But in the field, things get ugly. Things get personal. People die and the survivors want vengeance. Eliška's wanted her pound of flesh. Noble wasn't going to deny her. He dialed and put the phone to his ear.

Gwen picked up and said, "What's your status?"

"I've got Cermáková in custody," Noble told her. "And the location of the printing press. It's in a derelict torpedo factory in Rijeka. The phony cash is scheduled to ship tomorrow evening, but I just took out four of their guys. When Lucas figures out they're dead, he'll assume someone talked and move up the time table. We need to hit that factory with a Quick Reaction Force. What elements do we have in the area?"

"We'll pass that information on to the Secret Service," Gwen said. "Your job is to get Cermáková to Berlin. We have a team waiting there to receive her. There is a 2:30 a.m. train leaving out of Prague. You need to be on it."

"Are you even listening to me?" Noble said. "We have a chance to stop this, but we have to act now."

"Armstrong has called *three* times," Gwen told him. "She's breathing fire. She wants this tied off. We'll pass the intel to the Secret Service and they can liaison with a local SWAT team to investigate the warehouse, but your part in this mission is over."

"Lucas is a former Navy SEAL," Noble said. "You send a Croatian SWAT team in there, they're gonna get killed."

"Let us worry about Randall," Gwen said. "We'll do everything we can from our end. You did your job. It's time to come home."

When Noble didn't answer right away, she said, "Noble, are you still there?"

"I'm here," Noble told her.

Her voice took a hard edge. "Get Cermákova to the train station, Noble. That's an order."

He hung up and drove the Škoda up the side of the mountain.

Eliška sat in the gravel, elbows propped on her knees and blood dripping from her fingertips. She had on a thousand yard stare. The dead guard lay at her feet. His mouth was stretched in a silent scream. Noble ignored the body—it wasn't a pretty sight—and hunkered down in front of Eliška. "I'm sorry about your father."

She sniffed and ran one blood-streaked hand under her nose, leaving a trail of red. "He was a good man. He didn't deserve to die like that."

Noble nodded. There was nothing more to say.

Eliška went on staring into the distance. Her face was slack, emotionless. She said, "What now?"

"Now we've got a train to catch," Noble told her.

CHAPTER FIFTY-ONE

Lucas Randall felt the Cessna touch down with a gentle lurch and a long shiver. The private jet hurtled along the runway, wind shearing against the flaps as gravity reasserted itself. Cabin lights came on, accenting the dark walnut interior in a warm glow. Lucas sat slumped in a calf-skin leather seat with a glass of bourbon in one hand and his phone in the other. He was scrolling through a collection of pictures from Iraq and Afghanistan, looking at pictures of his old unit. Just having the photos was an operational risk, but they were the last remaining vestiges of his old life. He swiped a thumb across the screen. Jake Noble's grinning face and disheveled hair popped up time and again. Noble had been a First Sergeant with an A-team back in those days. Randall was a SEAL, but their paths had crossed, first in Afghanistan, then again in Iraq. Special Forces is a close-knit community of top-tier operators where everybody knows everybody. When Noble got sheep dipped by the CIA and placed in charge of a Special Operations Group,

Lucas had heard the rumors and asked for a spot on the team.

Lucas was between deployments at the time. He had been twenty-seven years old and spent his days working out and drinking. His nights were spent chasing tail. None of it seemed real. For Lucas, the months between deployments were the hardest. He struggled to fill up the time. In reality, he was just waiting. Waiting to get back to his real life killing bad guys in Indian Country. So when the call came from Noble, Lucas had jumped at the chance.

He had spent the next six months learning tradecraft at the CIA's top-secret training facility in Tidewater, Virginia —known to insiders as simply the Farm. After that, Lucas was always in the field. The world was his operating theater and every day was a mission. Operating in the black meant he was always on, even when he was home in America. Espionage doesn't recognize international boundaries. A threat can come anywhere, anytime.

Noble was his team leader back in those days, and he was one of the best. He had a natural gift for tradecraft, a talent for languages, and could think on his feet. Their SOG team had quickly gained a reputation for pulling off missions the desk jockey's back at Langley deemed impossible. They became Langley's go-to for high-risk operations that needed complete deniability.

All that changed when Noble gunned down a politician in an effort to liberate a bunch of human slaves. After that, the team was disbanded. Lucas found himself driving a desk at an embassy in Morocco, working under the most boring Station Chief in the world. The guy was more afraid of missions going bad than collecting useful intel. He wouldn't greenlight an operation unless the success probability was one-hundred percent, which was never. So Lucas spent his days shuffling papers.

When he finally had enough, Lucas quit the CIA and took work as a private contractor. That's when Keiser found him. The old man had opened Lucas's eyes to so many things. Keiser had shown Lucas that he was the pawn of a corrupt system that used young men with too much testosterone and too little experience to wage wars in far-flung places like Afghanistan, all to appease the big oil donors, who in turned filled the war chests of the politicians.

It all came back to money. And that was why, in the end, money would be their downfall. *Fitting*, thought Lucas, *almost poetic*. Keiser had developed a plan to take down the capitalists using the very thing they loved most: money.

Lucas sat staring at a picture of him and Noble together, smiling for the camera. It had been taken just before the fateful mission in Qatar. A lot of water had passed under the bridge since then. Lucas's eyes were open now. He was no longer wearing the rose-tinted lenses of patriotism that had blinded him to the truth for so many years. He understood that America wasn't the solution. It was the problem. The good old US of A—that shining City on a Hill—was nothing more than an imperialist oppressor. But Lucas still considered Noble a friend. He regretted giving the order to kill him. *What choice did I have?* Lucas asked himself. It was for the greater good. They were soldiers on opposite sides of the battlefield now. Noble was working for the enemy. *Simple as that.*

The thought left a bitter taste in his mouth. Lucas

downed the last of his bourbon in one long swallow. Eric was sitting across from him, apparently lost in thought. The former Captain had a boating magazine open on his lap, but he hadn't looked at it in more than thirty minutes. He was staring out the window at the tarmac.

As the Cessna taxied toward a private hangar, Lucas noticed his mobile had reception again. He used the opportunity to dial Müller. The phone rang a dozen times before going to voicemail. Lucas dialed again with the same results. The first hint of worry started deep in his gut. He dialed a third time.

Eric tossed the magazine into the empty seat beside him and leaned forward. "The team in Prague?"

Lucas nodded.

"Not picking up?" Eric said.

Lucas nodded again and fixed the German with a hard stare that said plainly, *Your boys screwed up.*

Eric pulled out his own cell and started calling the rest of the team. One by one their phones went to voicemail.

Lucas looked at the phone in his hand, as if staring hard enough would make it ring. He tried willing Müller to call him back, but the phone remained stubbornly silent. He told himself not to panic. There were plenty of reasons why they might not pick up. Maybe they're out of range of a cell tower? Or maybe they're busy working Noble for info and not paying attention to their phones? *Or maybe they are all dead,* Lucas thought.

If the team in Prague was out of commission, the operation in Croatia was compromised. Lucas carefully weighed his options. He had to assume Noble was alive and that he knew the location of the intaglio press. Everything Lucas had spent the last six months working for was in jeopardy. He shook his head and dialed again. Only this time, he was calling Keiser.

Keiser picked up and cut right to business. "Have our interests in Prague been settled?"

"We ran into a slight hiccup," Lucas said. "A guy I used to work with showed up in Prague. Walked right into the middle of the deal. He's working with the freelancer."

"I thought your people were taking care of it?" Keiser asked.

"The team has gone dark."

"You mean they aren't answering their phones," Keiser said.

"There could be any number of explanations. They might be out of cell range or just keeping a low profile," Lucas said, trying to put lipstick on a pig.

Keiser dropped all pretense and said, "If your team isn't answering their phones, they're dead. We need to move up the time table. Where are you now?"

"I just touched down in Rijeka."

"Shut down the operation and get the last of the cash ready to move," Keiser told him.

"It's too early," Lucas argued. "I've had that press running round the clock and we're still several hundred million short of our goal."

"Let me worry about the math," Keiser said. "If the Americans are onto us, the entire operation is at risk. Get the cash ready to move right away."

Keiser hung up before Lucas could argue.

CHAPTER FIFTY-TWO

NOBLE STOOD IN THE MOSTLY EMPTY TERMINAL AT THE Praha Smíchov Railway Station, staring up at the departures board. Smíchov station is south and west of the city proper, a lonely station separated from the city center by the Vltava River and seldom used except by businessmen passing through on their way to someplace else. The remote location meant less traffic and less security.

A loudspeaker announced the 2:15 train to Salzburg. Half a dozen American backpackers hurried for the gates. Their shoes made peeling noises on the grimy floor. Noble got a whiff of pot as they passed. American college students often add Prague to their European itinerary as a place to get high. Czech laws are pretty lax. Recreational use is against the law, but personal possession is not a crime.

Eliška stood with her hands in her pockets and her eyes downcast. She hadn't spoken a single word since they left the cabin. She had allowed Noble to load her into the Škoda and drive to the station without resistance. He kept expecting her to make a move, but all the fight had gone out of her.

Noble kept her in his peripheral vision while he inspected the board. There was a 2:30 train to Berlin and 2:45 bound for Zagreb, capital of Croatia. From there, it was a little over fifty miles to the coastal town of Rijeka. Noble chewed the inside of one cheek. Going to Rijeka was a direct violation of orders, but Lucas had been one of Noble's men, and that made it his responsibility. Special Forces operators are the best of the best, modern-day ninjas. America trains some of the most highly skilled fighters on the planet, and those sheepdogs are expected to use their skills for good. If Lucas Randall had gone over to the Dark Side, Noble considered it his duty to stop him. Even if that meant getting fired—again.

Eliška finally spoke up. "What are you waiting for?"

Noble said, "Still want to get the guy responsible for your father's death?"

A dangerous light kindled in her eyes. "You know I do."

Noble nodded. They stepped up to the ticket counter where a tired man with a five o'clock shadow grunted at them. Noble paid cash for a pair of first-class berths on the sleeper coach bound for Zagreb. The vendor pushed the change, along with the tickets, under the partition and grumbled, "Leaves in thirty minutes."

Noble led the way up the stairs to the platform where a gleaming blue and yellow train waited. An attendant greeted them at the door, shined a flashlight on their tickets, and directed them toward the first-class coaches. Noble let Eliška go first, wondering if he had made the right decision.

Armstrong would likely fire him the moment she found out. Noble pushed that thought aside.

Eliška found the cabin, slid the door open, and slipped inside. Noble crowded in behind her. A pair of bunks took up most of the space, along with a small table and a seat. A narrow door opened on to a private bathroom with a toilet and a shower stall.

Noble sat down in the seat next to the window where he could watch the platform. He was looking forward, toward the stairs. Eliška dropped onto the bottom bunk and watched the opposite direction. She was watching his six without having to be told. *We work well together*, Noble thought for the second time since meeting her. She was a natural. Too bad she was a murderer. He glanced at his wristwatch. It was 2:32. The train to Berlin was gone. He was officially off the reservation. He returned to his vigil. They waited in silence as the seconds ticked slowly past. At last, the train started to move with a loud chuffing of air brakes. The platform slid out of sight and the lights of Prague dwindled.

As soon as the train left the station, Eliška unzipped her leather jacket. A splotch of dark blood stained her T-shirt. She pulled at her collar for a look at the damage. Her face pinched.

"Is it bad?" Noble asked.

"I think the bleeding has stopped."

"We need to bandage you up," Noble told her.

CHAPTER FIFTY-THREE

NOBLE MADE HIS WAY ALONG THE CARRIAGE TO THE connecting corridor where he spotted a white plastic box emblazoned with a bright-red cross attached to the wall. He glanced around—the passage was empty—and jerked the box free with one sharp tug. The screws let go with a wrenching shriek. Noble tucked the medical kit under one arm and made his way back to the first-class cabin. He knocked twice to let Eliška know it was him before sliding the door open.

She hadn't moved from her place by the window. Her face was blank and her eyes were unfocused. One hand cradled her injured breast through the T-shirt. The blood had dried into dark copper stains. She didn't react when Noble entered. She might be going into shock. She had been through a lot, even for a hardened assassin. She had been captured, tortured, and watched her father die. It was enough to break even the toughest of soldiers. Eliška was made of stern stuff, but everyone had their limits. The stress of the situation was finally catching up with her.

Noble locked the door behind him and sat down next to her on the bunk. "We'd better have a look at that."

When she didn't respond, Noble laid a hand on her shoulder. "We need to doctor that wound."

Her eyelids fluttered, like she was coming up from a dream. She looked down at her chest. The palm of her hand was flecked with dried blood. She glanced briefly at Noble, before shrugging out of the jacket. She peeled off the Rolling Stones T-shirt and Noble got his first look at the damage. Müller had done a job on her left breast. Unfortunately, she hadn't been wearing a bra. The padding from a good pushup would have taken some of the damage. As it stood, her left breast had borne the brunt of the torture.

Noble popped the clasps on the cheap medical kit and lifted the lid. It wasn't much more than bandages, tape, disinfectant, and pain killers, but it was better than nothing. He sorted the contents, selected an alcohol swab, and ripped it open.

"This is going to sting," he told her.

Eliška gripped the edge of the table with bone-white knuckles when Noble touched the swab to the bruised and mangled globe. A scream caught in her throat. She clamped her jaw shut, cutting off the sound.

"Just breathe," Noble reminded her.

He used the disinfectant swab and tried to keep his mind on the task at hand. It wasn't easy. He worked quickly, first cleaning the numerous punctures and then tearing open a large bandage. Eliška had closed her eyes, making things easier on him. She was taking deep breaths in through her nose and out through her mouth. Sweat beaded on her forehead.

Noble placed the square pad over the worst of the injuries and said, "Hold."

Eliška pinned the bandage in place without opening her eyes. Noble wrapped clean white gauze around her chest. He passed the gauze under her arms and over her shoulders until she was wearing a crude linen bra. It wasn't much, but should be enough to prevent infection and keep the worst of the cuts from tearing open every time she moved.

Eliška's eyes fluttered opened. She looked down and nodded appreciation. Her hand found his. He was placing one last piece of tape. She trapped his fingers against her ribcage.

"Thank you," she whispered.

"Don't mention it," Noble said. He could feel her heart beating beneath her chest and noticed, for the first time, how close she was. A small fire kindled in his belly. His breath sounded loud in the confines of the cabin. He tried to take his hand back, but Eliška held tight. She leaned into him and her lips graced his check. The soft touch left a trail of fire on Noble's skin. He felt that old familiar stirring in his gut and, before he could stop himself, he was returning her kisses.

Their mouths melded together. She moved his hand down to her bare stomach. Noble felt porcelain skin beneath his fingertips. The fire in his gut blazed white-hot. He gathered her up in his arms, careful to avoid her inured chest, and Eliška tore at his clothes. He worked the button on her denims while she pulled his shirt over his head.

Eliška saw the ragged claw marks and stopped. She put

a hand on his chest and pushed him back. "Did you kill my dog?"

Noble paused with one hand on her zipper. "He's alive and well."

Eliška took his face in both hands and smothered him in kisses. Noble knew it was wrong. Eliška was a stone-cold killer. She had murdered P. Arthur Fellows and left him in a closet. She'd kill Noble given half the chance. But those facts dwindled to background noise. Right now, they were rocketing through the countryside on a collision course with Lucas Randall. They might not live through tomorrow. This moment, here and now, was all that mattered.

CHAPTER FIFTY-FOUR

OTTO KEISER WAS IN HIS OFFICE WATCHING THE STOCK tickers. Half a dozen aides were gathered around the long conference table, monitoring the markets from their tablets while sipping cups of organic free-trade coffee. The smell permeated the air. It was the only thing keeping the group awake. The sky outside the floor-to-ceiling windows was velvet black. American markets were getting ready to close and the dollar was strong. Both the S&P and the DOW were up.

"Short another five hundred million in US dollars," Keiser ordered.

The tension in the room was palpable. Several of his aides shifted in their seats. Yuri Popov cleared his throat.

Keiser grumbled, "What is it, Yuri?"

"Sir, with all due respect, the dollar is strong right now and the US economy isn't showing any signs of a correction. Are we sure this is the right move?"

Yuri was a good trader with a nose for unicorns, but

Keiser didn't like being questioned. He had built this fund from the ground up with his own money. He fought to keep his temper in check. "I know full well what the dollar looks like. I can see it right here in front of me. And I'm telling you to short another half billion."

Yuri keyed the trade into his tablet without another word. Over the course of the next hour they watched as the price of the dollar showed a slight tremor. Other investors were taking notice of Quantum's position and reacting, but it wasn't enough to start a correction. Not yet. That would come later.

Keiser leaned back in his wheelchair, propped his elbows up and laced his fingers together. He had already arranged for an exposé on the 2.1 trillion in counterfeit currency. When the time was right, one of Keiser's secretaries would leak the story to a trusted source in the newsroom at CNN, and the price of the dollar would plummet.

Not long now, Keiser told himself.

In a few days, America would be brought to her knees. The juggernaut of the West would finally crumble. For decades now, America had forced its morals on the other nations of the world through the violence of capitalism. The free market economy was a system of oppression, a weapon the rich used to exploit the working class for profit. To Keiser, America represented slavery, racism, and bigotry—a country of wealth built on the backs of the working man.

But that will all change, thought Keiser. When the dollar collapsed and the economy crumbled, America would descend into utter chaos. There would be rioting and looting in the streets. *Stoke the fires of rebellion so that the world can be reshaped*, Keiser told himself. It was a Fabian principle. The idea was to implement democratic Socialism gradually through the slow and careful manipulation of world economies. Fabians understood that people had to be brought slowly and, more importantly, voluntarily to the freedom of Socialism. It could not be forced on a society. First the capitalist systems of oppression had to break down. Only then could the machines of social reform take over. For that to happen, is was necessary to break the American economy.

Keiser had been striving to reach that goal for decades. All the money and power he had built had been accumulated in pursuit of a singular purpose: destroy America and finally end the free market. He would use their own system against them. When America had collapsed under its own weight, the new order could begin.

The closing bell signaled the end of the trading day. Keiser dismissed his staff with a few curt words of encouragement and an admonition to be back at two o'clock sharp for opening bell. They collected their tablets and filed out of the room, headed home for a few hours of sleep before it all began again. Keiser pushed away from the long conference table and wheeled himself to the windows for a look at the glittering lights of Bern.

Not long now.

Soon, everything would change. Soon, America would be just a memory, a failed experiment. And once that lumbering behemoth of bigotry and oppression was finally out of the way, the Fabian Society would lead the world into a better tomorrow.

CHAPTER FIFTY-FIVE

THE MORNING SUN WAS JUST A WARM YELLOW RUMOR bleeding into the dark horizon when Armstrong's secretary handed her a folder stuffed full of urgent cables. She carried the stack, along with her second cup of coffee, to her office where she leaned back in her executive leather chair and paged through the documents. Most of it was boilerplate stuff. With the situation in Prague finally under control, Armstrong was able to turn her attention to other matters. Tensions between Iran and America were mounting. The radical factions running Iran had fired on American merchant ships. The president was rattling his saber. Half the nitwits in the mainstream media voiced the opinion that the president should back down, give concessions, and defuse the situation. They didn't understand a move like that would only embolden the Iranian regime. Armstrong had a team full of experts on the Middle East who assured her the only thing they respected was force.

She kicked off her flats as she read through the reports

and shrugged out of her pinstriped jacket. Nothing in the folder came as any surprise until she got to the end. Out of curiosity, she had asked Farnham to keep an eye on the financial news. The very last page was a reprinted article from Investopedia.com titled, *"The Man Who Broke the Bank of England Sets His Sights on the US Dollar—and Investors Are Starting to Panic."*

It was like a lead weight dropping into her belly and pinning her to the seat. Armstrong scanned the article, and all the puzzle pieces—the counterfeits, the assassin, the United Front—started falling into place. Why hadn't she seen it before? Yesterday's edition of *Investor's Business Daily* was still laying on the coffee table, the headline facing up. Armstrong put two and two together. A counterfeiting ring capable of producing untraceable bills and a billionaire shorting the dollar. The idea sent a shiver tip-toeing up her back. If she was right ...

She shook her head. She didn't want to think about the fallout. She pulled her jacket back on, took the reprinted article along with the *Investor's Business Daily*, and hurried down the hall to the operation room.

Both analysts turned at the sound of the door. Witwicky's hair was a frizzy mess and Cook had dark bags under his eyes.

"Has Noble arrived in Berlin?" Armstrong asked.

"We're waiting to hear from him," Witwicky spoke through a yawn.

Armstrong dropped the IBD onto their cluttered workstation. "An investment banker named Otto Keiser is short-selling US dollars."

"Never heard of him," Witwicky said.

Cook reached for the paper and scanned the headline. "Maybe he's just betting on the wrong pony. Investors make bad decisions all the time."

Armstrong paced back and forth. "That's a hundred billion dollar bet against the market."

"He'll lose his shirt if he's wrong," Witwicky remarked.

"Men like Keiser don't make billions backing the wrong horse," Armstrong said. "In fact, they don't make a move without rock-solid information."

Cook looked up at her. "What are you thinking, boss?"

Armstrong stopped her pacing. "The economy is booming. The dollar isn't showing any signs of a correction. Short-selling the dollar doesn't make any sense."

Witwicky was nodding along as Armstrong spoke. She said, "Unless you have reason to believe the dollar will take a hit."

Armstrong nodded.

"You think he's involved?" Witwicky asked.

"I think at the very least he's got insider information," Armstrong said.

"What do you want us to do?" Cook asked.

"Dig into Otto Keiser's background," Armstrong told them. "Find out everything you can about him. I specifically want to know if he's got ties to the United Front."

CHAPTER FIFTY-SIX

Noble lay huddled next to Eliška in the tiny bed, feeling the rhythm of the train as it clanked along the tracks. He was on his back, staring up at the overhead bunk. One hand was stuffed under the flimsy pillow. The other arm was trapped beneath Eliška. She was draped along his side, her back to the wall, her fingertips lightly tracing the lines of his chest. Noble enjoyed the press of her body against him and her touch. It had been a long time. So long in fact, that Noble had nearly forgotten what it was like. It was good, but now that it was over, a nagging sense of shame crept up and took hold.

Noble couldn't place it at first. He had no hang-ups about sex. He certainly wasn't a prude. He liked sex and would do it more often, but his lifestyle didn't exactly jibe with long-term relationships. Special Forces operators had an incredibly high divorce rate. The CIA wasn't much better. But that wasn't what was bothering Noble. He wasn't in love with Eliška. He certainly didn't have any intention of marrying her. She was a killer for hire and he was the guy sent to stop her. Fate had thrown them together. Neither harbored any illusions about love or fidelity. They were just two lonely people hurtling toward a deadly confrontation. Both of them knew it might be their last night on Earth. There were no guarantees. They might die tomorrow, and wanted to feel another human's touch before checking out. It was as simple as that. So it was a moment before Noble realized what was bothering him. It wasn't the cheap, desperate act of two lonely people on a train facing uncertain odds.

It was Sam.

Sam—like Noble's mother—had been a born-again, bible-quoting Christian. A true believer. *Let all God's children say amen*, Noble thought with a heavy dose of irony. Hell, when Noble first met Sam, she had been running a shelter for abused women. She didn't believe in sex before marriage and had made that fact perfectly—painfully—clear to Noble during their first encounter. What would she think of him sleeping with a murderer?

It was like a barbed arrow straight to Noble's heart.

What if she could see him right now? What if there really was an afterlife? Noble swallowed hard. Was Sam up there right now looking down on him? *Did she know?* Noble felt hot with shame and self-loathing. He felt certain that Sam, wherever she was, knew. He felt that he had defiled her memory for a moment of pleasure. The idea left a bitter taste in his mouth.

Eliška propped her head up on a fist and whispered, "What is her name?"

The question jerked Noble from his reverie. He craned his neck up for a look at her. "What are you talking about?"

"You were thinking about a woman just now." There was no accusation in her tone, just curiosity.

He put his head back down on the pillow. "How did you know?"

"A woman always knows." A knowing smile played on her lips. "What is her name?"

"Sam," Noble admitted.

Eliška's fingers stopped. She placed her hand flat on his chest and pushed herself up to look him in the eye. "This is a man's name."

"Short for Samantha," Noble told her.

Eliška relaxed and her fingers went back to exploring his body. "She is your wife?"

"No," Noble said.

"Your girlfriend?"

"It's complicated," Noble said.

"You will tell her about us?" Eliška asked.

"I can't." Noble swallowed a knot in his throat. It took him a moment to say the words out loud, as if speaking it made it true. He licked his lips and croaked out, "She's dead."

"I am very sorry for your loss," Eliška said and sounded like she meant it.

Up until now, Noble figured she was motivated entirely by greed and vengeance. It was strange to think of an assassin feeling remorse. He felt the armor around his heart shift. Hairline fractures formed in his defenses. Noble knew it was a mistake. She was a killer. It was a mistake to get too close, to let her under his skin.

"She was very lucky woman," Eliška said.

Noble shifted on the bunk, putting some space between them, and gave her a hard look.

Eliška read his expression and hurried to explain. "She was loved by a very good man before she died. Yes, she was very lucky, I think. I will never know this type of love. I have never been loved by a man."

"Your father loved you," Noble said.

"Yes, my father loved me," she said and laid her head on his chest. "Only, he is dead now."

Noble didn't have any response to that. Piotr Cermákova had lived a hard life and met a bitter end. Nothing Noble or Eliška did now could bring him back. They could only avenge him. Noble felt a drop of wet on his skin and realized Eliška was silently weeping. Tears spilled down her cheeks onto his chest. He wrapped his arms around her and let her cry.

"We'll get 'em," he whispered. "We'll make 'em pay."

CHAPTER FIFTY-SEVEN

"WE FOUND A CONNECTION BETWEEN KEISER AND THE United Front," Ezra said. He pushed a thumb and forefinger into his eyes in an effort to stay awake. He didn't remember what sleep felt like. He was operating inside a thick fog. He had to check all his numbers twice. His thoughts came slow and trudging, like petulant children reluctantly settling down to their homework. All he wanted to do was curl up on the sofa and drift off, but he forced himself to stay awake. Red Bull helped. He said, "It's nothing we can prove in a court of law, but it's there all the same."

Armstrong crossed her arms and nodded for him to continue. "Impress me."

Ezra waved a hand at his computer screen. "After leaving the CIA, Lucas Randall took a job working for Global Security Solutions. Global Security is owned by a parent company called First Initiative Holdings."

"Let me guess," said Armstrong. "Owned by Apollo Fund?"

"Close," said Gwen. "Owned by a legal entity which is owned by Apollo Fund."

Armstrong nodded understanding. "Suspicious but not necessarily criminal. He might be doing it for tax purposes."

"That's the way Keiser runs all his businesses," Gwen said. "He controls literally hundreds of corporations, but he doesn't technically *"own"* any of them," She put the word in air quotes. "He's just the primary shareholder of the parent companies."

"So you're telling me Lucas Randall worked for Otto Keiser?" Armstrong asked.

"That part's not in question," Ezra said. "Randall definitely worked for Keiser. He spent six months at Global Security Solutions before he was tapped to run Keiser's personal security detail. Only, he was no longer going by the name Lucas Randall. He disappears from Global Security's payroll and reappears under the alias Luke Ralston."

"You're kidding?" Armstrong uncrossed her arms.

Ezra shook his head.

"How did you find that out?" she wanted to know.

"Found a picture of Keiser attending a fundraiser for candidate Helen Rhodes in 2016." Ezra drew her attention to a picture on the screen. "That's Keiser in the wheelchair, and standing right behind him ..."

"Lucas Randall," Armstrong finished for him. She leaned over his shoulder to scan the photo and Ezra caught a glimpse down her blouse.

He turned his face away. His ears went red. He said, "Randall, aka Ralston, spent a year as Keiser's head of security before pulling another vanishing act. The United Front committed their first terror attack on an oil pipeline in the Sudan just three months later."

Armstrong straightened up and crossed her arms again. "A guy like Randall doesn't decide out of the blue to start his own terror organization. He had funding. Can you link Keiser financially to the United Front?"

"No," Ezra admitted. "But that's where things get interesting. We went over Global Security's employee records from the last ten years. Lucas Randall wasn't the only employee who suddenly vanished from their payroll. Twenty-seven other security specialists have worked for Global and then pulled a Houdini. They dropped off the face of the planet. No job records, no known addresses, no phone bills. It's like they all fell into a black hole."

"More like they got recruited," Armstrong said. "So it's entirely possible that Keiser is using the security company as a recruiting ground for the United Front?"

"That's what we suspect," Ezra said. "And that's hardly the worst of it."

Armstrong fixed him with a look. "What's worse than a billionaire funding a terror organization?"

"You asked us to crunch the numbers on Keiser's bet against the US dollar," Ezra said.

"What did you find?"

Gwen took up the narrative. "Assuming even a ten percent devaluation in the dollar due to an influx of counterfeits, Keiser's bet against US currency would result in a complete financial meltdown."

Armstrong's face froze. She stared at them for several

seconds before she found her words. "How is that even possible?"

"Imagine untold billions in counterfeit bills flooding the market," Ezra said. "It would cause a steep devaluation in the dollar. All of a sudden, the money in your wallet is no good, because you don't know what's real and fake. Banks have no way of knowing if the stuff they have is any good either. The stock market would crash and the economy would come to a screeching halt. It would be worse than Black Tuesday. We'll be back to the barter system, exchanging chickens for gas. It could take decades to recover from something this big."

"That's impossible," Armstrong said. She shook her head. "It would take—"

"Just over seven-hundred and fifty billion in counterfeit bills," Gwen said. "We ran the numbers twice."

Ezra delivered more bad news. "Assuming they only have one press and they've been running it since Lucas Randall dropped out of sight, they could have printed just over one trillion in supernotes. That's with nights and week-ends off."

Armstrong breathed a curse.

"It gets worse," Gwen said. "The dollar is the world's reserve currency."

Armstrong looked around for something to sit on. Her only option was the sagging, threadbare sofa. She leaned against the wall instead. "Hit me with it."

"If the dollar collapses," Gwen said, "China could cash in on our debts and send the economy spiraling further down. With the reserve currency suddenly unreliable and our stock market in shambles, supermarkets would run out of food in just three days."

"Three days?" Armstrong said.

Ezra nodded. "America doesn't produce our own food anymore. We get most of our food from Mexico. Without a reliable currency, the trains stop running, and the store shelves would be bare within three days. A week, at most. Lifesaving medications would run out in two to three months."

"Heaven help us." Armstrong scrubbed her face with both hands. "Death toll?"

"Hard to get an accurate estimate," Gwen admitted. "The sick and elderly would be the first to go. That's nearly a third of the American population."

"Who else knows about this?" Armstrong asked.

"We had to consult with the people in financial to be sure our numbers were correct and a specialist in economics."

"Get on the phone with them," Armstrong ordered. "Make sure they don't spread any rumors. We don't want to start a panic. Then figure out how the United Front plans to move the money. Look for any commercial shipping companies owned by Apollo Fund or any of its subsidiaries."

"We're on it," Ezra said and both analysts turned back to their computers.

CHAPTER FIFTY-EIGHT

ARMSTRONG ORDERED HER SECRETARY TO CALL AN emergency meeting with the president and the head of NSA, then stopped at the open door to Wizard's office. She hesitated before rapping her knuckles on the frame. The old spymaster stood with his hips against his desk and a cigarette dangling from his mouth. He was staring at the cluttered wall of newspaper clippings and red string. A cloud of smoke gathered around his head, stirred slowly by the current from the air vent. He turned at the sound of her knock. "Something on your mind, Director? Or are you just checking to make sure I made my appointment this morning?"

Armstrong stepped inside, glanced around at the explosion of paperwork and said, "We found the printing press. It's in an abandoned torpedo factory in the port town of Rijeka."

"You didn't come here to tell me that," Wizard spoke from inside the cloud of smoke.

Armstrong thought about whether to tell him the rest. It would only fuel his paranoia. Then she thought, *Why not kill two birds with one stone?* Wizard needed a boogeyman, and Otto Keiser was trying to crash the dollar. It was a match made in heaven. She said, "There is an investment banker named Otto Keiser. He runs—"

"Apollo Fund in Bern, Switzerland," Wizard finished for her. "I'm familiar with him."

She held up the paper. "He's been short selling the US dollar."

Wizard reached out a hand. A frown creased the lines of his face.

Armstrong brought him up to speed on everything they had learned. She finished with, "Investors are starting to panic. They're afraid Keiser knows something they don't."

"Maybe he *does*," Wizard said. "Maybe he knows a few billion in counterfeit bills are about to flood the market and crash the dollar."

"The Secret Service is coordinating with local law enforcement in Croatia to take down the warehouse," Armstrong said.

"And if Jake is right?" Wizard asked. "If Lucas Randall is running the United Front? The Croatians are walking into an ambush."

"Have you got a better idea?"

"Jake Noble may be our best option."

"You think he stands a better chance than a Croatian SWAT team?"

"Jake was Special Forces. He knows the way Randall thinks," Wizard said. "He can anticipate Randall's moves."

"It's too late for that," Armstrong said. "Noble is

halfway to Berlin by now. Besides, he's saddled with the assassin. She can close the book on a dozen murders. We can't just cut her loose."

"I wonder," Wizard said to himself. His attention went to the wall and his eyes tracked the lines of red string.

Armstrong almost regretted knocking on his door. The old spymaster had slipped back into his web of conspiracy theories. If she let him, he would wander in the wilderness of mirrors for hours, maybe days. Armstrong said, "I'm meeting the president in thirty minutes to discuss damage control. The DNI will be there, along with the SecDef and the Joint Chiefs." She reached over and tapped the article still clutched in Wizard's fist. "I need someone to oversee the operation in Rijeka."

A smile worked its way onto his lined face. "Is this your way of apologizing for shutting down my op and suggesting I'm crazy?"

"You started this," Armstrong told him. "I thought you'd want to finish it."

CHAPTER FIFTY-NINE

Noble and Eliška laid tangled in each other's arms as the first rays of sunlight crept in through the window. Noble was the first to stir. His bladder threatened to burst if he didn't empty it soon, and he couldn't remember the last time he ate. He needed food, but nature's call came first. He slowly extricated himself from Eliška's embrace, eased off the narrow bunk, and stepped into the cramped lavatory. The door closed with a soft *click*. Noble took care of business, turned on the sink and splashed water on his face. Cold drove the last of the sleep from his brain. He raked both hands through his shaggy hair before inspecting himself in the mirror. A gaunt wraith with haunted eyes stared back. One hand went to the stubble on his chin. He muttered, "You've looked better."

He used liquid soap on his face and under his arms. The bird bath washed away the worst of the grime. At least he no longer smelled like a dead carcass rotting on the side of the road. His stomach informed him it was time to eat by way of a loud rattle. He opened the door and let himself out.

Eliška was already dressed. She hurriedly stuffed her foot into her shoe and sprang for the opening. Noble let her slip past and reached for his pants, which were crumpled on the floor of the cabin. He dressed in silence while Eliška used the toilet. When she emerged, Noble held out her short leather jacket. "Put that on."

"We going somewhere?" she asked as she shrugged into the coat. She zipped it closed to hide the bloodstain.

"Restaurant car," Noble told her. "I'm starving."

They passed along the train to the dining car. The mouthwatering aroma of sizzling sausages enveloped Noble as he stepped through the door. His stomach tied itself in knots. A dozen high-top tables lined both sides of the carriage. Dust motes danced in the soft warm glow of morning sunlight spilling through the windows. A smiling waiter in a clean white apron motioned them in with a wave of his hand. They were his first customers of the day. He greeted them in Italian and then switched to English. It's uncanny how often Europeans can pick out an American on sight. "Please sit wherever you like."

They took a table near the door and ordered from the menu. The waiter returned shortly with two plates piled with food and a stainless-steel carafe of steaming hot coffee. Noble picked up his fork and speared fluffy scrambled eggs into his mouth. His belly welcomed the chow with open arms and begged for more. Noble wasted no time filing that request. He wolfed down half the plate, pausing just long enough to fill a cup with strong black coffee.

Eliška was listless, poking at her food, mostly pushing it around the plate.

"Eat," Noble told her. "You'll need your strength."

She put her fork down and stared out the window at the fiery red disk of the rising sun. "I never even told him I loved him."

That statement hung in the air for what seemed like an eternity.

Noble picked up his coffee cup and cradled it in both hands, enjoying the warmth. He said, "My father died while I was overseas. By the time I got back to the States, he was dead and buried. I didn't get to say goodbye. Sometimes, I think maybe it was better that way."

He didn't bother to explain it. He couldn't even if he wanted to.

Eliška didn't need an explanation. She nodded. "Did he know that you loved him?"

"I think so," Noble said and added, "I hope so. Anyway, it all happened so fast. At first, it didn't feel real. By the time the shock set in, I was busy taking care of Mom. That helped."

"I never knew my mother. She died when I was very young. My father was all that I had left," Eliška said. She took her eyes off the rolling countryside and looked at Noble. "The American? Lucas? You knew him?"

"Yeah," Noble admitted. "I know him."

"He is a friend?"

"He was," Noble told her. "Once."

"Will you be able to kill him when the time comes?"

Noble thought about that. He tried to imagine pointing a gun at Lucas and feeling the sudden kick. His lips pushed together. He had killed plenty of bad guys—so many he had lost count—but he had never killed a friend. "If he's intent on destroying the United States," Noble said, "I'll do what I have to do."

Eliška nodded. "You and I are very much alike. We both do what we must."

He eyed her over the rim of his mug. She was a remorseless killer, and she didn't do it for anything so noble as country or creed. She killed for money. It was one step above killing for sport. Noble lowered his cup and placed it gently on the tabletop. He spoke in a voice barely above a whisper. "You're wrong about that. I fight for my country. You kill for money."

"You do it for country. I do it for money. But we both thrive on the adrenaline. We both like what we do." She flashed her teeth in a humorless grin. "Don't bother to deny it. You have the same darkness within you, Jakob. I can feel it."

He stared out the window. The sun was above the horizon now, casting the rolling green countryside in a brilliant gold light. He thought about Sam and about the terrible darkness eating away at him—it felt like a black hole in the center of his chest pulling in all the warmth and leaving only bitterness in its wake—and he wondered if Eliška was right. Maybe they weren't so different after all? Maybe she was just further along the path? That idea rattled him. How many more deaths, Noble wondered, how many more Samanthas, until he was a remorseless killing machine?

He drained the last of his coffee in one long gulp that burned his throat. The dining car was slowly filling up around them. The sound of silverware clinking against dishes and friendly conversation made him feel out of place. He looked around at the other patrons. None of them knew that a pair of trained killers sat in their midst. He dropped some cash on the table and said, "Let's get out of here."

CHAPTER SIXTY

ARMSTRONG WAS ON THE PHONE WITH A SPECIAL investigator from Secret Service named Ron Hinson. He sounded tired but alert as he brought Armstrong up to speed on the situation. Hinson had taken a red-eye to Croatia, landing just after five in the morning. He was acting as liaison with the head of Rijeka's *Specijalne jedinice policije*, or SJP for short—Croatia's version of a SWAT team. The head of the local unit had the abandoned torpedo factory under surveillance. His spotters claimed the place was empty. Sharpshooters stationed on nearby rooftops hadn't seen any signs of movement and nothing showed up on thermal.

"It looks like they're long gone," said Hinson. "If they were ever here to begin with. You might have gotten bad intel. I've got a team of people taking water samples from the beach about ten miles south. They'll be able to tell us if it matches the forensics we took from the supernotes."

"How long will that take?" Armstrong wanted to know.

She sat hunched over her desk with a pair of reading glasses riding low on her nose and her hair gathered up in a plastic clip.

"A day or two, at least," Hinson told her.

Armstrong felt any hope of a quick resolution draining away. She had spent two and a half hours in the Oval Office, with the president, his Chief of Staff, the Joint Chiefs, the head of the FBI, and the head of the Federal Reserve. They had argued different courses of action—everything from military intervention to a freeze on the markets—but in the end everyone agreed it would be best if they could stop the money from ever reaching the United States, which threw the ball back in Armstrong's court. She was now working hand in hand with the Secret Service. The president had made it clear that they were to use any and every tool at their disposal.

"Local SWAT is getting ready to probe the building," Hinson was saying. "If everything looks good, they'll breech. I'll let you know what they find, but it doesn't look hopeful."

There was a knock at the door and Wizard stuck his head in.

"Just a minute, Ron." Armstrong covered the phone with one hand and waved Wizard in with the other. "What have you got?"

Wizard crossed the floor to her desk as he tore the cellophane off a new pack of smokes. The Deputy Director of Operations seemed to have an endless supply. Armstrong wondered how much of his income went to cigarettes. He rasped out, "Jake Noble never made his meeting in Berlin."

"Has he made contact?"

Wizard shook his head. "The phone he was using is no longer in service. Whoever he stole it from must have had it disconnected."

"Think he's in trouble?" Armstrong asked.

Wizard shook a cigarette loose from the pack. "I think he's headed for Croatia."

Armstrong looked up at the ceiling and shook her head. "I'm starting to regret reinstating him."

Wizard flicked his lighter and cupped the flame. "That kid is like a dog with a bone."

"That's why you put him on to this," Armstrong said. "You knew he'd see it through no matter where the evidence went."

Wizard waved away a cloud of smoke. "I suspected it would get hairy and wanted one of my best people on the job. Jake might be an emotional wreck right now, but he's still the best field officer I've got. The kid can think on his feet and he's not afraid to take chances."

Armstrong bit back an angry reply. Wizard had run this op from the very beginning. He seemed to know what was going to happen before it happened. It was like he could see around corners. She figured the old spymaster could stare a hole through a brick wall, given enough time.

Wizard said, "Might be good to have Noble on hand in Croatia if things get loud."

Ron Hinson was saying something on the phone. Armstrong took her hand away from the receiver and said, "Sorry, what was that, Ron?"

"I said they are getting ready to breech."

"Tell them to hold on," Armstrong said.

"What's shaking?" Ron asked.

"Tell the local commander to put his people on hold," Armstrong said. "I've got a, uh ..."

"Consultant," Wizard interjected.

"Consultant," Armstrong said. "He happens to be in the area. Tell the local commander I'd like him to work directly with my guy."

"I don't think that's going to be possible," Hinson said. "They aren't exactly taking orders from me. In fact, they've made it clear that I'm only allowed to sit in on the operation as a favor to our government."

"Did you tell him this operation directly effects American interests?" Armstrong asked. "Did you explain to him that if the American economy crumbles, Croatia won't be far behind?"

"I did."

"And?"

"And he doesn't seem to care."

Wizard said, "Tell Hinson I said hello."

Armstrong didn't even bother to ask Wizard how he knew the name of the Secret Service Agent in charge. One look was enough to know Wizard had a card to play. Armstrong said, "Your old friend Albert Dulles says hi."

"Is Al there now?"

"Yes, he is."

"I suppose your *consultant* is working closely with the old Wiz?"

"That's right," Armstrong said.

Hinson breathed heavily into the phone. "Okay, I'll see what I can do. Tell Al he owes me one. When will your consultant be here?"

"I'm not sure exactly," Armstrong admitted. "Not long. He's en route."

"How will we know him?"

"He'll answer to the name Jake," Armstrong said. "And he may be traveling with a companion."

"Okay," Hinson said. "I'll keep an eye out for him."

Armstrong hung up the phone and turned her attention to Wizard. She said, "What if that money's already gone? What if we are too late? What if it's already headed toward the United States? Hell, it might already be in circulation?"

Wizard breathed smoke and shook his head. "It's not. Keiser wouldn't risk it. He has to time it just right in order for him to profit from the collapse of the dollar. He needs that money to hit the market shortly before his puts expire."

Armstrong passed a hand over her face. "God, I hope you're right."

"Me too." Wizard breathed smoke. "More importantly, I hope Noble is right. We won't get another crack at this."

"So all our hopes are pinned on a grieving drunk?"

Wizard hitched up boney shoulders. "It's an imperfect world."

Armstrong buzzed her secretary. "Make a pot of coffee, will you?"

CHAPTER SIXTY-ONE

THE TRAIN PULLED INTO THE STATION AT ZAGREB A few minutes after eight o'clock. Noble and Eliška passed along a line of cars in the parking lot looking for something without an alarm system. Noble pointed to a dented yellow Citroen. Eliška nodded. There was no time for subtlety. He glanced around the lot before using his elbow to hammer out the rear-passenger window. Eliška gave a loud fake sneeze at the same time. It wasn't much in the way of camouflage, but nobody was close enough to hear the jingle of breaking glass anyway.

Noble reached in and unlocked the passenger-side door, which he then held for Eliška.

"Such a gentleman." She seated herself in the old clunker with all the grace of an English princess stepping into a carriage and then reached across to unlock his side. By the time he piled into the driver's seat, Eliška had already pried apart the steering column. Noble flicked open the SpyderCo knife he had taken from her weapons cache back in Prague. Eliška indicated which wires to cut. Noble sawed through them with the blade and Eliška twisted them together. The exposed ends sparked and the engine came to life with a loud knocking.

The fuel needle pointed to half a tank. Better than Noble had hoped for. Most people drive around with their car on empty. He said, "How far to Rijeka?"

They had purchased a map of Croatia from the station. Eliška measured the distance using the stub of a pencil she found in the center console. "Maybe one hundred and sixty kilometers."

Noble made the conversion in his head. It was about a hundred miles. He pulled the Citroen out of the parking lot and followed signs to the freeway. The E65 runs west along wooded mountain roads all the way to the coast. Noble pushed the speedometer up to eighty miles an hour and cranked his window down. A cool breeze filled the car and helped clear his head. He had been torturing himself about last night—about Eliška—and wondering what Sam would say if she knew. It was an exercise in futility. Sam was dead, and if there was a heaven, she was in it. And Noble doubted very much if he was going there when he died. *And if there was no heaven?* Then Sam was just dead and it didn't matter either way. Torturing himself wouldn't change a thing.

He shelved those questions for the moment and focused on the road ahead. He needed to find the torpedo factory and stop that money from reaching the United States. And he decided it was time to check in with Langley. There was nothing they could do to stop him at this late stage. He might as well give them an update on his position. He had been on the road nearly thirty minutes. A sign up ahead advertised gas, beer, and cigarettes, first in Croatian, then Italian and English. Noble eased off the pedal and put on his blinker.

Eliška had been slumped in the passenger seat, staring out the window at passing trees. She sat up a little when Noble started to slow. "Stopping for gas?"

Noble nodded and dug his wallet from his back pocket. He flipped it open and passed his company credit card to Eliška. "We're going to need a mobile phone with GPS."

Noble pulled into the filling station and nosed the Citroen up next to a tank. He got out, twisted off the gas cap, and slotted the nozzle while Eliška went inside. He watched her disappear through the glass doors and turned his attention to the digital readout, watching the gallons tick. Petrol fumes filled his lungs as he listened to the pump. The auto shutoff valve clunked and Noble wracked the nozzle.

Eliška emerged from the station as Noble was screwing the gas cap into place. A plastic shopping bag swung from one arm and she carried two cups of coffee. She hauled open the passenger door with a squeal of rusting hinges and climbed in beside him as he touched the wires together. Noble got them back on the road while Eliška worked open the plastic clamshell and booted up the phone. The screen came to life and a call came through seconds later. Eliška's eyebrows went up.

"That will be for me," Noble said.

———

Gwen and Ezra had been working furiously to figure out how Keiser planned to move the money. First, they had to calculate the space requirements. Since they didn't know how much money Keiser had printed up, the best they could do was estimate, but even a conservative guess of one trillion dollars would require something the size of two or three football fields.

Running on coffee and Red Bull, they had crunched the numbers twice. Assuming one hundred million dollars on a standard shipping pallet, they calculated it would take ten thousand pallets stacked with cash. That ruled out cargo jets. It would take a fleet of them. Instead, they focused their attention on container ships. Keiser had several commercial shipping interests. His conglomerates controlled three different shipping companies in the area around Rijeka, but that didn't answer the question of how he was clearing the shipments through customs. He couldn't just stack the money on pallets and load it into shipping containers.

Gwen had her feet stacked on her desk, staring up at the fluorescents, while she tried to imagine all the ways someone could hide money. She was painfully aware of Ezra. He was on the couch with a thick packet of papers, reading through Secret Service reports on counterfeiting schemes in the hopes of finding something that would help. Every few minutes, his eyes would flick to Gwen and then back to the stack of reports. An hour ago, he had timidly brought up a new movie arriving theaters this weekend. Gwen wanted to see it, but she didn't want to give Ezra false hope and had made up an excuse. The tension in the room had been palpable since.

Gwen felt horrible. It was just a movie. But that wasn't all. That was never all. If she said yes to the movie, then it would be dinner, then roller skating, concerts, and eventually he would be shopping for a ring. She wondered if there was some way to explain it all without crushing his feelings. She had just made up her mind to try when she heard the gentle chirp from her computer and saw the notification appear on screen. She took her feet off the desk and sat up.

"Noble just used his credit card," she announced.

Ezra set aside the Secret Service reports and pushed himself off the couch. "Where?"

"Croatia," Gwen said.

"I knew it," Ezra said. "That guy ..."

He never finished the sentence.

Gwen was already on the phone with Armstrong. The Director appeared in the situation room seconds later. Her pinstripe suit and pressed white blouse had picked up a few wrinkles, but she still conveyed a sense of poise. Blonde hair had worked loose from the plastic clip and a few loose strands framed her face. Wizard was right behind her, looking like he always did: a brooding vulture with beady eyes and a cigarette dangling from his beak.

"Where is he?" Armstrong wanted to know.

"A gas station about sixty miles east of Rijeka," Gwen told her. "He bought gas, coffee, a couple of protein bars, and a cellular phone."

She expected Armstrong to rant and rave. The Director had been livid when she learned Noble missed the connection at Berlin. Instead of being angry, Armstrong seemed relieved. "Have you got the number of the phone?"

Ezra said, "Working on that now." He consulted his

computer, grabbed a pen and an empty candy bar wrapper. He tried writing on the smooth surface of the wrapper, but the ink wouldn't take. Gwen passed him a crumpled napkin. He scribbled the number, leaving little rips in the paper, and passed the napkin back.

"Call him," Armstrong ordered.

Gwen put the phone on speaker and dialed. The first attempt got a recorded message, telling them the phone was not in service. They tried again.

"He may not have activated it yet," Ezra said.

It started to ring on the third attempt.

Noble's voice came on the line. "Goodman and Associates. Goodman speaking."

Armstrong had her arms crossed under her breasts. Her mouth was a strict line. She said, "Noble? This is DCI Armstrong speaking. You're supposed to be in Berlin."

"Berlin is so depressing this time of year," Noble said.

"Is Cermáková with you?"

"Affirmative."

Armstrong's nostrils flared. She glanced across at Wizard.

The Deputy Director of Operations jumped into the pause. "Jake? Albert Dulles here. How far are you from Rijeka, son?"

"Thirty minutes, sir. Maybe a little longer."

Armstrong nodded.

Wizard said, "Jake, there is a Secret Service Agent on sight by the name of Ronald Hinson. He's working with the local police. They're expecting you. I want you to link up with Ron and assist the SWAT commander in any way you can. Understood?"

"Hooah," Noble said.

Ezra looked at Gwen, who only shrugged. She didn't know if that was code for "Affirmative" or some obscure curse word.

Wizard seemed to take it in stride. He said, "Hinson and the SWAT team have set up shop in a used tire outlet a few blocks east of the torpedo factory."

Noble said, "Let them know I'm driving a beat-up yellow Citroen. I don't want to catch a bullet."

"I'll do that," Wizard said. "And Noble, listen to me—we need Lucas Randall alive."

"Sir, you know as well as I do that may not be possible," Noble said. "Lucas is a SEAL. He's not going down without a fight."

"Randall is our only link to the man behind this counterfeiting scheme," Wizard said. "We believe his name is Otto Keiser, but we can't prove the connection. We need you to bring Randall in for questioning."

There was a long pause and Noble finally said, "I'll do everything I can to bring Lucas in alive."

CHAPTER SIXTY-TWO

Noble clasped hands with Ron Hinson. The agent was medium height and medium build. He belied the myth that all Secret Service agents were big, burly men who protect the president. Hinson could pass for an insurance adjustor or a city planner. He pumped Noble's hand and said, "Thanks for coming on such short notice."

"I was in the neighborhood," Noble lied.

They stood in the dim confines of the tire factory, breathing in rubber fumes. Refurbished tires were stacked in steel rafters fifteen feet high. The handful of employees went about their jobs, sneaking glances at the team of men in dark-blue combat fatigues with submachine guns strapped to their chests. American law enforcement would have cleared out the employees and locked down the buildings on either side as well, but this wasn't America.

The shop was just three blocks from the abandoned torpedo factory. The large bay door stood open, letting in the sunlight and a cool breeze tinged with the fresh scent of saltwater. The loud rattle of pneumatic drills and the constant hum of machinery made it hard to hear anything below a shout. The local SWAT team had erected a pair of plastic folding tables in one corner. On the tables sat dozen ruggedized laptops with closed-circuit feeds from various cameras stationed around the abandoned factory.

Hinson directed Noble's attention to a short, powerfully built man with iron-gray hair on a head shaped like a bullet. Blue combat fatigues were stretched taut across an expanding belly. Hinson said, "This is Captain Vuković. He's running the show."

Noble put out his hand. Vuković tried to crush it in a pointless display of male dominance. He had stubby fingers that felt like iron bands. Noble endured the bone-crushing grip with a straight face. "Good to meet you, Captain."

"And your name is?" Vuković asked.

"Jake," Noble told him.

"Do you have a last name?"

"Just Jake."

The muscles at the corner of Vuković's jaw tightened. "Okay, Just Jake. So long as you understand who is in charge."

"It's your rodeo, Captain."

His gray eyebrows knotted. "What is rodeo?"

"It means you're in charge," Noble said. "I'm just here to offer advice."

"If I need advice, I'll be sure to ask," Vuković told him. His eyes went to Eliška. He was obviously waiting for an introduction.

Noble said, "Meet my chauffeur, Ellie."

They all shook hands. Noble thought he saw a flash of

recognition in Hinson's eyes, but the Secret Service agent was too well-trained to give anything away. He favored Eliška with a tight smile.

Noble returned his attention to Vuković. "What's the situation, Captain?"

"Situation is American Secret Service department call me and tell me Germans run counterfeiting operation out of old factory. I put factory under surveillance, but nobody home. Place is empty." He waved stubby fingers at the laptops on the folding tables. "I'm just about to breech when Americans tell me I must wait for consultant. So tell me, Mr. Just Jake. What is your expert opinion?"

"It's empty," Noble agreed. He hooked his hands in his pockets and chewed the inside of one cheek. The torpedo factory was a crumbling structure of brick and steel that dated back to 1930. The manufacturing side of the factory hugged the sea wall and adjoined the launch house, a three-story structure thrusting out over the cobalt waters of the Adriatic and topped by a weathered observation post. The SWAT team had their cameras pointed at doors and broken windows. Nothing moved in the dark labyrinth of abandoned halls. One of the feeds came from a thermal camera. It revealed inky blacks and deep blues. In the center of the launch house sat a large, dark angular shape. The size and shape was right for a printing press. At its base, Noble eyed a few muted blobs of lighter blue, edging toward green. He pointed, "But it hasn't been empty long. Someone has been there recently. Your thermal camera is registering heat. See it?"

Vuković shrugged, unconvinced. "Is rats maybe?"

Noble conceded that point with a shrug. He indicated the shape to Hinson. "You see what I'm seeing?"

Hinson narrowed his eyes. "I think so."

"Could that be the intaglio press we're looking for?"

"It's the right size," Hinson said. "Can't say for sure until we go in and have a look."

Vuković said, "Is settled then. We go in."

Noble shook his head. "I don't like it."

Vuković turned to the knot of officers in combat fatigues. "Mr. Just Jake doesn't like."

They grinned appreciatively at their commander's joke.

Noble said, "Captain, have you got bomb-sniffing canines?"

"Canines?" Vuković questioned.

Eliška translated from English to Italian which, given the proximity, is widely spoken in Croatia.

"Zagreb has K9 units," Vuković said. "It's takes one and a half hours."

"Make the call," Noble told him. "We can wait."

Vuković gave a humorless laugh and shook his head. "I'm not waiting hour and a half, Mr. Just Jake. This is our job. This is what we train for. We go now."

Noble said, "Captain, you send your men in there, they're going to get killed."

Vuković snorted. "Don't tell me how to do my job."

He barked orders and his men filed outside to a waiting van.

Noble cursed and circled around in front of Vuković. "Captain, listen to me. The man we are dealing with his is highly trained. He'll be expecting this. Your men are walking into a trap."

"*You* listen to *me*, Mr. Just Jake." Vuković planted his fists on his hips. "Americans aren't the only ones who know how to deal with terrorists. My men are also highly trained and experienced. They can handle any situation."

"Then at least let me go in with them," Noble said.

Vuković threw his head back and laughed. "You? With your long hair? You look like journalist. Do you even know how gun works?"

"I've spent some time on the range," Noble assured him.

"This is real life, Mr. Just Jake. In shooting range, targets don't shoot back. Besides"—he waved a hand at the cameras—"factory is empty."

"That's what worries me," Noble said. He turned to Hinson, who only shrugged.

Eliška stood off to the side, shaking her head.

Vuković raised a walkie-talkie and issued commands. The unmarked van pulled away from the curb. Several more laptop screens came to life with video feeds from the SWAT team's helmet cams. Noble turned his attention to the displays and tried to ignore the sinking feeling in his gut. Inside the van, the SWAT team checked the action on their weapons, topped off mags, and tested their microphones. Vuković said "Now you see how we do things in Croatia, Mr. Just Jake."

CHAPTER SIXTY-THREE

Noble felt like a caged animal. He paced back and forth in front of the monitors, a restless lion eager for the hunt. He wanted to be in on the action, not watching it on a television screen. He thought about jogging the six blocks to the torpedo factory and linking up with the *Specijalne jedinice policije,* but Vuković would no doubt arrest him if he tried. So Noble paced, throwing dark looks at the monitors.

Ron Hinson stood off to one side, his hands buried in the pockets of a gray windbreaker. He caught Noble's eye and communicated understanding with a slight nod. His expression said, *What can you do?* He didn't like it any more than Noble, but this was Croatia. The local police had jurisdiction.

Eliška looked on in sullen silence. Her face was impassive. Noble watched her as much as the monitors.

The taciturn SJP Captain stood with his arms crossed over his barrel chest and a wireless radio nestled in the crook of one arm. His eyes bounced from monitor to monitor as he tracked the team's movements. The van had stopped a block from the torpedo factory and idled at the corner. The Captain took one last look at the warehouse, thumbed the talk button, and gave the green light.

The van was moving again, picking up speed. A dash-mounted cam gave a front-seat view as the vehicle raced up to the main doors of the abandoned torpedo factory. The monitors had visuals but no audio. It was strange to watch without sound, like watching a movie with the volume turned off.

The van braked hard in front of the warehouse. The camera feed blurred and pixelated as the back doors of the van were thrown open and the team leap out. Another feed showed the view from a sniper perched on a roof two doors down. He followed the team's progress through his scope. One of the SJP officers lugged a steel battering ram up to the weather-beaten doors. He squared up on the bolt while the other men stacked up to the side. The SJP officer reared back with the heavy door knocker and swung. His body cam turned to snow with the impact. The ancient timbers held fast. Hard to believe time and the elements hadn't rotted the doors right off their hinges, but the oak barricade stood firm. It took two more swings.

Noble's eyes flashed to the thermal monitor. If anything happened, he would see it on thermal first. But the image was all dark blues and heavy purples. Five bright red and orange heat signatures filed through the door, moving fast.

———

Lucas Randall stood in the pilothouse of the ULCV *Maersk Minerva*. The 400 meter long triple-E class container ship floated off the port of Rijeka, surrounded by blue waters and bright sunshine. Over thirteen thousand containers of various colors, mostly rust red with some blues thrown in, covered the deck. The pilothouse looked like the deck of a crude starship. There was a pair of seats for the pilot and the navigator, and a control panel covered in dials, levers, and hundreds of blinking lights. Hospital green paint was flaking off the walls in patches, revealing fire engine red beneath and, below that, primer gray. A small fire extinguisher hung next to an exterior hatch and a pinup calendar was tacked to the back of the door. Ms. April was a curvy brunette in a polka-dot bikini.

Sunlight glinted off the windows, turning the interior of the pilothouse into an oven. Lucas had a mobile phone clutched in one hand as he watched a tablet computer. It showed the inside of the torpedo factory and the intaglio press. *Not long now*, thought Lucas. He tugged at his shirt in an effort to cool off while he watched the tablet. He knew what was coming. Hee didn't like it, but it had to be done. He wondered if it would be Noble or someone else. A QRF from a carrier group stationed in the Atlantic, maybe? Fellow soldiers. Brothers-in-arms. The idea left a bad taste in Lucas's mouth.

Erik sat with one arm slung over the back of the pilot's seat. He wore a pistol in a shoulder rig over a checked flannel shirt and work-stained chinos. He glanced at the tablet screen and then to the torpedo factory in the distance. They could just make out the shape of the launch house jutting out over the water. "Go ahead and blow it," Erick said. "Why wait for the police? No one else needs to die."

"I don't like it any more than you," Lucas told him. "But we're still waiting for port clearance. If I blow it before we get permission to leave, the authorities might shut down the harbor. Then where would we be?"

Erik made a face but said no more.

What was taking so long?

Lucas wanted to be under steam before anyone found the press. Once they were on the open ocean, they would turn off all transponders, change course, and meet up with a Feedermax. The counterfeits only made up the top layer of containers. The rest of the *Minerva*'s cargo was regular consumer goods. The feeder ship would offload the counterfeits for the trip across the Atlantic. After that, it would take a miracle for anyone to find the money before it hit the US market.

The speaker on the control panel gave a loud squawk, followed by a high-pitched squeal. A voice came over the airwaves, giving them permission to depart. Lucas snapped his fingers at Erik, but the navigator was already working the controls. The metal floor vibrated beneath Luke's feet as the engines came to life. A moment later, the massive container vessel started to move, churning up water in her wake.

Lucas lifted the phone and started to dial when he noticed movement on the tablet screen. His mouth turned down in a frown. He saw a five-man team in dark fatigues, armed with MP5 submachine guns, file into the launch house and fan out around the abandoned intaglio press.

Erik had his hands on the controls, but he was watching

Lucas. Sweat was beading on his forehead in large wet drops that trailed down his face. He didn't have to say a word. His eyes said everything. He shook his head and looked away.

Too late, thought Lucas. *Too late to back out now.* He had spent too much time. Too much effort. He was too close to his goal. America had to die if the world was going to be reborn. There were going to be casualties. He punched in the last three digits and hit send.

Noble breathed a sigh of relief as the SJP team swept through the launch house without incident. He had been waiting for some trap. If Noble had been running the counterfeiting operation, he would have left a greeting party or an explosive charge at the very least. And he figured Lucas would do the same. But maybe Lucas had been forced to clear out quickly and didn't have time to cover his tracks. He had left behind the press. That certainly pointed to a fast exit.

The SJP team had cleared the factory and now gathered around the intaglio press. The machine was the size of a small truck and took up most of the launch house. Shredded sheets of misprints lay on the floor and unused paper stood on pallets around the edge of the room. Shelves were cluttered with mostly empty ink containers. Noble watched the screen as one of the SJP officers stooped and picked up an uncut sheet of hundred dollar bills. The sheet had run through the press at a bad angle. The print was off.

Someone had marked a large red X on the page before tossing it to the floor.

"That's it," Hinson said. "That's what we've been looking for."

All four of them had gathered around the laptop computers for a look at the machine.

"Where is the printing crew?" Noble asked. "That's what I'd like to know."

Vuković nodded in agreement. He raised the wireless radio and pressed the transmit button but never had a chance to speak.

Noble felt the explosion before he heard it. The ground trembled beneath his feet. It felt like the faint rumor that runs through the earth before a massive quake. An earsplitting *bang* rent the air. Noble flinched and pulled his shoulders up around his ears in an unconscious gesture. His hand was halfway to the pistol in his waistband before he stopped himself.

The lights winked out and fluttered back to life. The computer screens showed a confusion of movement. Noble thought he glimpsed a body tumbling through the air, before all five helmet cams turned to static. Only the thermal and sniper cams remained online. The thermal showed a bright-white bloom. From the sniper's cam, they watched as the launch house deflated like someone had let the air out of a child's bounce house.

————

Lucas heard a faint *pop* as the charges attached to the underwater pylons detonated. The water beneath the launch house leapt up like a volcano boiling over. The support pylons buckled and the torpedo factory crashed down into the sea. It would take the authorities days to sift through the wreckage. By the time they started piecing the puzzle together, America would be in an economic tailspin. He turned to Erik and said, "Get us out of here."

"*Da*." Erik throttled the *Minerva* up to twenty-three knots.

It would take just four days for the money to reach Miami. From there, it would be trucked to various cities along the East Coast where associates waited to introduce the fake cash into the money supply. Within days, the American financial system would crumble. *Taking all the money-hungry bureaucrats in Washington down with it*, Lucas told himself. Nothing could stop them now.

CHAPTER SIXTY-FOUR

VUKOVIĆ SPRINTED TO THE FACTORY, STUMBLED OUT into the surf, and started clawing through rubble. He heaved aside large slabs of broken concrete and tortured steel, shredding his hands in an effort to save his men. Noble caught up moments later and tried to stop him.

"They're dead," Noble said.

Vuković spun around, catching Noble with a wild haymaker. The surprise blow put Noble on his butt. Vuković went right back to digging.

Noble, more surprised than injured, climbed to his feet and wrapped Vuković up in a bear-hug to stop him from hurting himself. "They're gone," Noble said. "They're gone."

Vuković struggled, thrashing and cursing, but finally relented. Noble felt bad for him. He had lost men in combat before. It was a crushing feeling that no words could accurately describe. It left a large empty space right in the middle of your chest, and nothing would ever fill the void.

But Noble had never lost an entire unit. It had to be devastating. Noble was able to hoist thee Captain back onto dry ground by time the sirens and flashing lights converged on the scene.

———

What remained of the launch house lay on the ocean floor. Demolition charges had taken out the supports and dropped the whole structure into the surf. The roof of the observation deck was visible above the waves, a jigsaw puzzle of twisted steel, shattered brick, and weathered timbers. Broken pylons jutted up through the wreckage like skeletal fingers. Saltwater crashed over the jumbled heap and turned to foam. A fine silt filled the air, stinging Noble's eyes and scouring his throat. He turned his head to the side and spat.

Emergency crews combed through the wreckage, looking for any sign of survivors. Police and EMS workers in hip waders stumbled around the broken pile, while rescue divers searched the ocean floor. The chances of finding anyone alive were slim to none—unless one of the SJP officers had been lucky enough to be trapped in an air bubble underwater. And Noble doubted that. The launch house had collapsed and the roof had come down on top of the team, sealing their doom.

Poor bastards, thought Noble. *They didn't stand a chance.*

The walls of the manufacturing plant ended abruptly at the seawall, as if a giant's axe had hacked off the end of the building with one powerful swipe. Noble stood at the opening, gazing out over the jumbled heap. Beyond the hump of broken stone and rebar stretched an azure sea dotted with merchant vessels and cargo ships. Somewhere out there, a ship was steaming toward the United States with a cargo hold full of counterfeit cash. Noble's lips pressed together in a grim line.

Vuković sat with his back against a wall. His face was a mask of stunned disbelief. His eyes stared, unfocused, into the distance. Blood was drying on his fingertips. Gashes covered his forearms and two of his fingernails were missing.

Ron Hinson and Eliška had come along minutes later. The assassin was handcuffed to the Secret Service agent. They stood off to one side, watching the emergency crews work. Noble considered telling Hinson that he was hand-cuffed to one of the world's most deadly assassins, but decided against it. Hinson probably already knew and he'd done it anyway. Noble's respect for the agent went up a few notches.

While the rescue personnel worked to clear the rubble and recover the bodies, Noble turned back into what remained of the torpedo factory. He spotted a frayed scrap of gold and white cordage. He had noticed the pieces of rope scattered around the floor of the factory as he raced to catch up with Vuković. He picked up a piece and turned over it in his hands. Something about it was very familiar, but Noble couldn't place it. He scowled at the strip of fabric and tried to imagine what it had belonged to.

"Mattress," Vuković mumbled.

Noble turned to him. "What did you say?"

Vuković motioned to the length of frayed rope. "Is mattress seam."

Noble looked again at the cord in his hands and tried to imagine it attached to bedding. Vuković was right. It was the seam from a mattress. He dug the burner phone from his pocket and dialed.

Gwen picked up after two rings. She sounded exhausted and defeated. "Hey, Noble. Any survivors?"

Noble turned away from Vuković and dropped his voice, "Never mind that. I think I know how they're moving the money. The floor of the factory is covered in mattress scraps."

"You think they are hiding the money inside mattresses?" Gwen asked. She sounded fully awake now.

"It would make the perfect camouflage," Noble said.

He heard Gwen snapping her fingers at Ezra. She said, "Okay, we're on it."

"Let me know what you find."

Gwen hesitated.

"What now?" Noble asked.

"Armstrong has already laid in the pipeline for an extraction," Gwen said. "She wants you to get Cermáková to the wharf five miles south. A team will be there by five o'clock—your time—to pick her up."

Noble glanced at Eliška and said, "Fine, but I want to know as soon as you find anything, understood?"

"No way, Noble," Gwen said. "Your part in this operation is over."

"Gwen, this may be our last chance to stop that money from reaching the States," Noble told her.

"I know that," Gwen said. "But even if I wanted to, I

couldn't pass the information to you without Armstrong finding out."

Noble bit back an angry reply. He wanted to unload on her. He turned and spotted Hinson. He said, "You can send the information to Hinson's phone. Armstrong won't be monitoring that."

She sighed. "*If* we find out anything, I'll *try* to pass the information on. No promises."

CHAPTER SIXTY-FIVE

"I think I found it," Ezra said. All he wanted to do was curl up and drift off, but he kept plugging away in a feverish race to find the money. He said, "Yeah, I think this is it."

"What have you got?" Wizard asked. The DDO had spent the last twenty minutes smoking one cigarette after another until the situation room slowly filled with thick gray smog. He hunched over Ezra's shoulder. The glowing tip of his cigarette bobbed in Ezra's peripheral vision.

"It's a complicated series of connections. The links are buried in shell companies, but it all traces back to Keiser in a roundabout sort of way," Ezra said.

Gwen stopped what she was working on and turned to him. She looked like Ezra felt, exhausted and harassed, barely able to keep her eyes open.

"Walk me through it," Wizard said.

"Keiser's Apollo fund owns controlling shares of an emerging technologies firm called FabianFirst.org. Keiser sits on the board of directors. FabianFirst acts as an umbrella firm for over two dozen different shell companies that do everything from disease resistant GMO foods to space exploration technologies. Fingers in many pies." Ezra waggled his fingers. "One of their holdings is a commercial shipping outfit named Inter-Ocean Couriers. Nine months ago, IOC acquired the *Maersk Minerva*, a Triple-E class cargo container ship. It's four hundred meters long and can carry over eighteen thousand shipping containers.

"FabianFirst's other holdings include a discount bedding outfit based out of China that goes by the name of Hangzhou Trading Company. Five months ago, Hangzhou Trading got an order for four hundred and fifty thousand queen-size mattresses, which were delivered to another of FabianFirst's shell companies, a hotel chain with locations up and down the East Coast."

Gwen was nodding along as he spoke. She said, "You think they shipped the mattresses to the warehouse in Rijeka? The money goes into the mattresses, the mattresses go into cargo containers, and the containers are loaded onto a ship bound for the United States."

"That's the way I see it," Ezra said.

Wizard blew smoke at the ceiling. "Are you sure about this? We may only get one shot at that money."

"The *Maersk Minerva* received port clearance at 2:43 p.m.," Ezra told him. "Exactly one minute before the torpedo factory was scuttled."

Wizard plucked the cigarette from his lips and jabbed the smoldering tip at the computer screen. "Find that ship."

Ezra and Gwen went to work while Wizard smoked. Ten minutes later, Gwen was shaking her head. "The

Maersk Minerva's GPS went dark thirty minutes after she left port."

"Too bad Jake Noble doesn't have a description of the boat," Wizard said in an offhand sort of way. "He's our only asset in the area. Might be the only man who can stop this. I'm going to update the Director on our progress. You two keep working the *Minerva*. I want to know how much fuel she was carrying, an estimate of every American port she can reach, and how long it would take to get there."

They bobbed their heads in unison.

Wizard walked out of the situation room and Gwen turned to Ezra. "Do we tell Noble?"

Ezra thought for a minute and said, "I'm pretty sure Wizard just ordered us to."

Gwen grabbed her phone and texted Ron Hinson's cell.

———

Eliška Cermáková was still handcuffed to Ronald Hinson. The Secret Service agent was nobody's fool. As soon as Vuković had taken off at a sprint for the destroyed torpedo factory, Eliška had decided to exit stage left. Any hope of catching up with Randall had vanished when the factory sank into the ocean. Eliška decided it would be better to disappear for a while. She could always put out feelers on the underground network. Lucas would eventually resurface and Eliška would be waiting for him. But before she could slip away, she had felt the metal bracelet lock down on her wrist.

Without missing a beat, Hinson said, "Stay a while, Ms. Cermáková. You and I have a lot to talk about."

Eliška could have killed him then and there, but the thought of Noble stopped her from simply breaking Hinson's neck. Noble was a good man and he had saved Eliška's life. She owed him. Killing another American agent right under his nose was a poor way to repay, so Eliška waited, looking for another opportunity.

When Hinson took the buzzing phone from his pocket, Eliška saw the opportunity she had been looking for. She said, "Noble? We have the name of the boat."

Hinson held up the phone. Noble and Vuković both came over. The Secret Service agent said, "Your guess about the mattresses was right. The money is aboard the *Maersk Minerva*."

Noble turned to Vuković. "Does your team have a helicopter?"

The Captain's eyes turned to hardened steel. He nodded. His mouth worked into a determined frown. "*Da,* we have helicopter."

"Anyone left who can fly it?" Noble asked.

"I can fly," Vuković assured him.

Hinson said, "What's your plan, Noble? You going to land a chopper on the deck of a container ship?"

"I just need to get close enough to drop down onto it without breaking an ankle," Noble told him.

Hinson started to chuckle. He stopped when he realized Noble was serious. "Wizard said you were one of his top guys. He failed to mention you were crazy. That's suicide."

"You got a better idea?" Noble asked.

When Hinson didn't answer, Noble thrust his chin at Eliška. "I'm going to need help."

The Secret Service agent pressed his lips together.

Noble said, "I can't do this alone."

Hinson hitched a sigh, brought the key from his pocket and unlocked the bracelet. "You take chances, Noble."

"Have you got a weapon?" Noble asked.

Hinson shook his head. "They wouldn't let me bring it into the country. I'm here as an observer only."

Vuković said, "You are going to kill the ones who did this? Kill the men who murdered my boys?"

"Every last one of them," Eliška assured him.

The Captain took the MP5 submachine gun from around his own neck and looped the single-point sling over Eliška's head. "You know how to use?"

In answer, Eliška dropped the mag and checked the chamber, before reseating the magazine.

"You coming?" Noble asked Hinson.

The Secret Service agent only shook his head. "It's more than my job is worth, but shoot one for me."

As Vuković led the way through what remained of the torpedo factory, he mashed the talk button on his radio and barked commands in Croatian. By the time they got to the unmarked SWAT van, the SJP sniper was waiting for them. Vuković slipped into the driver's seat, twisted the key, and shifted into drive. A moment later, they were racing through the streets of Rijecka.

Eliška bounced off the steel-reinforced wall of the truck as Vuković slewed around a corner. She reached for safety strap and tried to relax, allowing her body to absorb the sudden jerking movements. The MP5 felt good and solid against her chest—four pounds of cold, hard retribution.

Noble clung to a safety belt across from her.

Eliška said, "Are we really attacking a container ship full of terrorists?"

"I haven't got a choice," Noble told her. "If that money reaches the United States, the economy will crumble. A lot of good people will die."

The man was a patriot, Eliška realized, like her papa. Maybe that's why she liked him. He was ready to risk everything for his country. There weren't a lot of people like him left in the world. At least, Eliška didn't know any.

Noble said, "It's not too late for you to back out."

"Lucas betrayed me and murdered my father," Eliška said. "I'm going to kill him if it's the last thing I do."

CHAPTER SIXTY-SIX

Ezra and Gwen were working feverishly to find the boat, but without GPS it could be anywhere between the Adriatic and the Straight of Gibraltar. The United States Navy had been put on high alert. A carrier group in the Atlantic, and another from the Mediterranean, were steaming toward the Rock of Gibraltar. A pair of drones had been scrambled out of Tripoli. They were checking every container ship headed west, but hundreds of commercial vessels transit the passage every day. It was like looking for a floating needle in an ocean of floating needles.

While Ezra focused on locating the *Maersk Minerva*, Gwen worked on the crew manifest. It took her fifteen minutes, but she finally managed to obtain a complete roster. She had just finished when the electronic lock on the door chirped. Armstrong and Wizard crowded into the cramped situation room to demand an update.

"Any luck finding the boat?" Armstrong wanted to know.

Ezra shook his head. "Given the *Minerva*'s load and fuel capacity, it couldn't even reach America before Keiser's puts expire."

Wizard's wiry gray brows pinched. "Are you saying we're chasing the wrong boat?"

"Not exactly," said Ezra. "Inter-Ocean Couriers has dozens of feeder ships that operate around the area. They're smaller, faster, and equipped with cranes. I think it's highly likely they plan to offload the containers onto a second ship —a ship already bound for America and not under suspicion."

"Can they do that?" Armstrong wanted to know.

"Easily," Ezra told her. "That's what feeder vessels are designed for. They side-load containers from larger ships and then ferry them into port. They don't normally cross the Atlantic, but it's not unheard of."

"Clever," Wizard said. He brought out a bottle of pills and tossed a pair back. "Even if we figured the connection to the *Maersk Minerva*, we'd be chasing the wrong boat. Keiser's smart. He left nothing to chance."

"I've got more bad news." Gwen swiveled in her chair to face them. "I've been running background checks on the crew of the *Minerva*. There are nine crew members listed. I've managed to pull up profiles on six. So far, every single one of them has ties to Baader-Meinhof."

"So it's possible every member of the crew is in on the plot," Wizard said.

"Looks that way," Gwen said.

Armstrong said, "Call Noble and let him know what he's up against."

Gwen and Ezra exchanged a look. Gwen shook her head. "I'm not sure what—"

"Spare me, Ms. Witwicky." Armstrong and held up a hand. "I was born at night, not *last* night. I know Noble is on his way to intercept the ship. I want to know as soon as he has it in sight. At least we'll have a fix on its location. And he might as well know what he's walking into."

"Yes, ma'am." Gwen turned back to her computer and dialed Noble's burner.

He picked up after a half dozen rings. Gwen adjusted her headset and heard the long whine of a helicopter gearing up for takeoff.

"Make it fast!" Noble yelled into the phone. "We're about to lift off."

"Jake," said Gwen, raising her voice. "We suspect the *Maersk Minerva* is going to make contact with another ship, a feeder ship, and off-load the cargo. A feeder ship—"

"I know what a feeder ship is," Noble interrupted her. "I live on a boat."

"Once they off-load the cargo, we won't have any chance of finding that money," Gwen said. "There are at least nine people on board the *Maersk Minerva*. Every single one of them should be considered suspect."

His voice was tight with tension. "Understood."

"And Jake?"

"Yeah?"

"Armstrong wants a location as soon as you have the ship in sight."

"If we find it, we'll alert port authority." Noble had to shout over the thunderous *chuck-chuck-chuck* of the helicopter blades. "They can relay the position. I'll try to hold the boat until the Navy can get a get a QRF aboard."

"Hey, Jake?"

"What?"

"Good luck," Gwen said.

"Say a prayer," Noble said before hanging up.

Gwen scowled and pulled the headset down around her neck. His last statement had caught her off guard. Gwen did not take Noble for the religious type. She turned to the others. They could see by the look in her eyes that something was wrong.

Armstrong said, "What's up?"

"I think he's scared or nervous."

"Probably a bit of both," Ezra remarked.

"No," Gwen shook her head. "Something's wrong."

"What makes you say that?" Wizard said.

"He asked me to say a prayer."

Armstrong's eyebrows danced up her forehead.

Wizard said, "Kid's got guts."

"What are you talking about?" Armstrong asked.

"Less than two months ago, Samantha Gunn was killed on a boat," Wizard said. "Noble watched her die. Now, he's in the same situation with a different girl. I'm sure that fact isn't lost on him."

CHAPTER SIXTY-SEVEN

THE OH-58A KIOWA SCOUT HELICOPTER FLEW LOW over a bright blue ocean reflecting hot afternoon sunlight. The Kiowa was powered by an Allison T63-A-700 turboshaft and cruised along at 100 knots with the cabin doors open. Noble felt the heavy *chuk-chuk-chuk* of the rotor blades deep in his chest. The single-engine observation craft had been manufactured by Bell for the United States military in the late sixties and has seen action in every war since Vietnam. In the early nineties, the military started phasing out the aging Kiowas for the newer, smarter AH-64 Apache attack helicopters and the battered OH-58s found their way into the hands of countries like Croatia. Judging by the look of this one, it had been running operations against the Vietcong long before Noble was even born.

Wind whipped his hair into a cloud around his head. A bulky pair of headphones helped keep the shaggy locks out his vision. He was strapped into one of the back seats, scanning the ocean for any sign of the *Maersk Minerva*. Eliška was strapped in next to him, staring out the port side. They were headed south, toward the boot heel of Italy. Noble could just make out the Italian coastline in the distance. The sun was a fiery bronze disk cutting into the horizon.

Vuković would swoop down for a low pass anytime they spotted a cargo ship. They had been in the air for over an hour and buzzed dozens of cargo vessels, without spotting their prey. Noble was just starting to think they had passed it when Vuković came over the headset and said, "I'm at almost half a tank. We must turn back soon."

He twisted around in the pilot's seat for a look over his shoulder at Noble. His face was an apologetic frown.

Jake nodded but held up his hand, fingers splayed. He shouted into the headset. "Five more minutes?"

"*Da*," Vuković said. "I give you ten."

The OH-58A Kiowa sped south toward the Mediterranean as the sun slowly melted with the horizon, leeching the light from the sky and turning the waters black. Once the last of the light was gone, any hope of finding the *Minerva* would be gone with it. Noble's jaw muscles bunched and released as he scanned the vast blue expanse. He was painfully aware of each passing second slipping away. A hard fist gripped his guts and was starting to squeeze, tighter and tighter. He needed to find that boat.

Find the boat! Noble told himself.

The SJP sniper, riding in the copilot's seat with his rifle between his legs, sat up and narrowed his eyes. He pointed and spoke into his headset. "Cargo ship. Starboard side. Two o'clock. Might be one we look for, *da*?"

Noble had to squint. All he could make out was a small black spot amid the dark waters. It could be a boat. It might be an island. Or just a reef. Noble couldn't tell from this distance.

Vuković angled the stick and the Kiowa banked in that direction. The long shape of a massive cargo freighter gradually took shape. The deck was easily four football fields long and covered in shipping containers stacked six high. The pilothouse jutted above the bed of containers like a high-rise apartment building rearing above a squalid shantytown. Noble decided the SJP sniper had good eyes. Of course, he was also a decade younger. The sniper aimed his rifle at the stern. It was a tricky maneuver. He had to stick the barrel of his weapon out the window to get enough room to peer through the scope. "*Da*. Is *Minerva*."

Vuković adjusted his lip mic and relayed the coordinates to harbor patrol. There was a brief conversation and then Vuković said, "Harbor patrol is sixty minutes away."

Noble said, "Can you get us over the stern?"

Vuković looked at the freighter and then back at Noble. "You'll have to jump."

"Fine," Noble told him. "Just get me close."

Vuković worked the pedals and eased forward on the stick. The nose of the old Kiowa dipped. The craft shot forward. Vuković said, "That pilothouse has three-hundred sixty degree view. They will know you are coming."

"Life's imperfect," Noble told Vuković as he checked the action on his pistol. His hands were shaking hard. His stomach was a mass of butterflies with razorblade wings. It would be him and Eliška against nine guys, all of them armed and ready for a fight. *Long odds*, Noble told himself.

Vuković said, "I have less than half a tank of fuel. Once

I put you down, I will be forced to turn back. I will not be able to provide air cover. You are understanding?"

Noble licked his lips, tried to ignore the fear turning his guts into a hot runny mass, and nodded. "Understood."

The sun was just a half disk shimmering on the horizon as the Kiowa closed with the shipping freighter. The massive cargo vessel loomed up out of the ocean like a floating mountain with sheer granite walls, churning up white foam in its wake. They were still several hundred meters out when a deckhand stepped onto the rear deck from the narrow alleyway formed by the cargo containers. He spotted the incoming Kiowa and sprinted to the gunwale. He was a heavyset man in a denim shirt and a faded red jacket, clutching an AK47 with a collapsible stock.

Eliška shouted into her microphone. "Shooter! Shooter!"

CHAPTER SIXTY-EIGHT

THE DECKHAND RAISED THE AK47, SIGHTED ON THE nose of the chopper, and pulled the trigger. A tongue of fire leapt from the muzzle. The little automatic burped out a stream of bullets. Noble took a deep breath. There was nowhere he could go and nothing he could do. He was strapped into the seat with the side door open. Lead blistered the nose of the chopper in a series of sharp, ear-splitting bangs. A round screamed past Noble's shoulder. The sound was muffled by the steady, hard beat of the rotor blades, but Noble felt the sonic boomlet as the bullet zipped past.

Vuković shouted something in Croatian. Noble didn't think it was anything he'd use in polite dinner conversation.

The SJP sniper pulled his knee up to his chest, balanced his rifle on top, and eased off a shot. The weapon kicked. Noble watched the deckhand bend over double and clutch his belly. The sniper sent another round downrange and the deckhand fell.

321

Noble reached forward and patted the kid on the shoulder. "Good shot!" he yelled. To Vuković he said, "Get us on the deck!"

The SJP Captain was already angling the Kiowa toward the bed of shipping containers. A crosswind forced him to come in sideways. Noble clung to the safety belt as the chopper swooped low over the heaving deck of the freighter. The rotor blades caught the spray from the stern, whacked it into a fine mist, and Noble felt the saltwater on his cheek. All at once, he was back in Paris, aboard the river barge. He could feel the icy spray and the pitch of the deck rolling under his feet. He saw Sam. She was trying to speak, but Noble couldn't hear what she was saying. He yelled out a warning. He willed her to move, to get the hell out of the wall, but all he could do was watch. He was a passenger and nothing he did could change the past. He heard the *whipcrack* of the pistol. He saw her jerk with the impact. Her eyes went wide. Then she was falling.

Grief, so terrible it was a physical pain, assailed him. Noble felt that dark chasm at the center of himself growing, expanding, until it threatened to consume him whole. His throat choked shut. An invisible weight settled on his chest until he was struggling for air. He watched Sam die. Watched her fall. Heard the shots. It happened over and over. And every time, the darkness claimed a little more of Noble's soul until he was certain he was going mad ...

He felt a hand on his arm, shaking him. Noble clawed his way back to the present, heard the heavy *whomp-whomp-whomp* of the helicopter blades, saw the deck of the *Maersk Minerva* growing large beneath him, and smelled the ocean air. He turned and saw Eliška gripping his sleeve.

She said, "Are you okay?"

Noble managed a nod.

She studied him for a long moment like she wasn't sure he was ready for this. The first hint of fear and doubt was creeping into her eyes.

Noble swallowed hard. *Get your mind back on the mission,* he told himself. But he could still see Sam. He could hear the shots that claimed her life and see her falling overboard. He knew the memory would cripple him if he let it. *You've got a job to do, soldier!* Noble gave himself another shake. Sam was dead, and he had a job to do. He said, "Let's get this over with."

Over the headset, Vuković shouted, "Happy hunting, Mr. Just Jake!"

The OH-58A Kiowa hovered a scant five feet above the bed of shipping containers. The updraft from the rotors threw dirt and dust into Noble's face. He narrowed his eyes, snatched the headset off, and grasped at the buckle on his safety harness. For a moment, his fingers fumbled at the catch. Adrenaline was turning his hands into flippers. He finally managed it, and the belt dropped away. Noble planted one foot on the skid and stepped out into space.

A puke-green container leapt up to greet him. Noble took the impact on his arches. His knees buckled and a shot of electricity went straight to his brain. He landed with a solid *bang* on the corrugated metal. His face pinched. He managed to hold back the grunt that tried to work its way up from his chest. A few years ago, a jump like that wouldn't have even phased him. Thirty-four was too young to be getting bad knees, but the Army had put a lot of hard miles on his body.

Eliška landed next to him with a hollow *clang*. She did it with more style and grace. She just buckled her knees to absorb the hit and then she stuck out a hand to help Noble up. She said, "You okay?"

It was the same thing he had asked Sam when they had fast-roped onto the river barge. Noble was struck with the awful certainty that one, or both of them, were going to die. He climbed to his feet, ignoring the creaking in his knees, and inclined his head. "I'm fine." Noble had to shout over the roar of the chopper. "Whatever happens, we stick together!"

Eliška nodded. She was already headed for the scaffolding between containers. The Kiowa's engines climbed to a feverish pitch. The chopper blasted them with air as it lifted into the darkening twilight, then it was banking away from the *Minerva*. Noble threw one look at the pilothouse, spotted the silhouette of a man in the large picture windows, and turned to follow Eliška.

———

Lucas Randall wheeled around at the loud crack of the automatic. He recognized the sound of the weapon. He would know the telltale *kak-kak-kak* of an AK47 in his sleep. He had outfitted the crew with the collapsible AKs because they were easy to operate, didn't take up much space, and were almost impossible to jam. The Russian weapon could take a lot of abuse and didn't need much in the way of maintenance. It was a perfect weapon for poorly trained troops who couldn't be bothered to clean and function-check their rifles.

Lucas heard the hard rattle of the automatic and peered out the rear windows across a deck piled high with shipping containers. An ancient Kiowa was coming in low and fast. Lucas saw sparks flash off the nose cone of the chopper. The last of the fading sun glinted on the fuselage and highlighted the Croatian law enforcement emblem emblazoned on the open side doors. The craft angled and a sniper took aim. Lucas heard the crack of the sharpshooter's weapon. There was a pause. Then a second crack.

Lucas cursed.

Erik was out of his chair. "What should we do?"

The Kiowa swooped low over the stern, hovering above the platform created by the containers. Two figures dropped from the chopper. One of them, a man with long hair and a lean frame, stumbled and fell. *Noble.* Lucas shook his head and bared his teeth in frustration. The other would be the Cermáková woman. She helped Noble to his feet and they disappeared between containers.

Lucas shouted another curse.

"What do we do?" Erik wanted to know.

Lucas grabbed him by the arm and shoved him back to the control panel. "Steer the boat. How far is the feeder vessel?"

Erik checked the navigation system. "About twenty minutes. We should be able to see her soon."

They both looked out the windscreen at the horizon for any sign of the smaller vessel, but the sun was sinking fast now and the waters of the Adriatic were dark fathoms of inky blackness. A few blood-tinged clouds still scurried across a bruised purple sky but did nothing to illuminate the waves. *That was the plan all along,* Lucas reminded himself.

Offload the containers full of cash under the cover of darkness and watch the OS-*CinCom* feeder sail away.

Twenty minutes, Lucas told himself. *Not long now.*

All he had to do was take care of Noble and Cermáková. That was easier said than done, of course. The Baader-Meinhof idiots crewing the *Minerva* were no match for Noble—most of them were full-time sailors and part-time crooks—but enough of them together could box Noble into a corner and riddle him full of holes. They just needed to work together. By now, they had all heard the shots. They knew the ship was under attack and they'd be scrambling in different directions, most of them wondering where in the hell they had left their guns.

Lucas snatched the microphone off the control panel and cramped down on the transmit button. "Stanz, Grinkov, and Ludwick to the pilothouse on the double!" His voice boomed out across the *Maersk Minerva*. It would tell Noble right where he was, but that couldn't be helped. All that mattered now was holding Noble at bay long enough to load the money onto the feeder vessel. Lucas repeated the instructions in German, racked the microphone, and then reached for a Bravo Company AR15 rifle standing in the corner. He hauled back on the charging handle and activated the EOTech optic attached to the top rail. *Ready to rock and roll.*

———

Noble and Eliška clambered down through the reinforced scaffolding. There wasn't much space—just enough for a man to shimmy up. Eliška, slimmer and younger, reached the bottom first and put her back to a metal wall, covering Noble while he climbed. He reached the deck a little winded. He had spent the last two months drinking booze, and it was catching up with him.

I'll start running again if I live through this, Noble promised himself.

Eliška said, "You know anything about tankers?"

"It's not a tanker," Noble told her. "It's a freighter."

"I'll take that as a yes," she said. "Which way?"

Noble motioned her starboard. Either way from here—it didn't really matter. They needed to work their way to the gunwale and then forward to the pilothouse. She had started in that direction when they heard Lucas's voice over the loudspeakers calling a trio of sailors to the bridge.

Noble said. "Three men is more than enough to hold the pilothouse against us."

"What about harbor patrol?" Eliška asked. "How long until they reach us?"

Noble shook his head. "Not fast enough. I'd estimate we're moving at a good twenty seven knots, with an hour head start. We need to stop this boat."

"Okay," Eliška said. "How do we do that?"

"Engine room," Noble told her. "We'll find a hatch and work our way into the bowels of the ship. If we can stop the engines, she'll be dead in the water until harbor patrol arrives."

A change came over Eliška. She chose that moment to turn on him. It was like she had been waiting for her chance. Her eyes screwed down to angry slits and she lunged at him.

CHAPTER SIXTY-NINE

PANIC TURNED NOBLE'S ARMS AND LEGS TO JELLY AS Eliška hammered him against the metal wall of a shipping container. She thrust the MP5 out to the end of its sling and mashed the trigger. Noble's heart crowded up into his throat. It took his brain a second to make sense of what was happening. He just had time to register the outline of a man, half hidden in shadows, when Eliška's stubby automatic peeled thunder. Noble turned his face away from the fiery breath and squeezed his eyes shut. He felt the heat from the barrel and the snap of displaced air against his cheek.

The MP5 spit empty shell casings against the opposite wall in a steady jingle of brass. The spray of bullets caught the deckhand full in the chest. His face twisted in a mask of pain and surprise. The automatic burst slammed him against a container and he collapsed in a jumble. A Kalashnikov clattered to the ground at his feet.

Smoke trailed from the barrel of Eliška's weapon. She said, "You're welcome."

Noble put one hand to his ear and made an unintelligible note at the back of his throat that came out sounding like, "Gah-aaah!" His hearing was gone, replaced by a high-pitched buzz in his skull that sounded like a dial tone from hell. Still holding his ear, he turned to Eliška and barked, "Really?! I'm probably going to have permanent hearing loss."

"But you are still alive," she pointed out. Her words sounded like they were coming up from the bottom of a well.

"What?" Noble shouted.

She put a finger to her lips. "You'll have the whole crew down on us."

It was hard to know how loud he was speaking. His adrenaline was racing and his hearing was knocked out. As a soldier he had experienced this before, but it had been a lot less worrying when he was in the mountains of Afghanistan surrounded by other tier one operators. Being aboard a boat full of German extremists, his only backup a cutthroat assassin, rebalanced the equation—and not in Noble's favor.

He flexed his jaw wide and rubbed at his ear. He'd have time to worry about hearing loss later. And he *would* worry about it. Right now, he waved for Eliška to follow and hurried along the lane to the fallen deckhand. The man lay with his head cocked against the side of a container at a cramped angle. Blue eyes stared up at them and pink bubbles formed at the corner of his lips. Blood was pooling around his bottom. He was still alive, but he didn't have long. Eliška had punched all five rounds right through the ten ring—dead center—puncturing both lungs.

Noble stooped to retrieve the fallen AK47. It was a short-barreled model with a folding stock and was in bad need of maintenance. Russia had probably still been fighting Afghanistan the last time the weapon had been cleaned. Noble locked out the shoulder brace and checked the action. Great thing about Kalashnikovs: you can pour sand down the barrel and they'll keep functioning.

He shouldered the weapon, checked the corners, and stepped out onto the gangway running around the outside edge of the freighter. He needed to find a hatch and make his way down to the engine room. He got Eliška's attention, pointed first to his own eyes and then motioned to the front of the ship. *Watch my back*. She nodded understanding. Noble moved around the corner, headed for the stern. Eliška followed, doing an ungainly sideways trot so she could watch their six. She gripped Noble's shoulder with her left hand, using it to steady her own movements.

With the Kalashnikov leading the way, Noble moved along the gangway, checking the cramped passages between containers as he went. Fifty meters of open deck separated him from the stern. His heart was trying to knock a hole through the wall of his chest. Sweat pasted the shirt to his back. He strained to see everything at once because all he could hear was the terrible ringing in his ears.

The ringing is good, Noble told himself. *It means your ear drums still work.*

With his hearing on the fritz, his other senses were dialed up to ten. He could make out the tiniest details in the dented metal containers and smell ocean brine. They reached the last of the stacks and rounded the corner. A short stair led to the castle deck. Noble started up the risers, going slow, his front sight sweeping the top step for any sign of a threat.

They were halfway up when he felt Eliška's fingers cramp down on his shoulder. It was a signal every operator recognized. *Contact rear!* An electric shock propelled him up the steps two at a time. His thigh muscles bunched and released. Giddy panic informed his movements as the first bullets hissed past his ear. He heard Eliška's MP5 cough three short bursts. Noble reached the castle deck and spotted a hatch right where he guessed it would be. He was already moving in that direction when the latch turned and the trap door swung open. A deck hand stuck his head up and spotted Noble. Both men opened fire at the same time.

CHAPTER SEVENTY

NOBLE NEVER STOPPED MOVING. HIS FINGER JERKED back on the trigger and a loud ripping noise split the air. It sounded muffled to Noble's buzzing ears. The AK47 bucked and rattled in his hands, chewing out spent shells and smoke. Bullets pinged off the metal hatch and skipped off the deck in a spectacular shower of sparks.

The deckhand thrust his pistol over the lip of the hatch. He wanted no part in a close-quarters gunfight. He triggered a blind volley, completely missing Noble, and tried to haul the trap door closed at the same time. The hatch banged shut and the latch twisted into place with a screech of rusting steel.

Noble threw himself behind a low wall that separated the castle deck from midships. The waist-high gunwale protected his flank, but gave no cover from the hatch. Noble trained his front site on the opening in case the deckhand worked up the courage to take another shot.

Eliška landed next to him a second later. She slammed

her back against the wall, breathing heavy. Red blotches colored her pale cheeks and smoke drifted from the barrel of her weapon. She saw the hatch and thrust her chin at it.

Noble shook his head. "Blocked."

She cursed.

"You okay?" he yelled. There was no sense trying to hide. The whole boat knew they were on the castle deck.

"Think so," Eliška said and looked down at her body. Soldiers sometimes get hit in combat without knowing it until minutes—sometimes even hours—later. Adrenaline dulls the pain and they don't realize they're leaking blood until after the fight. She leaned forward and Noble patted her back. She didn't have any new holes, which seemed a minor miracle given the amount of lead in the air.

She returned the favor. Her hands roamed over his back and shoulders. He didn't feel any pain. Then she indicated a dime-size hole in the sleeve of his windbreaker. Noble's eyebrows went up. He inspected the rip. The bullet had missed his arm by a fraction. A little to the left, and it would have blown through his elbow.

"Lucky," Eliška muttered.

Noble only nodded agreement. A long burst of automatic gunfire erupted behind them. Bullets splatted against the metal gunwale at their backs. It wasn't directed fire. The Baader-Meinhof goon was just trying to keep them pinned. It worked. Noble shrank at the loud ding of bullets against metal. He cocked a thumb over his shoulder. "How far?"

"About a hundred meters," Eliška said.

"Think you can hit him if I provide suppressing fire?"

She indicated the stubby automatic in her hands. "Not with this."

The MP5 is a good weapon for close-up work, but it's not made for long distances. Neither was the short-barreled AK clutched in Noble's hands. He bared his teeth in a frustrated grimace. "Well, we can't sit here," he said. "They'll gang up on us and make a push. We'll be overwhelmed. We need to move."

"Where?" Eliška said. "We're out of boat."

It was true. There was nowhere to go. To Noble's left lay the dead man who had taken a shot at the helicopter. He was sprawled on his back. A folding AK lay near his outstretched hand. Beyond him was another stair leading back down to midship.

"Keep an eye on that shooter," Noble said and hurried across the castle deck in a crouch. He was halfway to the body when a Baader-Meinhof goon stuck his head around the head of the stair and squeezed off a burst of automatic fire. Bullets skipped along the deck and hissed overhead. Noble threw himself down behind the dead body. A half dozen slugs impacted the dead man's side. Noble levered his rifle over the chest of the corpse and cramped down on the trigger. The automatic breathed fire, forcing the Baader-Meinhof thug behind cover. Noble reached for the fallen weapon.

The dead man had fired off half his mag before catching the sniper's bullet, but it was a half mag more than Noble had had a moment ago. He rocked the magazine loose from the weapon and grasped it in his left hand as he steadied his weapon site on the far stair, waiting for the German to try again. He was using the dead body as a shield. It wasn't perfect cover, not by a long shot, but any port in a storm.

Behind him, Eliška was trading shots with the shooter

midship. She had switched to selective fire. She was trying to conserve ammo. She leaned out around the short wall, squeezed off a single round and ducked back. A long, rattling buzzsaw of thunder answered her. Bullets went ricocheting off the gunwales of the castle deck. Sooner or later, one of those rounds would take a bad skip and end up planted in Noble's skull. His testicles tried to crawl up inside his pelvis as he waited for the ricochet with his name on it.

The goon at the head of the steps leaned out and sprayed angry lead bees in Noble's direction. The swarm stung the side of the corpse with hard, wet ripping noises. Noble answered with a short burst.

"I'm running out of ammo!" Eliška hollered over to him. "We have to do something."

"Any ideas?" he shouted back.

"You stand up and draw their fire," Eliška said. "When they run out of ammo, I'll kill them."

"Any other ideas?"

She shook her head, leaned out, and fired. The MP5 spit a single round before the bolt fell with a hollow *clack* on an empty chamber. Eliška cursed and dropped the weapon on the deck. It landed with a clatter.

Noble grabbed the dead man's AK47, jammed the half mag back in, and slid the weapon over the deck to Eliška. "You got half a mag," he shouted. "Make it count."

She scooped it up and jerked back on the charging handle.

———

Schafer used the scaffolding to reach the top of the containers. A veteran Baader-Meinhof soldier, he was a big man with a bushy salt-and-pepper beard. He had served the cause since the early '80s and spent time in Stadelheim Prison. He had the tattoos to prove it, including a swastika over his heart. He knew how to deal with a bothersome American spook and a Czechish whore.

Randall, leader of the new Baader-Meinhof wing called the United Front, had filled the boat with sailors. They were good Germans, one and all. They believed in the cause, but they weren't soldiers. Most had never shot anything but paper. They were seafaring men recruited for their knowledge of the ocean and ships. Schafer was a killer. He had murdered his first man at the age of seventeen in a drunken brawl. He still remembered the feel of the man's windpipe crushing beneath his meaty fists.

He walked across the tops of the containers. His boots made hollow clonks on the corrugated steel. One of the Russian-made automatics was cradled his work-calloused hands as he worked his way toward the back of the freighter.

The last of the light had faded from the sky and stars appeared like diamonds in the deep blue vault of heaven. The wind was picking up, tugging at the collar of Schafer's work-stained coveralls. He went carefully over the metal scaffolding between containers. One bad step and he'd go tumbling down through the rafters. He'd be dead long before he hit the deck.

The sounds of the gunfight reached a fevered pitch and then settled to brief spats of back and forth. Schafer smiled.

Both sides were running out of ammo. He reached the last row of containers, crept to the edge, and peered over.

Night cloaked the *Minerva* in deep shadow, but Schafer could just make out the form of a man stretched out on the deck. The foolish American was clearly outlined against the lighter paint of the ship. Schafer shouldered his weapon, sighted on the prostrate form of the American, and fired.

———

Noble scrambled to his knees for a peek over the waist-high wall. It was a twenty-foot drop to a narrow strip of deck that separated the castle deck from the last row of containers, but at least it would get them off the stern and out of the line of fire. Just thinking about the jump made his knees ache.

Better than waiting around for them to overwhelm us.

There was a deafening roar overhead and bullets chewed into the corpse at Noble's feet. He lunged away from the wall, lifted his AK47, and sighted on the shadowy silhouette of a man outlined against the night sky. His weapon rattled off an angry reply. Bullets sparked against the container wall in deadly yellow flashes before the bolt slapped against an empty chamber.

CHAPTER SEVENTY-ONE

Noble cursed and crowded against the wall, trying to make himself as small as possible. In his haste, he had fired low and shot up the side of the container, missing the man. His AK47 was empty. He let the Russian rifle clatter to the deck and dug the CZ pistol from his waistband. Noble wasn't a fan of the Czech-made handguns. The triggers were too gritty with a long travel for his taste. He could probably make the shot, but not before the Baader-Meinhof soldier plugged him full of holes, so he pressed himself against the wall and looked for some way to escape.

Eliška was pinned down on his right. Another shooter controlled the stair on Noble's left. And now they had someone atop the containers as well, controlling the high ground. Once the Germans realized they had the invaders boxed in, they would draw the net closed.

Think of something fast, Noble told himself.

He could sprint to one of the capstans. It would give

him a better angle on the three shooters, but he doubted he would make it across the castle deck before they cut him down. Noble imagined himself halfway across the deck when they caught him in a deadly triangle of fire.

Not going to happen.

He pressed flat against the wall as another deadly spray of bullets blistered the ground inches in front of his feet. The German on his left leaned out at the same time and hosed the castle deck. The dead body caught most of the rounds. Two lead wasps buzzed past Noble's face. He angled the CZ pistol in that direction and triggered a round. He wasn't really aiming, just trying to drive the German back behind cover. It worked. The man disappeared around the head of the stair, buying Noble a few precious seconds.

Schafer shrank back from the edge after the first loud burst of machine gun fire from the deck below. He hadn't noticed the figure crouched against the wall in the dark. He cursed himself for being so sloppy. He had wasted the element of surprise and poured rounds into a dead body instead.

Some of the bluster had gone out of him. The American had nearly shot his legs off. Schafer was in no hurry to expose himself again. He hunkered atop the container, holding his rifle out in front of him with the barrel angled down, jerking the trigger. He couldn't see what he was shooting at. He shot off half the magazine and then chanced a peek.

A bank of clouds hid the moon. The deck lay in gloomy shadow. All he could see was a small bit of one shoulder, or maybe it was the top of the American's head, behind the low wall. Schafer knew he could make the shot if he could get the angle right, but it would require him to lean out over the edge and expose himself. He dug a spare magazine from the pocket of his coveralls and reloaded. The mag seated with an audible *click*. He took a deep breath to steady his nerves, then stood up and leaned over as far as he dared, aiming for the dark wedge of shoulder.

———

Noble knew he had to do something. The longer he waited, the more these guys would start working together and his chances of survival would plummet. Someone had to take out the shooter overhead. Noble could do it, but it would require moving away from the wall and exposing himself to the other two.

A Jim Morrison lyric leapt into his head: *"Five to one, baby. One in five. No one here gets out alive."*

He felt a *whomp-whomp-whomp* deep in his chest and mistook it for his own heartbeat. There was a chance—an astronomically slim chance—he could shoot the tango over-head and then pivot and get the guy at the head of the stairs as well, but it wasn't very likely. There was a far better chance Noble would die taking out the shooter atop the containers. His death would give Eliška a fighting chance.

"Five to one, baby. One in five ..."

The thought of catching a bullet didn't scare him. If the German on the stairs was any good at all, he would hose the deck the moment Noble exposed himself. A few seconds of pain and then it would be over. *Then what?* The thought of the unknown used to leave Noble in a cold sweat, but Sam had crossed over. Maybe she was on the other side waiting for him? *If I die*, thought Noble, *let me be with Sam. Let me go wherever she is.*

He didn't know if it was a prayer or just a passing wish offered up to whatever mindless force set the gears of the cosmos in motion, but a sense of peace settled over him—a peace so profound that Noble felt the anguish of her death leave him for the first time. His hands stopped shaking and the metal bands around his chest relaxed. He couldn't hear anything, but he could feel the rhythmic chug of the engines. The smell of exhaust mixed with salt water filled his lungs. It was now or never. He took two big steps away from the wall and started to pivot when a single hard *crack* rose above the ringing in his ears.

CHAPTER SEVENTY-TWO

Noble's shoulders cranked up around his ears and his head pulled in like turtle trying to hide inside its shell. All the muscles in his back went rigid. He waited to feel the bullet punch a hole between his shoulder blades and explode out his chest. He was still moving, but time had slowed to a crawl. Fractions of a second seemed an eternity. Noble pivoted on his heels and pushed the CZ pistol out with both arms, looking for a target.

He spotted the figure atop the containers, limed by starlight, but the man seemed to be melting—shrinking down into the container like a wax statue in a microwave. It was surreal. Noble's brain struggled to make sense of it. Then he heard the heavy *whomp-whomp-whomp* of the Kiowa and realized it wasn't his heartbeat he had been hearing but the heavy beat of the chopper coming back to lay down suppressing fire.

Noble shifted his front site to the top step and fired. His fingered tightened on the trigger and the weapon kicked at the same time the deckhand leaned out for a shot. Noble's bullet caught the man in the face and snapped his head back. Chips of broken teeth exploded like shrapnel. A shock of blood and pulpy red matter splattered the gunwale. The German's body went limp and tumbled down the stairs.

Noble turned. He saw the OH-58 hovering sixty meters off the port bow. The chopper was just a black shape hanging in a dark sky. The single rotor beat out a steady rhythm. Noble thought, or maybe just imagined, he saw the sniper wave once before the Kiowa banked hard and headed for the coast. They had to be almost out of fuel by now. They'd never make it all the way back to Croatia. They would have to make an emergency landing in the Balkans. A Croatian surveillance helicopter landing on foreign soil would cause a stink, but Captain Vuković had done his good deed for the day—for the *year*, so far as Noble was concerned. He lifted a hand in farewell, then hurried to the top of the steps where the deckhand's weapon had fallen.

The Captain and his sniper had bought Noble a few precious seconds. He grabbed the gun and checked the chamber as he jogged back to the hatch. Eliška met him halfway. She was unarmed and said, "Are we going below?"

"Anything is better than waiting up here for them to box us in again." Noble motioned to the hatch with the barrel of the AK47. He took a firm grip on the weapon and positioned himself in front of the opening. His finger took up the slack on the trigger.

Eliška gripped the latch, gave it a quick twist, and hauled up on the metal portal.

The hatch swung open with a ponderous groan. They were greeted by the roar of engines running full throttle.

Noble hunkered down and thrust the AK47 out in front of him, looking for any sign of movement. Instead, he saw a dark red smear, like old paint, on the watertight seal. His finger eased off the trigger.

"I must have hit him," Noble whispered. At least, he thought he whispered. His hearing was coming back slowly. He crept to the edge and peered down the ladder. Another splash of red, this one bright and wet, painted the bottom of the railing. Noble dropped to one knee and bent over, nearly double, so he could clear the blind angles created by the hatch. When he was sure nobody was waiting to bush-whack him, he sat down on the lip, swung his legs over and scrambled down the ladder to a corrugated catwalk.

Eliška scampered down behind him and pulled the hatch closed.

Noble pointed out the splash of blood. Eliška nodded.

The path leading to a bulkhead door was smeared with a bloody handprint. Noble had scored a hit alright. But the deckhand had enough life left in him to make a run for it. Noble wondered how far the man went before he collapsed. He was bleeding pretty heavily. He couldn't have made it very far.

One side of the catwalk was open to the engine room below. Noble could see the giant motors propelling the massive *Maersk Minerva* through the water. The sound was deafening. Noble had to yell to be heard. "All we have to do is shut down the engines and wait for the harbor patrol."

"I didn't come here to sabotage a boat," Eliška said. "I came to kill Lucas Randall."

Noble caught her elbow. "We take out the engines and

let law enforcement deal with Lucas," Noble said. "He'll get his. I promise."

She looked like she wanted protest but said, "Fine. Lead the way."

Noble started down a long flight of stairs to the engineering deck. He went slow, trying not to make any noise on the metal risers, watching every shadow. He was halfway down when he realized Eliška was no longer behind him. He turned in time to see the bulkhead door swing shut with a soft *clang*.

CHAPTER SEVENTY-THREE

ELIŠKA EASED THE BULKHEAD DOOR CLOSED AND SPUN the wheel. The bolts shot into place. It wouldn't take Jake long to figure out she had slipped off—he probably knew already—but he was driven by an unerring sense of duty to his country. He would stop the engines before following after her, and that gave Eliška all the time she needed.

She was in a long hallway complicated by pipes and valves. The passage ran on, more or less straight, toward the front of the ship. *The bow*, Eliška corrected herself. *Sailors call it the bow.* She was following blood splashes on the walls and floor. She needed a weapon and figured the guy leaving behind all the blood hadn't gone far. He was leaking fast. The human body is basically a hydraulic machine. Rupture the system and the fluid starts to leak. The faster the leak, the sooner the machine breaks down. Eliška didn't know anything about boats, but she knew a lot about the human body. More importantly, she knew how to destroy it. And this guy was running on borrowed time.

Several side passages intersected the main one. Eliška paused at each to look around for dark red smears. She crept along the confusing web of corridors with her heart tripping along inside her chest. A film of sticky sweat gathered on her forehead and turned her T-shirt into a damp rag hugging her breasts.

The wounded man had made it a lot farther than Eliška would have guessed. It took her ten minutes. She finally found him sitting with his back against a large metal pipe. He was still alive. A dark stain covered his chest like a greasy bib. His eyes were open. One hand held onto a model 19 Glock, but he didn't have the strength to lift it. His eyes went to Eliška and he made a strange gurgling sound at the back of his throat. He was drawing on the last of his strength just to keep his eyes open and focused.

Eliška hunkered down in front him and reached for the Glock. "Mind if I borrow this?"

He tried to talk. A line of dark blood dribbled from his mouth instead.

Eliška thumbed the mag eject and pressed down on the hollow point rounds. *Mostly full.* She could tell by the feel. She slipped the magazine back in the weapon and seated it with a hard slap.

"Lucas Randall," Eliška said. "Is he aboard?"

The deckhand managed a nod.

"On the bridge?" Eliška asked. "Pilothouse? Whatever it's called."

Another nod.

"How do I get there?"

His head turned a fraction and his eyebrows went up.

Eliška pointed to her left. "This way?"

He nodded and then looked at the gun in her hand. The question was written on his face.

"Oh, don't worry," Eliška told him. "I'm not going to shoot you. That would be too noisy."

She wrapped one hand around his neck and squeezed. His eyes opened wide and his hand came up, fueled by one last burst of adrenaline from his failing heart. Dumb fingers swatted at Eliška's forearm with all the strength of a dying bird flapping around on the ground after a cat has ripped out its guts. Eliška choked him until his eyes rolled up and then counted to thirty.

When it was over, she patted his pockets and found a small folding knife. She clipped the knife to her waistband at the small of her back, gripped the Glock pistol in both hands and followed the passage, looking for a way to the pilothouse. She hadn't gone far when the loud chugging rhythm of the engines stopped.

Noble had managed to cut the power.

Silence settled over the *Maersk Minerva* and the sudden quiet was unnerving. Suddenly, every sound seemed amplified, like her hearing was turned up to ten. She listened to waves lapping against the hull and the groan of welding plates rubbing together. Her own breath sounded like thundering bellows. The rumble of the engines had helped mask her movements. From here on, she would have to go slow. She adjusted her grip on the Glock and told herself to relax.

Slow and steady wins the race, Eliška told herself.

CHAPTER SEVENTY-FOUR

THE FEEDER SHIP WAS IN SIGHT. LUCAS COULD SEE THE running lights winking in the darkness less than two hundred meters off the starboard bow. Ten minutes, maybe fifteen, to reach the other vessel. Another thirty or forty minutes to load the containers. An hour tops, and the operation would be successful. Nothing Noble did at that point would make any difference.

Stanz, Ludwick, and Grinkov were guarding the only two approaches to the pilothouse. All three looked jumpy and tense. They gripped their weapons with white knuckles, ready to shoot anything that moved. Anyone coming up the stairs would be met with a hailstorm of lead.

Lucas grabbed a satchel full of flares and a pair of heavy leather work gloves. Someone had to be up top to mark the right boxes and help attach the guide cables for the transfer. With Noble keeping the crew busy, Lucas would have to do the job himself. He slung the satchel over one shoulder and his battle-rifle over the other.

Erik asked the obvious. "You going to hook the boxes?"

"There's no one else to do it," Lucas pointed out.

He was about to say more when the engines cut out. There was no fanfare, no fireworks. One minute, the heavy diesel motors were chug-chug-chugging away; the next, they quit. Lucas rounded on Erik. "What happened?"

He spread his hands in a hopeless little gesture. "I don't know. The engines are offline."

"Get them back on," Lucas ordered.

Erik jabbed at the control panel, flicked several switches and worked a lever. He shook his head. "We are dead in the water."

"Noble." Lucas said and followed it with a curse. "He must have sabotaged the engines."

Lucas gazed out the windows at the distant lights. The first real hint of worry started deep in his belly. His hands curled into tight fists. He wanted to find Noble and kill him, but that would have to wait. He needed to get the money onto the feeder ship before harbor patrol arrived. The OS-*CinCom* was so close. Lucas turned to Erik. "Radio 'em. Tell them to come to us."

Erik shook his head. "If we do that, every ship in the Adriatic will know right where we are."

Lucas went to the large picture window. *So damn close.*

Stanz was on a knee in front of the portside door, his weapon trained down the stairs leading to the pilothouse. He spoke up for the first time. "I say we take the fight to them."

"Stay put," Lucas ordered. Stanz was good, probably one of the best men Lucas had, but Noble would have the engine room locked down by now.

Maybe not, thought Lucas. He might be injured and low on ammo. *Who knows what kind of hurt he's already taken just getting belowdecks?* Noble was human, after all, and it sounded like the crew of the *Minerva* had put up a hell of a fight. Noble could be on his last leg, just hoping to hold the *Minerva* until the Navy could arrive.

And then what? The Baader-Meinhof soldiers crewing the boat couldn't fend off a coordinated attack from a trained fighting force. They were never meant to. The *Minerva* was supposed to sail without anyone ever knowing about the counterfeit cash. The Čermáková woman had blown the lid on the whole operation.

Lucas had to get the cash aboard the OS-*CinCom* before harbor patrol—or worse, the US Navy—arrived. He turned to Erik. "Signal them."

"How?"

"You're a sailor, right?"

Erik nodded.

"You know Morse code, right?"

"Yes, but ..."

Lucas snatched a flashlight from a shelf full of supplies and hurled it. The heavy Maglite bounced off Erik's chest and clattered on the floor. Lucas said, "Get out on the bow and signal to them."

Erik scooped up the flashlight with a mutinous look on his face. He switched on the light, went to the door and hesitated.

"Go on," Lucas ordered.

Erik licked his lips and stepped through the portal like a man headed to the gallows.

"What are we going to do?" Stanz wanted to know. "We can't just sit here, Lucas. We have to do something."

When Lucas didn't answer, Stanz said, "We should go to the engine room and try to get the ship started."

"Quiet," Lucas told him. "I'm trying to think."

———

Noble stood in the quiet engine room, grease up to his elbows, listening to the big motors tick as they cooled. He had grown up on boats and knew his way around an engine. The *Maersk Minerva* wasn't going anywhere until a mechanic resealed the oil-pressure valves and replaced the camshaft.

Noble went to the foot of the stairs and watched the bulkhead door. He waited, gripping the AK47, but no one came. Minutes ticked slowly past. His training told him to stay put, hold the engine room. There were only two doors and Noble could watch them both from the bottom of the steps. He had disabled the ship. All he had to do now was wait for reinforcements. But as he stood there, Noble realized it wasn't about disabling the ship and waiting for reinforcements. It wasn't even about stopping the counterfeits from reaching the United States. Not anymore. It was about Lucas. It was about a member of his Special Operations Group who had gone rogue. And it was about Eliška. If she killed Lucas, the answers died with him.

CHAPTER SEVENTY-FIVE

LUCAS CHECKED HIS WATCH. THEY SHOULD ALREADY BE loading the money onto the other ship. Precious seconds were slipping away. Stanz kept bugging him about taking the fight to the enemy. Every few minutes, he would ask permission to go belowdecks. The others were in no hurry to shoot it out with a former Green Beret. They had more sense than Stanz. Lucas ignored the German and scanned the dark waters around the boat. He was looking for any sign of the harbor patrol. The only lights were the OS-*CinCom* still floating off the starboard bow. Lucas wanted to scream at them come get the money before it was too late. They *had* to see the *Maersk Minerva* sitting in the water. Why didn't they come? And what was taking Erik so long?

As if in answer to his question, a single loud *crack* carried across the deck. There was no mistaking the sound of a gunshot.

Closing time, Lucas told himself. *Last call.*

Noble had disabled the ship and ruined all of Keiser's

carefully laid plans. The operation was over. It was time for Lucas to cut his losses. He decided to make his escape while he still had a chance. He was the only one aboard with evidence linking Keiser to the counterfeiting operation. He needed to escape before he ended up in CIA custody. Try as he might, they would make him talk. Lucas had been on the other end of that equation and there was no holding out against those methods. Sooner or later, everybody talked.

He said, "Ludwick, you've got command. Hold the bridge."

"Why is he in charge?" Stanz wanted to know.

"Because I said so," Lucas shot back.

"Where are you going?" Ludwick asked.

"I'm going to signal the feeder ship." Lucas lied.

He settled the butt of his AR15 rifle into the socket of his shoulder as he moved to the open door. Stanz and Grinkov had their backs to him. They never saw it coming. Lucas shot Ludwick point-blank. His face disappeared in a shower of gore. His head snapped forward. He went over like a felled tree.

Before Stanz or Grinkov could react, Lucas pivoted and hosed them with a full-auto blast from his AR15. The rifle bucked against his shoulder, pumping rounds into the Baader-Meinhof soldiers. They jerked and danced. Lucas held the trigger until the weapon locked back on an empty chamber. He dropped spent magazine and pulled another from his back pocket before the bodies even hit the floor.

No sense leaving witnesses. The Baader-Meinhof thugs couldn't ID the old man, but they could put the finger on Lucas, and he didn't plan on spending the rest of his life in prison. He palmed the bolt release and felt the carriage slap into battery.

The hot copper smell of fresh blood filled the air as Lucas took out the cellphone he had used to drop the torpedo factory into the ocean. He dialed another number and pressed send. There was a heavy *whomp* and a tremor ran through the deck of the ship like the cold shiver of some sleeping giant. All the lights in the pilothouse winked out. Operations binders tumbled from the shelves.

The charge, placed directly under the engine room, had breached the hull. The *Minerva* started taking on water. Noble and Cermáková were both dead. The explosion would have seen to that. Anyone inside the engine room was shark food. A few Baader-Mienhof soldiers were undoubtedly still alive, but there was nothing Lucas could do about that. He would have to trust the sinking ship to do the rest of his work.

It was time to go.

He took the stairs to the deck and worked his way through the maze of boxes to a wench operated emergency dinghy secured to the port gunwale. The *Minerva* was already listing heavily to starboard. Lucas let his AR15 dangle at the end of its sling and went to work on the safety straps. One of the latches refused to budge. Saltwater had rusted the catch. Lucas pushed his weapon around in back of him so he could get better leverage on the stubborn clasp. That's when he heard Cermáková say, "Going somewhere?"

Lucas let go of the rusty catch and started to reach for his rifle.

Eliška said, "Don't bother."

The AR15 was riding against his butt. To get it in

action, he would have to reach back, grab the weapon and bring it forward while turning around. No one was that fast —not even Lucas. Cermáková would gun him down long before he could turn and bring the weapon up to fire. He stopped with his hands halfway back, fingers spread. Sweat broke out on his forehead.

"Keep your right hand where I can see it," Eliška ordered. "Take off the sling with your left and drop it overboard."

"This rifle has been with me for nearly fifteen years. I carried it rifle in Iraq and Afghanistan," Lucas told her without turning around. "It's killed bad guys all over the globe."

"Its killing days are over. Take it off and drop it overboard."

"Alright," Lucas said. He was biding his time. Looking for an opening. He said "Alright, whatever you say."

He reached up with his left, lifted the sling over his head, and held it out at arm's length. His prized AR15 dangled above the black depths of the Adriatic. Lucas took one last look—the AR had been a steady friend through some of the worst of times—then he dropped it.

The rifle hit the water with a *plop* and sank out of sight.

"What now?" Lucas asked.

"Walk backwards," Eliška told him. "Slowly."

He put his hands up and shuffled backward. Cermákova was looking for payback. She wanted her pound of flesh. She wanted to make Lucas bleed before it was all over. She should have just shot him. Lucas walked backward until he felt the barrel of her pistol press against his neck. It was still warm from the shot that had killed Erik.

Too bad, really. Lucas had liked Erik. The rest of the Baader-Meinhof crew could rot, but Erik was okay.

Eliška warned him not to move, not to even breath, then reached forward to pat him down. Lucas felt her hand jam into his armpit and she worked down his left side toward his hips, down the outside of his leg and up into his crotch. She knifed her hand up between his legs. A sour ache flooded his belly and threatened to bring his lunch up. Lucas grunted but managed to stay upright. His face turned beet red. He let her search his left side completely, and then she started on his right.

She was still using her left hand, crossing over in front of her body, tangling up her free hand with the hand holding the gun. That's when Lucas made his move. He spun around with all the speed of a coiled viper. His elbow knocked the Glock askew and his fist crashed down on Eliška's head. He meant to hit her square in the temple but missed and connected with her ear instead. It was enough to ring her bell.

The Glock clapped and Lucas felt the bullet scream past his ear. A molten-hot shell casing kissed his cheek before jingling over the deck. Then he and Cermákova were tangled together, both struggling for control of the gun. It was a bitter fight, but never in doubt. Eliška was a hissing bobcat up against a boa constrictor. She was mean in a fight, but Lucas had fifty extra pounds of muscle. While she punched and kicked, he wrestled her to the deck and wrapped her up in a strangle hold. He trapped her wrist in his armpit and caught her left hand in a viselike grip, then jammed his forearm into her throat and levered his weight down on her until her eyes started to roll up.

The ocean was boiling around the sinking ship and the deck was listing heavily. Welding plates popped and groaned as water filled the compromised hull. Lucas could hear the contents of the shipping containers shifting. The containers themselves shrieked and jerked as the ship slowly settled to starboard. A few more degrees, and they would start tumbling into the ocean. Cermákova held on to the gun as long as she could and then it slipped from limp fingers.

CHAPTER SEVENTY-SIX

NOBLE HEARD THE HARD RATTLE OF AN AUTOMATIC overhead and drew up short. An eerie sort of silence had settled over the freighter. It wasn't the kind of pleasant absence of noise that lulled him to sleep aboard his wooden schooner every night. That silence was easy and comfortable, broken by groaning timbers and creaking hawser lines. This was a heavy silence, and it was punctuated by the sinister pop of foot welds and the hollow slap of water against the metal hull.

Noble had been moving along an empty corridor toward an open stairwell when the rapid *ratta-tat-tat* shattered the quiet. He put his back to the cold steel wall, listening and waiting. It sounded like it had come from the top deck. There was no answering chatter. After a moment, Noble moved on. He hadn't gone far when a shuddering explosion rocked the ship.

There ran an earth-rending *bang*, followed by the unmistakable roar of water filling the hull. Lucas had scuttled the ship. The explosion sounded like it had come from the engine room. A few minutes earlier, and Noble would have been caught in the blast. The deck started a slow-motion tilt beneath his feet. The *Minerva* was sinking and Noble guessed he had maybe ten minutes before the whole thing surrendered to the watery depths.

He hurried to the steps. Metal grates allowed him to see up through the risers. The landings were clear and Noble took the steps two at a time. He reached the pilothouse and eased up to the door with the stubby AK47. An open hatch and a short flight of stairs led to the bridge. Noble went slow, checking the corners as he crept to the opening for a peek.

A deckhand lay flat on his back. His brains were blown all over the cracked window. The pulpy red mass was slowly working its way down the glass in long red streaks. The copper stench of blood and offal hit Noble as he stepped onto the bridge. Empty shell casings rattled and flattened under his feet. Two more dead men lay on the other side of the room. Someone—Noble was guessing Eliška—had caught the first man point-blank and then hosed the other two. It was neatly done. It looked like they never saw it coming.

He noticed one of shell casings and bent to pick it up. It was a 5.56. The Germans were using old Kalashnikovs chambered in 7.62mm. Eliška would be armed with whatever she could scrounge. And unless she had managed to find an AR, someone else had killed the three Germans on the bridge.

Noble nodded slowly as he pieced together the clues. The solution was simple really: Lucas had turned on his own crew. The boat was dead in the water and the plot to destroy the dollar had unraveled. Authorities were scouring the ocean for the *Maersk Minerva*. Lucas had decided to tie off loose ends. That included the crew. He had gunned down the three Germans in the pilothouse before scuttling ship.

Noble should have seen it coming, really. He studied a diagram attached to the wall. Emergency exit routes were marked in red and pointed to a lifeboat on the port side. Lucas was probably in the water already, rowing for shore. If he made it to Italy, he would disappear.

Noble bit back an angry curse and crossed to the control panel. Seconds were slipping by. His pulse was a galloping pony, urging him to get off the ship before it listed far enough that cargo containers started falling. Once that happened, the sudden shift in weight would cause the *Minerva* to break apart like a child's toy. He took a moment to study the dials and then powered up the GPS system. The light blinked red several times, then turned steady green. Noble opened a radio channel and placed a call to Croatian harbor patrol, requesting immediate assistance. When that was done, he switched frequencies and radioed the Italians as well. Within minutes, half the countries on the Adriatic had a fix on the *Minerva*. In fifteen minutes, give or take, there was going to be a regular flotilla out there.

Noble dropped the mic, grabbed a fresh Kalashnikov off one of the dead Germans, along with two spare magazines, and went in search of the lifeboat. He made his way back down the stairs to a closed exterior hatch. There was sonorous *boom*, followed by a rattling *clang* from somewhere deeper in the ship. Water was filling the stern, stressing the welds, and ripping the boat apart. Time to get out. Noble spun the hatch wheel and shoved. A breath of ocean air cooled the sweat on his face into a sticky shell. He turned to his left and followed the gunwale in search of the lifeboat. He found it still shipped the deck, the safety straps only partway removed. A moment later, he saw why.

Eliška was on her knees and Lucas had a gun pressed to her head. His face was a mask of uncontrolled rage. The muscles in his forearm flexed as he tightened his finger on the trigger.

"Lucas!" Noble shouted and raised the Kalashnikov. He should have fired. He meant to. He had a clear line of sight. But he couldn't. His finger started to ease the trigger back and faltered. His head told him to finish it, but his heart screamed for him to stop. Noble said, "Don't do it, Luke."

Lucas hauled a dazed and bloodied Eliška up by her shirt, looped an arm around her shoulders and screwed the barrel of the Glock into her ear.

Her face pinched. She said, "Finish it, Jakob. Blow him away!"

"He's not going to do that," Lucas said, shielding himself with Eliška's body. "Are you, Jake?"

Noble could only see one side of Luke's face now. He squared the front site on his friend's forehead and let his finger rest lightly on the trigger. He could take the shot, but it meant killing Eliška as well. He was aiming at a target the size of a baseball and the deck kept shifting under his feet.

"Do it, Jakob," Eliška insisted. "Kill him!"

Noble hesitated.

One side of Lucas's face twitched in an unsteady grin.

He said, "Put the gun down, Jake, or I'll splatter her all over the deck."

"And then what?" Noble said. "You kill her, and I'll kill you. Where does that get you?"

Lucas laughed. "I know you better than that, Jake. You aren't going to let me kill her. Put the gun down."

"It's over, Luke," Noble heard himself saying. "Give up."

But in his heart, he knew Lucas was right. He wasn't going to sacrifice Eliška. He couldn't. He had watched too many people die. Torres and Alejandra and Sam. All dead. His finger left off the trigger, but he kept the front site on the visible half-moon of Lucas's forehead.

Lucas sneered. "What? Do you want me to count to ten, like in the movies? Put it down, or I kill her."

"Okay," Noble said. "You win. I'm dropping the weapon."

He let go with his right hand and started to lower the AK to the deck with his left hand.

"Think I'm stupid?" Lucas said. "Throw it over."

"Don't do it," Eliška said.

"Shut up!" Lucas screamed in her ear.

Noble's mouth pressed into a strict line. He had no choice. He tossed the rifle. It landed in the dark waters with a *kerplunk*. His stomach felt like it was somewhere down around his knees. His tongue stuck to the roof of his mouth. He waited for Lucas to turn the Glock on him.

"Now be a lamb and undo that last latch for me," Lucas said and used the gun to motion to the safety strap.

Noble went to the lifeboat and tried the latch. It was rusted shut. Hhe had to lever all his weight against it before it finally shrieked open. He said, "Who's bankrolling you, Luke? You didn't put this outfit together. Someone with a lot of capital is behind this scheme. Who is it? Is it Keiser?"

Lucas said, "Now the wench."

Noble found the controls and set the motor in motion. "How did he talk you into this?" Noble asked. "What did he promise you?"

There was an ominous groan as cargo containers inched to starboard under the shifting weight of all those tennis shoes and cellphones. The back end of the ship was taking water fast and rode low. The bow was now several inches higher. Noble found himself on the low ground, looking up at Lucas.

"He promised me nothing," Lucas said. "He opened my eyes."

The crane swung out over the gunwale with a whirring of gears and the cable started down, lowering the lifeboat.

"He brainwashed you," Noble said.

"Bullcrap," Lucas said. "You're the one who's brainwashed, pal! You still believe in American exceptionalism. All those years, we were fighting for freedom and democracy while the bureaucrats in Washington played games. They sent us off to die in wars they never intended to win. Then they dishonored our sacrifice by lying about it on national television. You know where I was September 11, 2012? I was in Tripoli, Jake. I was a few hundred miles away while our men, our brothers, fought and died. We begged—*begged*—to help. And for thirteen hours, the White House told us repeatedly to stand down. Told us the situation was under control. When it was over, they went on CNN and told the nation they did everything they could."

Lucas turned his head to the side and spat. "They let our boys die, and they lied about it. That's when I knew American was too corrupt to survive. I knew I could no longer go on protecting a system that was rotting from the inside. The only way to save America is to tear it down and start again. Don't you see? We need to hit the reset."

"You're wrong," Noble shook his head. "America isn't perfect. No country is. America is what the voters make of it. We choose our leaders, and we get exactly what we vote for. Sometimes that's great. Other times, it's a nightmare, but the system works. Americans learn from their mistakes and course-correct. That's the way it's always been. That's the way it's meant to be."

The lifeboat had settled into the water with a solid *thump* and a splash. Noble knew his time was up. He said, "This operation is over, Luke. The Navy will be here any minute."

"I'll be long gone by the time they arrive." Lucas leveled the gun at Noble.

"You going to shoot me, Luke?"

"Nothing personal, Jake," Lucas said. He even managed to look apologetic. "If it makes you feel any better, I'll raise a glass to your memory, brother."

"Gee, thanks."

While they were talking, Eliška's right hand was creeping toward her waistline.

Lucas started to tighten his finger on the trigger just as the first cargo container lost its precarious perch. The metal box went crashing into the water and other boxes started to slide and tumble. The sound was a deafening cacophony of thundering booms and shrieking metal. The deck of the *Minerva* bucked like a stallion.

Noble stumbled.

Lucas pinwheeled his arm like a tightrope walker trying to maintain balance. It gave Eliška the opening she was waiting for. She produced a folding knife with all the speed and skill of a magician plucking a rabbit from a hat. The blade licked Lucas's wrist in one quick flash. His eyes opened wide and his fingers lost their grip on the weapon. The Glock clattered across the deck, and a lurid red splash of blood hit the wall of containers.

CHAPTER SEVENTY-SEVEN

Eliška spun around and steel flashed. She made two quick cuts, opening Lucas's belly with all the efficiency of a can opener. Ropey guts spilled out all over the deck, landing with a sickening *plop*. Lucas lurched backward, spilling a fresh gout of blood. His face turned a deadly shade of white. He tried to scoop up coils of intestines with his hands and stuff them back in, but they kept slipping through his fingers. "Jake," he moaned. "Help me, Jake."

The sight left Noble sick to his stomach. He fought down a wave of nausea that had nothing to do with the heaving deck. His first instinct was to help, but there was nothing he could do. Eliška had killed Lucas just as surely as if she had put a bullet through his heart. It was only a matter of time. Noble stumbled across the sloping deck for the gun. He scooped it up and said, "It's too late, Luke."

Lucas went on trying to push his guts back in. His face went from white to an unhealthy shade of blue. His breath came out in ragged gasps full of pain and shot with fear. His eye bulged from their sockets. It was agonizing to watch. Lucas was a SEAL, one of the best of the best. A tier one operator. He had fought beside Noble and sacrificed for his country. Now, he sat with his guts in his lap, begging for help.

"Help me, Jake," he said. His voice was barely a whisper. "Help me."

Noble knelt down in front of him. In that moment he would have moved mountains to save his friend, but Noble could no more save Lucas than he could stop the ship from sinking. He said, "Close your eyes and count to ten, Luke. It will all be over soon."

Lucas shook his head, flinging drops of sweat. "I don't want to die, Jake. I can't die like this. God, help me!"

"Close your eyes," Noble said. "Count to ten."

Lucas was hyperventilating now. His shoulders hitched with every panicked gasp. Noble laid a hand on his shoulder and told him again to close his eyes. It was another minute, but Lucas closed his eyes and started to count. He got to six before his strength gave out. He slumped sideways. His head landed on a rope of intestines. His eyes rolled up, but his lips kept moving, kept counting.

Eliška watched. She held the knife in one bloodstained hand and waited for the end. It came fast. Lucas had lost so much blood. The deck seemed to be drenched in it. Noble struggled to his feet and tried not to look, but his eyes kept going back to the grisly spectacle. Lucas let out one last, rattling breath—the death rattle—and then it was over.

———

Eliška looked down at the knife in her hand like she wasn't quite sure how it came to be there. Lucas Randall was dead. His organization was destroyed. She had expected to feel relief. Instead, she just felt hollow. Killing Lucas hadn't brought her father back. And it didn't make Papa's death any easier to accept. He was dead and gone and the man who killed him was lying in a puzzle on the deck of the *Minerva*. Eliška had won, but it was an empty victory. She dropped the knife. It landed amid the gore.

Noble grabbed her elbow and shoved her toward the side. "Go!"

The *Minerva* was leaning hard to starboard now, like a drunk stumbling home after an all-night bender. Containers continued to tumble off the deck. Eliška struggled up the incline to the gunwale. She swung one leg over the railing and pushed off the side. There was a short drop, and warm saltwater enveloped her in a rush of sound. She pulled with her arms and kicked with her feet and broke the surface. The lifeboat bobbed a few meters away. Eliška paddled over and pulled herself over the side.

A few minutes later, Noble clambered in next to her.

The *Minerva* pitched onto its side and spilled its cargo. Containers crashed down in the ocean with a mighty roar. A wave picked the lifeboat up and nearly tossed them out. Eliška clung to the side. The *Minerva* settled on the ocean floor with half the bow thrusting above the waves and the life boat eventually stopped riding the swells. Eliška started to thank Noble for saving her life and found herself staring down the barrel of the Glock.

"What now?" she asked in a tired voice. She mopped

water from her face and said, "Are you going to turn me over to the CIA?"

"You're still wanted for murder."

"You know why P. Arthur Fellows was killed," Eliška said. "Isn't that enough?"

Noble shook his head. "The United States government wants his killer."

"What does Jakob Noble want?" Eliška asked.

Jake hesitated.

"I thought we had something," Eliška said.

"Maybe we did," said Noble. "Doesn't mean I'm going to let a killer go free."

"If you turn me in, I'll spend the rest of my life in a cage."

Noble chewed the inside of one cheek.

Eliška could see the struggle. She looked to the west. She could just make out the lights of Italy in the distance. She said, "The coast is right there."

"Letting you go is a capital crime," Noble said.

"No one would have to know."

"I'd know," he told her.

"Maybe you turned your back for a moment and I just ... disappeared?"

"I wouldn't turn my back on you for a second. You're too dangerous," Noble said, but the gun went down to his side. He gazed across at the lights and shook his head. It was a moment before he spoke again. His brows knotted together. "Far as I'm concerned, you made your escape back in the engine room."

Eliška grinned. She started over the side and paused there a moment, one leg dangling in the warm water. "Was it just two lonely people on a train?" she asked. "Or something more?"

Noble didn't answer right away. A Croatian Coast Guard vessel was closing in on the *Minerva*. He turned at the sound of the engines. Searchlights swept back and forth across the black waves. He said, "It was more than just two people on a train."

Something inside Eliška seemed to relax, like there was a deep knot in her chest that had finally let go. She would probably never see him again, but she felt better just knowing he was in the world. She said, "Thank you, Jakob."

He said, "Find a new job, Ellie. If we cross paths again—"

"If we cross paths again, I'll have to kill you," Eliška told him with a smile.

"Well, let's make sure that doesn't happen."

She dove into the water and paddled for shore.

CHAPTER SEVENTY-EIGHT

Otto Keiser sat in his wheelchair, staring out the windows of the Apollo fund at the lights of Bern. He was no longer interested in the candlestick charts on the computer screens or the stock ticker scrolling across the televisions. The volume was muted, and he didn't see the CNN Kyron that read, "Hedge Fund Billionaire Otto Keiser Loses Big in Bet Against the Dollar." The office was empty, except for Keiser. His liver-spotted hands twisted together over his bulging stomach and one eye twitched. His lips pursed and relaxed, like a man trying to form words. But there were no words. He swallowed with an audible *click* in his throat. All of his carefully laid plans were ruined. His empire was destroyed. The money was at the bottom of the ocean and Keiser's puts had expired, costing him trillions. His fund was bankrupt, and the United States, the imperialist giant, marched on without so much as a hiccup. In fact, it had been a good day on the market. The S&P was up nearly two hundred points and the Dow was up fifty.

Within hours of the news, the resignations had started. His loyal staff, so eager to hitch their wagons to Keiser's rising star, had abandoned ship. They tried to quietly distance themselves from the failing fund. Some of them were probably already discreetly asking after opening in other brokerages. *The bastards.*

Everything was ruined. His life's work lay in a thousand pieces, like the shattered remains of a priceless vase on the parlor floor. He couldn't put it back together again. He could try to rebuild from the ground up, but who was he kidding? Keiser was too old for that. It had taken fifty years of hard work to maneuver all the pieces. No, too late to start again. Too late for anything but revenge.

He grasped the wheels of the wretched chair and wrestled himself around to face the conference table. The chairs were all empty and would probably never be filled again. Keiser stabbed the intercom button with one arthritic finger and barked at Westley/Wexler, "Find out everything you can about an American Special Forces operator named Jacob Noble."

CHAPTER SEVENTY-NINE

Noble arrived home to Saint Petersburg three days later. It was late afternoon and hot enough to melt wax. Sweat glued his polo shirt to his back. He parked his '67 Fastback at the marina across from Straub Park and made his way along the docks to a forty-foot wooden schooner. *The Yeoman* was lettered on the stern in curving gold script. Noble had a bag of groceries in the crook of one arm. The brown paper sack was full to bursting. He made his way up the gangplank and heard a low note, like the throaty rumble of a diesel engine, as he stepped on deck.

He wrestled open the small door to the galley with his free hand. One hundred and twenty pounds of fur and teeth was there to greet him. The Czechoslovakian wolf dog went up on his hind legs and planted his front paws in Noble's belly. Noble nearly dropped the sack of food.

"Okay, okay," he said. "I'm happy to see you too. Let me put these down before I drop them."

The dog sat back on his haunches. His tail wagged. A long pink tongue lulled from one side of his grinning mouth.

Noble dropped the sack on the counter and went down on one knee. He threw an arm around the dog's broad neck and scratched behind its ears with his other hand. The animal draped one paw over Noble's shoulder in what could only be described as a doggie hug. It was nice to have someone to come home to. Noble didn't know how in the world he was going to care for a dog. Work required long absences, but he was determined to make it work.

"Hungry?" Noble asked.

The dog let out one huffing half bark.

Noble untangled himself from the mutt and started unloading groceries. He was stuffing the eggs in the fridge when he noticed a marionette laying on the galley table. Noble's stomach clenched. His hand was halfway to the pistol in his waistband before he stopped himself. The dog seemed to sense danger. It stood and let out a deep growl. Noble shushed him and picked up the Czech doll. There was a note attached. A feminine scroll said, *Take good care of my dog.*

CHAPTER EIGHTY

COOK AND WITWICKY SAT IN WIZARD'S CRAMPED AND cluttered office. The Deputy Director of Operations was hunched over his desk with an unlit Chesterfield dangling from his mouth. CIA Director Armstrong was there as well, dressed in a pinstripe suit with her hair up. She clutched a thin cigar in one manicured hand. Tendrils of blue smoke curled up from the glowing tip.

"And there's no way we can connect Keiser to any of this?" Armstrong was saying.

Wizard turned his attention to Cook and Witwicky.

They shook their heads in unison.

Ezra said, "Everything was done through shell companies and subsidiaries. We can make the case that Keiser owns controlling interests in the holding companies, but we can't prove he was directly involved. For all we know, those organizations were acting on their own."

"Not likely," Wizard rasped.

"No," Gwen agreed. "But that's what Keiser would claim."

Armstrong muttered a curse and put the thin cigar to her painted lips. The end flared briefly, then dimmed. Her lipstick left a sensual ring of red on the brown paper. "Any luck tracking down Cermáková?"

"None," Gwen said. "She vanished into thin air."

"Probably drowned," Ezra suggested.

"I highly doubt that," Wizard said but declined to speculate further.

Armstrong said, "Randall dead, Cermáková escaped, and no way to implicate Keiser in the whole affair." She shook her head. "Not our finest hour."

"Not a complete loss," Wizard said. He searched the clutter on his desk for a match and lit it with his thumbnail. Cupping the flame from a nonexistent draft, he said, "We saved America from economic collapse. That's enough for one day."

Armstrong agreed with a nod. She turned in her seat to face Cook and Witwicky. They both straightened up, like soldiers coming to attention. Armstrong said, "Make Otto Keiser your full-time job. I want to know everything about him. I want to know where he goes, who he talks to. I want to know if he secretly wears women's panties. *Everything.* Understood?"

"The J. Edgar Hoover package," Ezra remarked.

"We're on it," Gwen said.

Armstrong levered herself out of the chair and went to the door. She paused in the opening. "Ezra, Gwen, you both did real good. I'd put you in for a medal, but this whole thing is off the books."

"We're the CIA," Ezra said. "We don't do it for medals."

Gwen said, "Stopping Keiser is reward enough."

Armstrong favored them with a smile before walking out.

Wizard waited until she was gone, reached inside his desk and brought out an 8x10 black-and-white headshot of Otto Keiser. He cranked himself out of the chair with difficulty and tacked Keiser's picture to the center of the vast web covering the wall.

Ezra sat up a little straighter.

Gwen said, "All this time, you knew?"

"I suspected."

Ezra said, "What now?"

Wizard leaned his bony hips against the desk and stared at the wall. He smoked his cigarette in quiet contemplation. After a while he said, "Now I watch, and I wait. It's a long game he and I have been playing. The end is still a long way off. We dealt him a serious blow, but he's far from finished."

EPILOGUE

SHE OPENED HER MOUTH TO SCREAM AND ICY WATER poured down her throat, choking her. The pain was exquisite, blinding. Her body felt electrified. Her lungs screamed for air. It felt like a metal band closing around her chest. Her back and legs were piano wires stretched to the breaking point. Her hands, fingers numb with cold, churned water into foam. Blackness crushed in around her, threatening to drag her down into the fathomless depths. She needed oxygen. She needed to breathe. She clawed her way toward the surface, desperate for air. She could see light shimmering on the water in kaleidoscopic patterns. If only she could reach it...

She came awake with a start, a scream dying on her lips. Painfully bright fluorescents blinded her. She had to narrow her eyes and blink against the overheads. She wasn't in the water. She was in a hospital room, and there was a man sitting in a chair next to her bed.

He was balding and slightly plump. The blood vessels

in his nose were broken. His eyes reminded her of a sad looking basset hound. He wore a faded brown suit under a rumpled overcoat and leafed through a file folder.

She tried to sit up in bed. Pain rocked her body in crushing waves that slammed her back to the pillow. It was a moment before she realized her wrists were strapped down by leather restraints. She tried to speak, had to clear an obstruction in her throat, and tried again. Her voice was a tired croak. "Who are you?"

"I am inspector Laurent." He closed the file and regarded her with those sad basset hound eyes. "You are American?"

She managed a nod. The muscles in her neck sounded like rusty saw blades. With great effort, she said, "That's right. Where am I?"

"You are in Hôpital Européen Georges-Pompidou," he informed her. "What is your name?"

She licked dry lips and said, "Klein. My name is Vanessa Klein."

"A pleasure to make your acquaintance, Mademoiselle Klein." Laurent re-opened the file folder and scanned a page. His lips bunched together in a pout. "And what are you doing in France, Mlle. Klein?"

"I'm a member of the U.S. State Department. Why am I cuffed to the bed?"

His unruly brows went up. "You were brought in without any papers. No identification. And you have been shot. You say you are a member of the U.S. State Department? Where is your passport?"

"I must have lost it," she told him. "It must have come out of my pocket in the river."

"Ah, *oui*. Of course." Laurent flashed a warm smile. "This makes sense. Now, Mlle. Klein, perhaps you would be so good as to tell me how a member of the State Department came to be in the Seine with two bullets in her back?"

She shook her head. "I don't remember."

The smile ran away from his face. Laurent looked genuinely disappointed. "That answer simply will not do, Mademoiselle. I find it very hard to believe that an American on a diplomatic passport should end up shot, face down on the banks of the river. This is very odd indeed. Wouldn't you agree?"

"I need to contact my embassy," she said.

"Also very odd," said Laurent. "The Americans haven't reported any of their people missing. You have been here for two weeks. Surely the State Department would have made inquiries if one of their people went missing for two weeks? Unless, of course, you are, let us theorize, a member of the American Central Intelligence Agency."

She laid there in complete silence.

Laurent went on. "Of course, I don't need to tell you, international espionage is a serious crime."

"I want a lawyer," she told him.

"All in good time, Mlle. Klein. First, we will discuss what you have been doing in France and how you came to be in the river. Perhaps if you cooperate, I may convince the magistrate to offer leniency for your crimes."

To be Continued...

CAN'T WAIT TO FIND OUT WHAT HAPPENS NEXT?

Click HERE to read GUNN WORK, the first standalone novella in the Sam Gunn Series. This story is available exclusively to my readers absolutely FREE! Just click the link.

http://eepurl.com/gypmb9

DID YOU ENJOY THE BOOK?

Please take a moment to leave a review on Amazon. Readers depend on reviews when choosing what to read next and authors depend on them to sell books. An honest review is like leaving your waiter a hundred dollar tip. The best part is, it doesn't cost you a dime!

ABOUT THE AUTHOR

I was born and raised in sunny Saint Petersburg, FL on a steady dict of action movies and fantasy novels. After 9/11, I left a career in photography to join the United States Army. Since then, I have travelled the world and done everything from teaching English in China to driving a fork-lift. I studied creative writing at Eckerd College and wrote four hard-boiled mysteries for Delight Games before releasing the first Jake Noble book. When not writing, I can be found indoor rock climbing, playing the guitar, and haunting smoke-filled jazz clubs in downtown Saint Pete. I'm currently at work on another Jake Noble thriller. You can follow me on my website WilliamMillerAuthor.com

 facebook.com/authorwillmiller

 twitter.com/noblemanauthor

 instagram.com/wmiller314

Made in the USA
Middletown, DE
29 January 2020